Murder at the Nineteenth

When there is a violent murder at a historic home counties golf club, Superintendent John Lambert himself discovers the crime. For the first time in a long career, he finds himself conducting a murder inquiry among people he knows well. The victim is the Chairman of the Golf Club and a prominent local businessman, and it is soon clear that the members of the Club Committee are the chief suspects. They are all prominent members of the local community, and Lambert is saddled with a Chief Constable who is uncomfortably aware of the fact. Indeed, he seems more concerned with the media attention which inevitably focuses upon such a sensational murder than with the emerging detail of Lambert's investigation.

Events move quickly in the two days following the murder. Amid further startling developments, Superintendent Lambert, supported by the deceptively stolid Sergeant Hook, moves steadily towards a solution.

J. M. GREGSON

Murder at the Nineteenth

COLLINS, 8 GRAFTON STREET, LONDON W1

William Collins Sons & Co. Ltd
London · Glasgow · Sydney · Auckland
Toronto · Johannesburg

First published 1989
© J. M. Gregson 1989

British Library Cataloguing in Publication Data

Gregson, J. M.
    Murder at the nineteenth.—(Crime Club)
    I. Title
    823′.914[F]

ISBN 0 00 232223 4

Photoset in Linotron Baskerville by
Rowland Phototypesetting Ltd
Bury St Edmunds, Suffolk
Printed in Great Britain by
William Collins Sons & Co. Ltd, Glasgow

CHAPTER 1

Lambert very nearly ignored the telephone. It bleeped, distant but insistent, an intrusion at a moment when he least wanted intrusion.

He had been in the garden for no more than ten minutes at the end of a tedious day; on this still evening of heavy heat, the scents of late spring were at their incomparable best. He let the phone bleep ten, twelve, fifteen times. Then the habits of a working lifetime asserted themselves; he muttered a ritual curse, set down his secateurs, and trudged resignedly through the French windows to the source of his irritation.

'Lambert,' he growled.

'Superintendent Lambert?' A man's voice he did not recognize. Educated, heavy, used to the telephone. 'This is James Shepherd.' A pause: he expected to be recognized. Lambert racked a reluctant brain. 'Chairman of the Golf Club.' Now there was the irritation of vanity deflated: this man expected to be recognized, especially when he gave his name. Well, it had been a long day.

'I need to see you. Urgently.'

'Now?' Lambert heard even in his monosyllable the note of reluctance. Through the open doors the scents drifted intoxicatingly; all down the long garden the colours hung vivid in the last of the sun.

'Not immediately,' said Shepherd. 'But this evening. We're about to begin a short meeting of the Club Committee. Meet me after we've finished. Say ten-thirty. The others will be gone—the bar will close at ten.'

No 'please'; no 'could you?' A man used to being obeyed. Or a man frightened enough to forget the usual greasing of conversational wheels? The snatched, irregular breathing at the other end of the line was prompted by some strong emotion: a policeman's instinct divined fear.

'I'll be there,' said Lambert. He wrote '10.30 p.m.' and circled it on the pad in front of him, following a routine that on this occasion was quite pointless. 'I hope this doesn't indicate a crisis for the Greens Committee!' Lambert was Chairman of this, but whether his sally was an attempt at levity or a probe for information he was not sure himself.

'Nothing to do with the Greens Committee,' said Shepherd sharply, 'I wish to hell it was!' The phone banged down sharply. The last phrase would ring in Lambert's mind all through the next day.

Christine came back from her yoga class soon after ten. Her husband lowered his large frame into the driving-seat as soon as she slipped out. 'The good policeman never sleeps,' she intoned as he struggled to move back the seat. Though she had long since accepted the rigours of his occupation, she still went through the rituals of wifely protection. She had become more tender towards him as middle age began to threaten and he tired more quickly than he used to do. Heavy with rank and success he might be, but he was to her more vulnerable without the vigour of youth. It seemed inconceivable now that she could ever have thought of leaving him.

'Wrong again, Mrs Lambert,' he smiled. 'You're understandably confused by the number of hats I wear. It's Golf Club business this time. I won't be long.'

He was wrong on both counts.

Even at this hour, he drove through the lanes with the windows right down. Through the heavy heat, the scent of hawthorn flower swirled between the hedges: no place like Britain on evenings like this. He wished Christine was with him for another dose of his propaganda against holidays abroad.

In the dusk, the long, low bulk of the golf clubhouse seemed almost a part of that more ancient landscape in which it was set. Shepherd was right: by this hour, things were very quiet. Only two cars remained in the car park, the steward's Ford by his flat and, in the Chairman's reserved space at the other end of the tarmac, Shepherd's Rolls-Royce, almost invisible in the deep shadow of the wall of the changing-rooms. The clubhouse and its many extensions were mostly one-storey. In the side of them which faced Lambert as he got out of his car there was not a light to be seen. Against the last of the light in a clear western sky, the long walls stood black, silent, almost sinister. As quiet as the grave, thought Lambert, as he wondered where to look for entry.

The locker-room door was locked, as he expected. He walked under the archway which connected the professional's shop to the rest of the buildings and went round to the back. Now he found himself deliberately trying to avoid any appearance of stealth, walking noisily, trying to announce to any unseen observer that he had an innocent and warranted purpose in this quiet place. Had he not been summoned here by the Chairman of the Club? He must not be caught in the felon's crouch of popular imagination. He walked upright, dignified, aldermanic. If a Chief Superintendent was to be mistaken for a criminal, said his gait, let it be at least a fraudster rather than a common burglar.

The rear of the complex of buildings seemed even more deserted than the front had been. He had always seen this area busy with the movement of golfers, so that the stillness now seemed eerie. It was too dark now for him to see the flagstick on the eighteenth green, but on the practice putting green beside the long verandah he could just make out the nearest of the holes with their short metal flags. Beyond these,.the brook which skirted the eighteenth green caught the clear, soft light of a young moon, so that its motionless surface shone silver in the gloom.

To Lambert's surprise, there was no light visible in the clubhouse buildings on this side either. A small rectangle of soft orange at the extreme end of the dark mass was the only illumination; after an instant's computation, he recognized this as the kitchen of the steward's flat. For a moment, he wondered if Shepherd had forgotten their meeting after all: then he remembered the Chairman's car standing still in its allotted space at the front of the building.

There was a simple explanation, of course. Shepherd must be chatting with the steward in the privacy of his domestic quarters. Somehow, it did not seem his style: Lambert could see the Chairman chatting amiably enough to the steward across the men's bar, where master–servant relationships could be comfortably preserved, but scarcely venturing into the servant's own territory for social inter-course. Yet that, it seemed, was where Shepherd must be: Lambert felt a pinprick of irritation: having called him out at this hour, the Chairman should have been looking out for him when he arrived.

He took a deep breath and marched boldly through the darkness, still anxious to assert in his bearing his right to be out here at this hour. He knocked boldly at the door of the steward's flat. But when the door finally half-opened his voice was muted and apologetic. He could distinguish no features of the figure silhouetted against the suddenly bright light. Only the outline of the hair told him that it was female.

'Sue? It's John Lambert. Sorry to bother you so late, but the Chairman asked me to meet him at the club and I can't find him.'

'Come in, Mr Lambert.' The soft West Country burr, the cheerful light of the kitchen, were welcome relief from the dark silence outside.

'I thought Mr Shepherd might be chatting to Vic in your place,' he said. Her face showed that she thought that as unlikely an occurrence as he had. 'I can't find him anywhere else and there don't seem to be any lights on.' He sounded to himself like a young constable.

'Vic,' she called through to the further recesses of the flat. After a moment, her husband appeared, apologetic in a dark blue dressing-gown. 'Vic, Mr Lambert's looking for Mr Shepherd. He arranged to meet him here.'

Her husband shook his head. 'It's not like the Chairman, but he must have forgotten you, Mr Lambert,' said the steward. He looked oddly discomforted to be caught outside his normal working habitat and dress. 'I checked everywhere was locked up and all the lights were out not ten minutes ago and he wasn't about then. He had a meeting until about a quarter to ten. But I shut the bar at ten and they all went soon afterwards. He must have forgotten you, I'm afraid.' His patient addition of detail derived from long, polite dealings with a public who might have been expected to deduce such things for themselves.

'You may be right, Vic. But he only arranged the meeting earlier this evening. And his car's still outside. I suppose it's possible he got a lift home with someone else, but . . .'

'Never known him do that before.' The steward filled the gap Lambert had hopefully left in the conversation. 'Look, I think we'd better just check the premises and then ring his house to make sure he's got home.' Lambert was happy to find Vic Edwards suggesting exactly the course of action he had already decided upon. The steward brought his keys and led the Superintendent through a maze of passages, kitchens and fire doors, until they reached familiar territory in the club's main lounge.

The glasses had been cleared from the tables, but the furniture in the big room lay as it had done at the end of a quiet evening. They checked the men's bar, the snooker-room, the locker-rooms, the showers, even the ladies' lounge. All of them had for Lambert that extra stillness of communal rooms usually noisily occupied.

'Where else?' said the patient Vic Edwards. He had never believed the Chairman was still on the premises, and each new empty room seemed to give him a little extra satisfaction. 'Do we try the pro's shop, the trolley-room or the ladies' locker-rooms? I've got the keys to all of them.' He rattled them interrogatively while Lambert looked out into the darkness. As if to emphasize the futility of their quest, the only light in the greenkeeper's cottage a hundred yards away was suddenly extinguished.

'I don't think we'll bother with those, Vic,' he said. 'Now that we've gone so far, we'd better just check the Committee Room. Then we'll call it a day.'

The Committee Room was in the oldest part of the clubhouse, being part of the original mansion from which all else had grown. The steward had to open the Secretary's office to get the single big mortice key for the heavy oak door. Lambert, unlike most members, had seen the interior of this holy of holies, for his Greens Committee met here. With its oak panelling, its huge table and heavy chairs, the room always seemed to him to be frozen in the 'thirties; the impression was reinforced by the yellowing but evocative photographs of Jones, Hagen and Cotton playing at the club in that decade.

In the sudden harsh light this room seemed at first as empty as the others through which they had passed. They might have turned and left, had not Lambert noticed that the door of the small wall-safe in the far corner of the room was slightly open.

It was only when they moved around the big table to investigate the safe that they saw what lay upon the floor. James Shepherd, OBE, Chairman of Burnham Cross Golf Club, lay spreadeagled by the empty fireplace. His jacket was open; in the centre of the immaculate white shirt beneath it, the handle of a heavy knife protruded from an irregular patch of crimson.

Lambert's first, uninvited, thought was that the 'thirties room had acquired a 'thirties murder.

CHAPTER 2

In the moment of grand guignol discovery as they stood over the body, the roles of the two men were suddenly reversed. Vic Edwards, unflappable steward of Burnham Cross Golf Club, stared wide-eyed at the grisly scene and strove to collect his shattered calm. When he turned to the man he had been conducting with patient tolerance through the empty club, his face was ashen, his voice unsteady with shock.

'Do we ring 999?' he said. Then, as the realization dawned that he was looking into the face of a Police Superintendent, there came an involuntary nervous titter that was near to hysteria. 'Sorry, Mr Lambert!' He turned half away from the corpse and stared hard at the picture of Henry Cotton. Lambert realized that he had probably never seen violent death before. He moved across to the steward, carefully skirting the table on the side away from the body.

'I'll do the ringing, Vic. Better go and tell Sue. Sit with her and I'll be through to see you presently.' He led the steward out of the room and through the labyrinth which would take him back to his own quarters, putting on a series of lights as they went. Lambert took his arm and guided him like an elderly invalid instead of the man ten years his junior he had been only minutes earlier.

He switched on the light in the secretary's room and sat down at the desk. He rang the police surgeon, then the CID room where he spent so much of his life. It was impossible to shock either the world-weary medic or the Inspector who took his call. An obscure professionalism made both of them treat murder as routine, though the departure of a local dignitary raised a little well-dissimulated curiosity. There was even a little black humour about the occurrence of such a dark deed at their Chief Superintendent's golf club.

Lambert looked at his watch; it was now approaching midnight. He stared at the phone for a full minute, then reluctantly took up the instrument and pressed the digits. The ringing tone sounded only twice at the other end of the line. 'Garner,' the voice said, gruffly neutral despite the hour: Chief Constables were professionally cautious about their responses until they knew who was phoning them.

'Lambert here, sir. Sorry to disturb you at this hour but there's been a death which I thought you should hear about from me rather than anyone else. Almost certainly murder.' That 'almost certainly' forced from Lambert a grim, involuntary smile. He thought of what lay in the room next door and had so recently been a man: the eyes frozen wide with surprise; the right arm flung wide upon the floor, the left bent half beneath the heavy trunk; the shirt around the squat hilt of the heavy knife wet with still-fresh blood. There were questions from the rasping, breathy voice at the other end of the phone. As Lambert had expected, Garner's first thoughts were of public reaction and press sensationalism rather than the machinery of investigation. The Chief quizzed him about how many people already knew and how he proposed to break the news to the world at large.

'It's bizarre,' he said in seeming conclusion, 'Jim Shepherd was a member of my lodge.' Lambert considered the notion that a Masonic imprint should give some extra indemnity against murder. Then his Chief's tone became businesslike again. 'You'll take charge of the investigation, of course, John. Set up a murder room if you need to, grab yourself an inspector and a CID sergeant and anyone else you need. The quicker we have an arrest the better.' He was thinking in terms of headlines and PR again; he rang off before his Chief Superintendent could argue. Lambert had known it was almost inevitable that he would be assigned to the case, but he stared sourly at the phone before he banged it back into its cradle.

By this time, there were muffled sounds from the other side of the wall. Lambert went back into the Committee Room to find much activity. Two young constables were taking measurements, while the police photographer selected his angles and went about his work with relish. 'This is the kind of thing that made me take up this job when I read about it in books,' he said, chewing vigorously on his anti-smoking gum as he balanced precariously on a chair above the corpse. 'Not quite as good as the body in the library I've always wanted, but the nearest a sinner like me is likely to get.' The fingerprint officer had already finished his work upon the lifeless hands and was preparing to encase them in protective plastic. Soon the body would lose its last connections with humanity and become evidence, tagged, documented, registered along with the rest.

Lambert, looking at it with this thought, wondered if the patch of crimson around the knife had widened a little even since the discovery. He passed on the thought to the police surgeon as he arrived, but that veteran was as laconic as ever. 'Death recent,' he said grudgingly, revealing nothing. Dr Burgess spent information like a miser his money. 'No rigor yet. Tell you more later. PM, of course. Do you want the stomach contents analysed?' He might have been a husband reluctantly checking a shopping-list.

'Hardly seems necessary. But yes, I suppose we'd better have the lot.' Lambert was already thinking of officious coroners, even of hostile counsel. Thirty years of playing straight man to barristers with a taste for histrionics made you cautious.

The photographer was almost finished. Now the print officer moved to the furniture, covering table, chairs, mantelpiece with white dust, then moving cautiously in upon the clothing of the body. He treated the gruesome handle protruding from its dark stain as though it were some prize fish that might escape if it were not brought to shore with delicate skill. 'Don't forget the safe,' said Lambert. Four white faces looked up at him from different parts of the room, their concentration broken for a moment. 'No, sir, next on the agenda,' was all the scene-of-crime officer said, but Lambert heard in his tone the resentment of the implication that they might miss anything so obvious. It made him realize he had spoken only because he felt superfluous at this stage.

In the steward's quarters he found Vic Edwards trying to comfort a wife shivering with shock. He went wordlessly back into the bar, took two glasses from the neat rows and pressed the optic beneath the whisky bottle twice with each of them. He handed one to each of the shaken pair, insisting that Sue sipped from the glass she tried to refuse. She sipped twice with an air of distaste, then gulped like one determined to down unpleasant medicine. She coughed, brushed away a tear, burst into speech as the fire coursed through her chest. 'Vic says—' She couldn't bring herself to repeat what Vic had told her about the scene in the Committee Room. 'There's a madman roaming about, and I've two children asleep upstairs!' she burst out. Lambert pinpointed now the source of her terror and understood the fierceness of her fear.

'I don't think you need fear for your little ones,' he said. In the quiet room his phrasing sounded remote, almost biblical; perhaps it was too long since his own children were small. 'Whoever killed the Chairman had a specific victim in mind. He—or she—isn't roaming about killing people at random.'

'She?' said Sue sharply. Her dark eyes looked straight into Lambert's face for the first time and he saw with relief that curiosity was merging with apprehension.

'We can't rule out the possibility. And for what it's worth, my feeling is that whoever did this is miles away from here by now. We'll know better after the medicos have done their tests, of course, but my guess would be that Mr Shepherd was killed immediately after the meeting ended.' At the limits of his peripheral vision, he caught Vic Edwards's widening eyes, but he kept his gaze on the Steward's wife. 'The Chairman asked me to meet him here at ten-thirty. Yet he had not asked Vic to leave a door open or to direct me to the room he intended to use. It looks as if he was killed before he could make any arrangements of that sort.'

Sue relaxed visibly and took her husband's hand. The nightmare vision of a mad axeman seeking out her children was banished. 'Thank you,' she said, whether to Lambert, her husband or the world at large being not quite clear.

'My advice is to get to bed as quickly as you can, Vic,' said Lambert. The steward nodded his thanks. 'We'll be as quiet as we can out there. I'll make one more phone call and then be gone myself. A policeman will remain here all night, so you can feel quite safe.' There was no call to tell them that this was to protect the evidence from any disturbance, to guard against the remote possibility of the deliberate removal of some clue by murderer or accomplice.

As he went back through the labyrinth of passages to the central part of the clubhouse, Lambert mused grimly upon the frightened pair behind him. The steward and his wife would need to be on any list of suspects he eventually compiled: they had access to the Committee Room, easy and unquestioned. What lay there must be protected until the morning, from them as from other person or persons unknown.

Lambert looked at his watch and sank wearily into the office chair to make his last phone call of the night. The Club Secretary's phone rang eight times before he responded. His voice was that of a man caught between full consciousness and that deep rest we enjoy an hour into the night.

'Burnham Cross 3210. Parsons.'

'David, it's John Lambert. I'm at the Golf Club. It's five to one and I apologize, but I had to ring you. David, I'm afraid Mr Shepherd is dead.' He waited, every nerve alert for any sound from the other end of the line that might be significant.

'Dead?' said Parsons dully.

'Murdered. At the Club. In the Committee Room. Earlier tonight.' Lambert poured the details into the mouthpiece, hoping the sudden flood of brutal facts might produce some reaction that might be useful from the shocked recipient.

'But ... I was with him tonight ... We had a meeting ...'

If David Parsons had known anything, his performance as he received the news was perfect, with just the right degree of bafflement, just the right reluctance to accept reality, which is characteristic of the innocent. Of course, thought Lambert with a grim and rueful smile, in all probability he *was* innocent.

'Do you want me to come down there now?'

Lambert had considered this.' No. There really isn't much more to be done. But I'll want to see you first thing in the morning. I'm going to get some sleep myself now, but I'll be down to see you at the Club by nine at the latest. I'll be needing quite a lot of information from you.' Had he meant it to sound like a vague threat? If so, there was no reaction.

'Of course.' Then, belatedly: 'This is terrible!'

Lambert was left hoping that some among those he must question would react more revealingly.

It was a relief to be outside beneath the brilliant canopy of stars. He had never seen a clearer moon than the bright crescent above the professional's shop. Breathing deeply of the still night air, he cleansed his nostrils of the scents of death and evil he had left within the clubhouse.

A slight sound behind him made him turn. Shepherd's body was being transferred at last to the ambulance which had awaited it for two hours. The head and hands were sheathed in plastic and protruded beyond the sheet which convention demanded even at dead of night. But the knife protruded still from the corpse's chest, so that the sheet draped itself in a cone about the handle. As the body was tilted to accommodate it without disturbing the knife, the head was turned towards Lambert. The last Lambert saw of James Shepherd was a pair of open, unseeing eyes, grotesquely enlarged by the clear plastic. Then the doors closed quietly and the ambulance eased away.

It was those eyes he had to banish before he could get to sleep. Christine stirred but did not wake as he crept into bed. Inevitably, he reviewed the events of the evening. Something he could not quite pin down seemed to differentiate this from other deaths he had dealt with in a long career. Just before he sank into the relief of sleep, he realized the tiny thing that seemed unusual. He had broken the news of Shepherd's death to four people who had known him well: the Steward and his wife, his own Chief Constable, and David Parsons. All had been shaken with the terror that sudden death always brought.

But not one had expressed regret at his passing.

CHAPTER 3

'Don't keep watching me!' Lambert growled unreasonably. Christine was not even in the same room. She stole surreptitious glances at her husband from the kitchen while the coffee bubbled beside her. They were part solicitude, part natural curiosity about the night's bizarre crime: John as usual had told her the barest possible details. She switched on the radio with an abrupt gesture of impatience; a union leader stressed the modesty of his stance to an uncaring world.

When she took the coffee-pot through to the table to refill his cup, his chair was thrust back and the room was empty. The toast was unfinished, the knife clouded with the marmalade it had never spread. Beneath the flowering cherry by the front gate, she caught the merest glimpse of the disappearing number plate of his car. 'Like the *Marie Celeste*,' she said, surveying the trim little dining-room. Some husbands kiss their wives when they leave in the mornings. Lambert never had, never would, though the bond now was deep enough between them.

Lambert had to remind himself as he drove beneath the fresh emerald of new leaves of the macabre business which awaited him. He wound down the window and drew deep on the clean morning air; it was going to be hot again. 'Not like Shakespeare,' he said aloud to himself. In the bard, murders of kings and emperors compelled a decent obeisance from nature, so that violent weather presaged such deaths. Even an industrial mogul might have been given a few routine rolls of thunder by old Will. '"When beggars die there are no comets seen,"' he reminded himself as he turned into the short private lane which led to Burnham Cross Golf Club.

James Shepherd, though, had been no beggar. As if to remind Lambert of the fact, the maroon Rolls-Royce stood, massive in its isolation, in the Chairman's space in the car park. To a Superintendent whose mind was wrestling still with blank verse, it looked like some great dumb beast patiently awaiting the return of a master who had gone away for ever.

Lambert was immediately reassured by a more mundane image. He saw as he parked the broad back of CID Sergeant Bert Hook, the assistant he had commandeered on his Chief's authority. The Sergeant was adjusting a blackboard on an old-fashioned easel by the main entrance. Chalked in his careful capitals were the words: 'Clubhouse closed all day due to sudden emergency. Course open.'

It was barely half past eight but already Hook had implemented his Superintendent's first suggestion: Lambert was enough of a golfer himself to know how even the most curious of the breed could be diverted by the heady prospect of play.

Hook's rubicund face, tongue moving in sympathy with his hand as he underlined 'Clubhouse closed' was a picture of concentration. He was five years Lambert's junior, but his ponderous gait and demeanour made him seem often the older of the two. His village bobby exterior concealed a shrewd and active brain; people usually underestimated him, a factor Lambert could turn to advantage. He called, 'Well done, Bert,' as he passed, and was foolishly pleased as the Sergeant's face filled with a childish glow of welcome.

The first rosebuds were almost in flower in the sheltered bed by the double oak front doors. Lambert sniffed them appreciatively, passed briskly within, then checked his step with a mild access of guilt. He was arriving here with a livelier relish for the scent of death than he had the previous evening for a routine meeting. He knew now what he was about: however macabre the business of the day, he was operating within the machinery of a police investigation, with colleagues trained as he was to the impersonal pursuit of facts. There was a problem here, but a problem it was his business and his skill to solve. And perhaps his pleasure? That was more questionable.

'"'Tis my vocation, Hal. 'Tis no sin for a man to labour in his vocation,"' he said to Hook behind him.

'No, sir.' The Sergeant was firmly uncomprehending but totally unruffled.

'But would Falstaff spring to a corpse quite so readily?' persisted Lambert.

'Very likely, sir,' Hook stonewalled impassively. He blamed graduate entry for these literary pretensions in a senior officer who had been sound for years. But then his wife could testify that he blamed graduate entry for most of his life's small tribulations.

The uniformed constable stationed unobtrusively in the entrance hall had listened to this incomprehensible exchange between his seniors with increasing concern. He introduced himself with nervous stiffness when bidden; probably it was the first time he had had occasion to report to anyone as exalted as a Superintendent.

There was a gentle cough, scarcely more than a clearing of the throat, behind them. 'What can I do to help?' The voice tailed away at the end of the question: the Secretary was uncertain whether to use his normal 'John' in addressing the Chairman of the Greens Committee or the 'Superintendent' which the presence of lower ranks in a working situation might require.

There were not many people to whom Lambert had to look up, but David Parsons was one of them. He stood in the doorway of his office with his eyes a good two inches above Lambert's. 'That's good of you, David. I'm going to need quite a lot of information and assistance, I'm afraid. I'll be with you in a moment.' Parsons acknowledged the polite dismissal that was intended by withdrawing into his office, and Lambert turned back to Hook. 'Bert, would you take statements from Vic Edwards and his wife while I instal myself here?'

'The Steward?' said Hook. Of course, he knew no names yet; Lambert had to remind himself that this familiar territory would be strange ground to the rest of his team.

'Sorry, yes. Take PC Spencer with you. You can lock the doors, lad,' said Lambert as the youngster hesitated to leave his post. 'Better listening hard to Sergeant Hook than being a waxwork in the entrance hall. It's called the "efficient utilization of labour".' He'd known that week's course on 'Management in the Public Services' would come in useful somewhere.

When he went into David Parsons's small office he moved the waiting chair so that the Secretary rather than he faced the bright morning light. Ex-Colonel Parsons looked drawn and shaken, despite a night's rest and the time to assimilate the tragedy. For the first time in the four years Lambert had known him, he looked like a man in his late fifties. The lean frame drooped a little, and some of the grey of his thinning hair seemed to have seeped into the tanned cheeks. Did his sensitivity do him credit, or was this a curious reaction in a man who must have seen violent death many times in a military career of almost thirty years? Parsons had better be probed fairly quickly, before the busy routine of a golf club secretary's life reasserted itself and rehabilitated him.

'I've got to be a nuisance, I'm afraid, David,' said Lambert. 'Perhaps even more than you anticipated. We've decided to set up a murder room here.' The royal plural was an occupational hazard for Superintendents. 'That means clearing a room exclusively for our use and closing off that section of the clubhouse for as long as is necessary.'

'Which hopefully won't be very long,' said Parsons with a brave attempt at a smile. 'When and where?' Lambert could see now the Adjutant he had been for so long, efficient, unquestioning, glad to be of such obvious use at the centre of organization.

'Immediately. In the Committee Room,' said Lambert firmly. It had not taken him long to decide upon this. Because of its size, its privacy and the soundproof nature of its thick panelled walls, the room was eminently suitable. And although the notion had melodramatic overtones, he knew that the possibility of questioning a suspect within that quiet room where murder had been committed appealed to him. The perpetrator of last night's dark deed would need to be nerveless indeed to re-enter that individual and rather claustrophobic room without suffering a tremor.

'Do you need Golf Club permission?' said Parsons. 'I could ring . . .' He hesitated, embarrassed at his gaffe, and Lambert filled the space for him with a grim little joke.

'The Chairman will hardly object, David. No, we don't need permission. If anyone gives you any trouble, tell them I requisitioned the room and refer them to me. Even the

byzantine sensitivities of golf club officialdom can scarcely
be allowed to impede homicide investigations.' Beneath his
light manner, he was watching the Secretary closely, but
learning nothing. Parsons seemed unruffled by the news
that a murder room was to be set up within yards of
his office, an arrangement that would keep him under
permanent surveillance in the days to come. His eyes were
thoughtful, even cautious, but with no more than the concern appropriate in one making the necessary arrangements
to clear up the distressing and sensational mystery which
had so disturbed his work-pattern. He had seen the
Superintendent previously only as a club golfer, resolutely
detached from his work. Now he was watching him at work
for the first time, and Lambert felt that even as he tried to
sound out the state and working of David Parsons's mind
he was being assessed himself. If the Secretary had no
hand in the murder, he would be a shrewd support in the
investigation, providing much of the information he would
have to dig for without such inside help. If on the other
hand he was the murderer or an accomplice, his nerve and
resource would make him difficult to corner. He might look
shaken, but there was no trace of fear now in his speech or
bearing.

'You can have my extension phone,' said the Secretary.

'No need,' said Lambert. 'We're getting another line put
in now. Be installed within the hour. Standard procedure
in these cases: British Telecom know the drill,' he said
quickly. They both knew that anyone in the Secretary's
office could have overheard police calls under the arrangement Parsons had proposed.

'It seems then that there's nothing I can do to help,' said
the Secretary with a hint of pique. Perhaps he heard the
note himself, for he immediately said by way of conciliation,
'I suppose this must be routine stuff for you. You must have
handled scores of murders.'

'Not so very many,' said Lambert drily, 'and none of
them quite like this'. He could not carry on this little
bout of cat-and-mouse any longer. Soon he would sit down

opposite this cool military presence for a formal interview, but not just yet. There were urgent things to be done first.

'You're wrong, though, David. There *are* things you can do to help.' He looked round the Secretary's office. There were grey filing cabinets, a computer blinking mindlessly, a large desk. The notes of last night's meeting in the Secretary's neat longhand lay scattered across the desk. Everything as it should be in an office innocent of the violent event twelve feet beyond its far wall.

'I'll need details of everyone who was at your meeting last night. And of anyone else that you know was around the clubhouse at the end of your meeting.'

'There was no one else.' The words came too quickly, almost without pause on the end of Lambert's request. How could he be so certain?

'Time will tell,' said Lambert severely. There would be other sources of information to probe as well as Parsons; there was no harm in letting him know that now.

'I'll let you have names and addresses within ten minutes,' said the Secretary, opening the top drawer of the nearest filing cabinet and accepting the relief offered by action.

Lambert went back into the corridor and thence into the Committee Room which would now be the centre of his operations. He found Hook lecturing young PC Spencer, who sat flushed and embarrassed on the edge of a chair, his short fair hair looking as if it needed to be covered with a helmet if he were to preserve his authority. He looked eighteen but was probably twenty-three.

'. . . so it looks like lots of suspects, lad,' Hook was saying. 'Too many. How do we start?'

'Well, I suppose we question everyone. Look for the strongest motive—or motives . . .' Hook let him toil away; he was enjoying playing the old sweat.

'Certainly motive may be important—eventually. But it's a long step from motive to proof. Never start with motive, lad. Start with facts. No one can escape facts. Facts are the framework. If you get enough of them, the final fact becomes obvious, and the final fact is the solution. Where, when and

how come before why. In this case we know exactly where,
exactly when and exactly how, and we're not much nearer.
But before we worry about why, we need more facts. Who,
for instance. How many people could have been in the right
place at the right time with the right weapon? That's the
next set of facts we want.'

'Well done, Sergeant Gradgrind,' said Lambert quietly
to Hook's back: the start told him his colleague had not
heard him enter.

'Thank you, sir,' said Hook evenly, his knowledge of
Dickens as scanty as Constable Spencer's but his calm as
impenetrable as any sphinx's. Spencer was glad to have his
avuncular instruction suspended in the Superintendent's
presence, but he wondered if he would ever fathom the
mysteries of this eccentric double act.

Lambert walked round the huge oak table to the spot
where he had found the body some ten hours earlier. The
fingerprint experts had long concluded their work; the
measurements from all parts of the room to the body had
been taken; the results of the photographer's work were
probably already printed. He looked down at the chalk
outline on the parquet floor which was the caricatured
reminder of death: it was slightly smudged in two places
where last night's traffic had been careless. Someone's
agenda paper, overlooked when the meeting broke up, still
lay upon the table. Lambert saw that the owner had doodled
with a ball-pen through one of the meeting's more boring
items—had doodled in fact a revolver, he noted with
interest. It pointed like a bad joke at the outline on the floor.
Psychiatrists might read something into that. Well, the
fingerprint men would tell him soon enough who had
sketched that revolver, but he expected nothing significant
there. It would be an incompetent murderer who spread
Freudian detritus behind him, and any other sign of in-
competence in this business was distressingly absent so
far.

As Lambert turned back to the expectant faces of his
colleagues, there was a sound of sudden movement in the

office next door, then an urgent yell from the car park. Despite his bulk, Hook reacted fastest. He led the trio through the hastily unlocked front doors. David Parsons leant far out of his office window, shouting still and straining to see beyond the wall of the changing-room to the reserved spaces neatly marked for the cars of club officials.

The late Chairman's Rolls-Royce stood still alone in its glory. But both its doors swung open and its boot lid reared towards the azure sky. Of the perpetrator of this violation, there was no trace visible. A hundred yards away, where the golf club's private lane joined the public road, a car engine roared invisibly into the distance. The foot on that urgent accelerator might be that of a tardy commuter, or that of a fleeing murderer.

CHAPTER 4

'Had the car been examined?' Lambert knew the answer even as he asked the question.

'No, sir,' said Hook.

'Fingerprinted?'

'Not yet.'

As Lambert stalked back ill-temperedly to the clubhouse entrance, Parsons leaned still from his window.

'I suppose I shouldn't have shouted,' he said, 'but it was instinctive.'

'What did you see?'

'Nothing at all. You can't from here. And of course you'd locked the front doors.' It sounded like an accusation.

'What alerted you, then?'

Parsons thought for a moment. 'Noises. Nothing very definite.'

Voices?'

'Nothing so precise. Footsteps perhaps. Someone moving around Mr Shepherd's car. I opened the window to listen and heard them opening the boot. That's when I shouted.'

'Them?'

Parsons shrugged helplessly. 'I don't know. Maybe just he or she. Sorry.'

'Don't be. You may have disturbed them before they got what they wanted.' Or they may have got clean away with vital evidence, thought Lambert sourly. He turned to find Hook and Spencer following him warily, like hunters behind a wounded tiger.

'Doors haven't been forced,' said Hook, 'nor the boot. Whoever it was had a key.'

'Thus showing the proper respect for a Rolls-Royce,' said Lambert grimly. In a happier situation he would have expected such an observation from Hook.

He went inside and rang CID on Parson's phone, recalling the fingerprint duo to cover the car. 'We won't touch anything else until you've had your fling,' he said. 'We surprised whoever it was, so it's just possible you may get a few interesting dabs somewhere. We know the two front doors and the boot were unlocked and opened, and there may be others inside.'

He put down the phone and shook his head moodily. In truth, it was no one's fault but his. Had he demanded a bigger team, some of the men would have examined the car at the outset. Had he asked for the terrapin hut so often used as a murder room, it would no doubt have been set up in the car park and the Rolls would automatically have been under surveillance. In fact, he still felt the permanent team for this investigation should be as small as possible—basically himself and Hook—with other resources brought in as necessary.

He went into the Committee Room now. The Telecom men, with their usual efficiency on these occasions, were completing the installation of the temporary line. They glanced from time to time at the chalk outline on the floor and spoke in the hushed tones people normally reserve for churches. As they finished testing and left, Hook, who had plainly been waiting to report in private, came and stood by Lambert as he peered at the empty safe.

'Young Spencer's keeping an eye on the car for the moment,' he said, 'though it's probably just locking the stable door after the horse has departed with the evidence.' Lambert grunted and waited: Hook wouldn't have needed privacy to convey this.

'Your Steward and his wife seem to be in the clear. They were both behind the bar after the end of the Committee meeting, Edwards serving and his wife tidying up ready to close. We can check that in due course with the Committee members, but that very fact means it's certain to be true. One of their youngsters was in their own flat adjacent to the bar and the two of them chased him off to bed and settled him down upstairs as soon as they shut the bar. Unless we presume as unlikely family conspiracy involving the children as well, they seem to be in the clear.'

'Vic discovered the murder with me and then we went and told his wife,' said Lambert. 'Unless they're both in the Olivier class as actors, their reactions were those of innocent people.' He had never thought the Edwardses were involved, but his training meant they had to be eliminated with painstaking care. Hook's report gave him the tiny surge of satisfaction which action always brought; at least the investigation was under way and the focus being narrowed, however obviously.

There was a soft tap at the heavy oak door and David Parsons came into the room. If there was any pique at having to ask entry to realms which he normally controlled,. there was no trace of it in his demeanour. 'The list of the Committee you asked for,' he said. 'I'm afraid you'll have to excuse my scrawl, but my girl isn't in until ten today and I thought you'd like it quickly.'

'And confidentially,' said Lambert. He took the sheet from the Secretary; in fact, the writing was neat, unhurried and clear. 'Thank you, David. Do sit down for a moment. Was there anyone else apart from the Edwardses who was in the clubhouse after your meeting last night?'

'I've already thought about that,' said Parsons. 'No one

else that I know of. The bar was empty apart from us, because Vic only stayed open after our meeting in case we wanted a quick one. Only the front door of the clubhouse was open. I suppose someone could have been hiding somewhere, in the locker-rooms or the snooker-room or the ladies' lounge, quietly waiting his chance.'

'Unlikely,' said Lambert. 'Vic Edwards says he checked everywhere as he locked up just before your meeting finished. Unless we see him as an accomplice to some person unknown, it looks as if the possibilities are confined to your list.' He glanced at the two sheets of neat handwriting, then smiled into the calm, watchful face opposite him.

'This is just the kind of detail I wanted, David. Compiled with your usual efficiency and despatch.' He waited; they exchanged half-smiles and the Secretary prepared to rise and leave. 'There is just one embarrassing omission.' He paused to watch Parsons's interrogative look: he had anticipated this moment. 'You were present at that meeting yourself, David, so I must have the same details for you as for all the others.'

'Sorry. Guilty until proved innocent, I suppose!' With a grim little smile, Parsons took back the paper and began to write.

'Unless someone is helpful enough to offer us a confession, we shall proceed by elimination,' said Lambert lightly but firmly. 'I'm sure you wouldn't like to be overlooked, David.' The Secretary was not five feet away from him; he watched his hands carefully as he wrote. They did not tremble, as he had half-hoped, and the writing in the neat black script was indistinguishable from the previous entries. Indeed, Parsons as he stood to go looked in better control of himself, less grey and shaken, than he had an hour previously. An innocent and diligent worker revived by the restoration of his daily tasks, by his usefulness in assisting the police in this appalling business? Or a murderer elated by the early bafflement of those same police? Lambert shook himself free of such profitless speculation. 'God preserve me from amateur psychology!' he muttered.

'And so say all of us,' said Hook with feeling. 'If you could add the professionals as well, you could make that the daily prayer of every police force in the country!'

But Lambert was already busy with the material Parsons had brought in; he passed the sheet to Bert Hook as he completed his perusal.

COMMITTEE MEMBERS OF BURNHAM CROSS GOLF CLUB PRESENT AT THE MEETING OF 28th MAY

Name	Office	Age	Address
James Shepherd (the deceased)	Chairman	58	The Dower House, Burnham Cross, Bucks.
Michael Taylor	Captain	42	The Cedars, South Park, Tipton St Giles, Bucks.
William Birch	Vice-Captain	39	17, Oxford Road, Harford, Berks.
Mary Hartford	Lady Captain	49	Cherry Cottage, Chiltern Hill, Burnham Cross, Bucks.
Deborah Hall	Social Functions Secretary	35	Flat 11, Tipton Old Hall, Burnham Cross, Bucks.
David Parsons	Golf Club Secretary and General Manager	59	Troodos, Hill Farm Lane, Burnham Cross, Bucks.

NB Len Jackson (Greens Committee Chairman) and Douglas Jordan (Immediate Past Captain) are on the Committee but were unable to attend on this occasion. Both had sent apologies in advance.

Somewhere within these listed names their murderer lurked; these dull statistics masked a hate strong enough to erupt into the violent killing of a defenceless man. It was an unlikely context for a killer, probably something Hook was trying to express when he concluded his perusal with the lame thought, 'These are your friends, sir.'

'Hardly that,' said Lambert, a little defensively. Thirty years of training and experience made him shy away from any suggestion of personal involvement in an investigation. 'I know them all, of course. None of them well. I won't

discuss them with you at the moment: your own first im-
pressions of them, unclouded by your Superintendent's
prejudices, will be interesting.' He ignored his Sergeant's
obvious disappointment. 'Better photocopy this. One for
you, one for the fingerprint boys, one for the file. That's all
for the moment.'

He sat down and prepared to ring each person on the list.
He would have liked to visit them, so as to watch their
reactions to the news of the murder, but there was no time
for that now. He got work numbers from David Parsons for
those who had already left home. All of them except Bill
Birch already knew of the killing. Lambert remembered too
late that Mary Hartford, the Lady Captain, was Matron of
the local small hospital. Although Shepherd's body would
have been taken to Wycombe Hospital with a post-mortem
ordered, her ambulancemen had collected the body. A
few calls to fellow Committee members, contacts with the
Steward this morning; the grapevine of information in a
small community was one of its most efficient growths. He
was left wishing he had woken his suspects in the still of the
night, weary as he had been. It would have been valuable
to study the impact of the death upon each of them at that
most vulnerable of hours.

He concluded each call with 'We shall be collecting your
fingerprints some time today. Please don't leave the area
without ringing this number to let us know your movements.' If he hoped to rattle his listeners, he was unsuccess-
ful. There was nervous laughter, the little jokes about South
America he had heard a hundred times, even cool distaste,
but nothing that was not a perfectly normal reaction from
people involved in a murder investigation for the first time
in their lives. There was also the same unusual factor he
had noticed in those receiving the news of the Chairman's
death on the previous night. Even now, from Committee
members who had had time to condition and civilize their
first, raw reactions to the Chairman's murder, there was
shock, even fear, but no regret.

From one of them he could get no reply. He went back

to the Secretary's office, where David Parsons was dictating letters to the part-time typist who had just arrived. 'No reply from Debbie Hall,' he said.

'No,' said the Secretary, 'but she knows. She came in here not very long ago looking as white as a sheet. She's having a lesson with Alastair now. I persuaded her to go ahead with it.' Lambert nodded and wandered through the changing-rooms to view the fair Debbie. It was no hardship. Indeed, he wondered wryly whether he would have moved so readily to check the presence of a male member of the Committee in the same circumstances.

At the back of the clubhouse he walked into a different world. The sun was climbing a cloudless heaven and the club flag, now at half-mast, scarcely moved as he strolled to the putting green and looked out over the course. Sixty yards away on the other side of the river, Debbie Hall was well into her lesson with Alistair McBrain. Lambert watched appreciatively as the golden-haired Debbie, in white sleeveless top and light pink trousers, sliced a ball away into the light rough between the first and eighteenth fairways which served as a teaching area. Alistair, dour, professional and sixty-three, adjusted the position of her left leg in a way which might have been dangerous for a man without the insurance of his years and expertise. Debbie waggled her hips from side to side as she had been taught to do and settled into the new stance, movements which caused unhealthy excitement in a fourball of visitors on the first tee behind her.

This time she dispatched the ball straight, then held the club at the zenith of her follow-through, in the pose beloved of golfers the world over after a good shot. As she turned to set up another practice ball, she saw Lambert and gave him a wave of greeting that was almost casual. A little piece of bravado to protest her innocence and free conscience? It was possible, but Debbie was a good mover in any case, as was frequently remarked in the male section of the club. And like many women who attracted considerable attention from men, she had developed an unruffled exterior from her youth.

Behind his Superintendent, Bert Hook coughed with conscious discretion, and was rewarded by a little start as that worthy's contemplation of the scene was interrupted. In a mere sergeant it might almost have been guilt. 'Phone for you, sir. Dr Burgess with the post-mortem results.'

Lambert stole a last look at the course in its late spring glory before he turned reluctantly back indoors. He indicated the fair Debbie to Hook. 'You'll be happy to hear Miss Hall is a member of the Committee and will thus need assiduous investigation,' he said. They watched her hit one more shot, sighing together as her blonde hair flashed briefly in the morning sun. '"Much have I travelled in the realms of gold,"' said Lambert appreciatively as they turned their backs dutifully on the scene.

'Indeed, sir?' said Hook.

'Keats,' said Lambert, anxious as ever to educate his staff.

'Does she really, sir?' said Hook impassively. He marched ahead of his Chief: it would never do for his leader to see his smile of satisfaction at setting up a superintendent as a straight man.

The panelled Committee Room felt claustrophobic after the brilliant light outside. After the tiniest hesitation and a rueful smile at his sensitivity, Lambert settled himself into the chair James Shepherd had occupied until he became 'the deceased'. The pathologist had waited long enough to be impatient.

'Time of death between nine and eleven on 28th May. Cause of death insertion of sharp instrument to a depth of seven inches. A sharp, slightly downward blow, almost certainly by someone facing the deceased, piercing the left ventricle. Wound commensurate with knife, probably military in origin, found at the scene of the crime. Analyses of blood from that knife and the corpse confirm this. Nothing for you in the stomach contents. A normal meal and a little alcohol consumed an hour or two before death.'

There was nothing here for Lambert. Just a list of details which would be proof against a defence counsel probing for police carelessness. For once he could be more precise about the time of death than the medics; he already had it down as between 9.45 and 10.30. Hopefully he put the one question he had been waiting to pose. 'Could a woman have inflicted the death-wound?' His suspects might be reduced here from five to three at a stroke.

'Oh yes. No great strength needed with anything as sharp and heavy as that knife.' The pathologist's tones had the slight smugness of one who knew he was not making life easy for the listener.

Without hope, Lambert asked the only other question he had thought of. 'Just the one wound, and that instantly fatal. Does that imply specialist knowledge of armed combat?' There was a pause; from long experience, he could see in his mind's eye Dr Burgess pursing his lips as he weighed the thought.

'It's possible; an interesting thought. But a bit of medical knowledge would do as well or better. And it could easily have been a lucky strike by someone with no knowledge. I'd have to say so in court. That was a deadly weapon to have lying around. If it was, of course.'

That thought had already occurred to Lambert. 'Would you send it back here when your examination's complete?' he said. 'We'll take good care of it.'

'Wanting to play ghoulish psychological games with your suspects, John?' said Burgess. 'You senior CID men make us sawbones seem sensitive souls at times.' He hesitated, then spoke reluctantly, like one loath to give the help he was about to volunteer. 'There's one other thing about the murder weapon that will gladden your avenging heart. The dabs boys say there's one print, on the extreme end of the handle. By the end of the day, you'll know whether it belongs to one of your precious Committee!'

CHAPTER 5

Lambert put down the phone slowly and stared at the Secretary's neatly written list of the Committee of Burnham Cross Golf Club. Was it really possible that the murderer had been so obliging as to leave a thumb-print on the handle of his chosen weapon? It would be scarcely less surprising than the perpetration of a killing by one of these highly respectable people.

'I suppose we now have to presume our murderer is definitely one of these five,' he said to Hook. The names stared up mockingly at him, each seeming equally impossible.

'I'd be as certain of that as it's possible to be of anything outside a family killing,' said his Sergeant with some relish. He produced his notebook but scarcely needed to refer to it. 'The Steward and his wife we've already eliminated. The only other people who live on the premises are George Dawson, the Head Greenkeeper, and his wife. They were out for the whole evening visiting friends. I've checked the friends out. There were two other couples there as well. Both of them have been contacted by phone and confirm the Dawsons' presence until around midnight. The house they visited is six miles away; neither of them left the lounge for more than five minutes.'

Something stirred in Lambert's memory. Last night, and particularly the period before he discovered the murder, seemed now a long time away, but he dredged it up. 'There was a light in the Dawsons' house when I went round the back of the club at about 10.45,' he said, 'I remember seeing it put off.'

'Time-switch,' said Bert Hook, his boad face flickering for a moment with the pleasure of virtue unexpectedly exposed. 'I've been in and seen it. Apparently the Club bought three of them last year to protect club property after break-ins. As you might expect, one has found its way to the Dawsons' house by now.'

Lambert looked down again at what he must now consider his list of suspects. 'Two people on the Committee were missing last night. Len Jackson and Douglas Jordan. Better check them out.'

Now Hook's face glowed, his lips broadened in what in a lesser man might have been smugness. 'Jordan is safely in Brazil, and telexed in from there last night to prove it. Jackson I haven't yet located, but he was away from home on business in the Midlands. We've got the name of his hotel and Spencer's checking it out now.'

Lambert knew Len Jackson quite well. He was a quiet, rather intense man who took a lot of getting to know but repaid the trouble. He had a dry sense of humour, a lot of common sense and a refreshing tendency to see the best in people. Lambert had been surprised but delighted to see this rather retiring man installed as Chairman of the Greens Committee. It was scarcely the make-up of a killer; Lambert would be glad to see him eliminated from the periphery of the inquiry. But then who among these exemplary citizens on the list before him *would* have the temperament of a murderer? It was high time he began to find out.

As if in response to this thought, there came a sharp rapping on the door of the Committee Room. It was precisely ten o'clock, and Colonel Parsons, Secretary of Burnham Cross Golf Club, presented himself for interview at the appointed time with a punctuality born of decades of military life. He stood erect and confident now, his equanimity restored as Lambert had anticipated by the activity on which he thrived. The Superintendent had done everything possible to make Parsons feel a stranger in the familiar oak-lined room which he had entered for one reason or another on most days in the last four years. The stenographer, examining his pencils at the special small table on one side, scarcely glanced up. The two detectives looked friendly enough, but their formal upright postures and the blank white pads in front of them were reminders that they were about their business. The Secretary seated himself a little awkwardly opposite the man he had known until now as an amiable member and a useful member of the Greens Committee The six feet of oak table which stretched between them marked a new, regulated relationship in which he was the stranger.

Lambert saw a man used to command, to a brisk despatch of routine business, now a little awkward in a situation where he had to wait for others to make the running. Parsons had had a busy morning, dealing with golf club staff adapting to an emergency and acting as unofficial police secretary. In the face framed by greying temples, the colour had been largely restored; although Parsons still looked tired, it was possible again to deduce from the depth of tan that this was a man who had spent many years out of England and in less temperate climes.

In an era of informal dress and drip-dry convenience, Parsons maintained a standard which was not that of his own generation but the one before that. Under the light-weight grey suit his shirt was stiffly starched, his grey and red tie had a small, neat knot. The heat, which had already caused Lambert and Hook to drape their discarded jackets over the backs of chairs, had merely prompted Parsons to forgo the waistcoat he wore for most of the year. A small gold tie-pin flouted the modern fashion; matching gold cuff-links gleamed as he folded his arms. Lambert should have felt at an advantage with his informal, comfortable dress and posture; instead, he felt uncomfortable, as if he were about to be reprimanded for his presumption in discarding his jacket. This room, with its overtones of 'thirties stiffness, and the unmistakably military presence opposite him cast him back a quarter of a century to his National Service days, so that he had to resist an impulse to check the fastening of his shirt buttons.

He had been surprised to notice as Parsons came in that he wore suede shoes, as if making a concession not to the fashion of the day but to that of perhaps five years previously. Yet these clothes, Lambert felt suddenly, were worn almost like a uniform, as a defence against a world which demanded individuality: this was a man who had practised for thirty years the virtues of disciplined anonymity within a system which took care of its acolytes.

For the man within this sartorial conformity was less certain of himself than his dress implied. The well-manicured hands which emerged from those immaculate white cuffs trembled slightly; Lambert let his glance dwell upon them, and Parsons withdrew them awkwardly to his lap beneath the table's edge. The tired grey eyes were sunk deep within the tanned face, their pouches hinting at hours of worry. They met but could not hold Lambert's gaze, darted from him to the impassive Hook, to the pads in front of these quiet, patient men.

'Colonel Parsons—by the way, you still use the military title?' said Lambert.

'The Chairman likes—liked—me to use it.' There was a flicker of a grim, nervous smile at the correction, a quick glance at the chalk outline to his right which lay like a gross cartoon upon the parquet floor. 'He mentioned it when I was appointed and put it on the club notepaper. Of course, to the members I'm just David, and I never ask for the title. Breweries and bank managers seem to like it. My wife says our daily help loves to use it . . .'

He was going on too long, a shade too apologetically, about what had been little more than an aside from Lambert. Probably it was no more than a normal nervous reaction: people often talked too much when put under the police microscope. But there might just be something here; out of the corner of his eye Lambert saw Hook make a brief note on his virgin pad. He noticed with amusement that all Hook had written was Parsons's full name: he had merely noted the nervous pulse which Lambert himself had caught and chosen to stress it a little by a pretended note, this wily old fox in stolid policeman's clothes. Parsons caught the movement as he was meant to, and Lambert saw a fleeting anxiety in those too-mobile grey eyes. He would return to military matters later in the interview.

'Right, David,' he resumed. 'You will understand how important it is that we get from you every detail you can recall of the events surrounding this murder. It's particularly vital that you give us the fullest possible picture of your own movements and those of everyone else with whom you had any contact in the period following the end of last night's meeting.'

'Of course.' The phrase did not come as clearly as the Secretary intended and he cleared his throat nervously.

'I don't know how much you know of the evidence we have gathered already, last night and this morning. It has been mostly routine work, but successful in so far as it has eliminated many people as possible suspects. I should tell you, I think, that it now looks almost certain that Mr Shepherd's murderer is one of the five people who sat round this table with him last night.'

Parsons gave a little start of excitement, a shudder of horror, at the disclosure. He must have expected it, but this was a normal reaction. For all his experience, Lambert himself had felt the same frisson of excitement at the realization. Within the invisible lines of social interchange, he knew these five people tolerably well. One of them had hidden the black night of the soul under a friendly exterior and stabbed a defenceless man with the violent energy of hatred. He pressed on with the interview. 'Now. The meeting broke up at what time last night?'

'9.50. I noted it. Time for one quick one before the bar shut at ten.'

'Think carefully. What happened after that is crucial. Who left the room first? In particular, when did the Chairman leave and where did he go?' Lambert expected the Secretary to pause and reflect, but Parsons needed no time to tease out an answer from his memory: he had obviously anticipated the question.

'Mary Hartford and Debbie Hall disappeared together. Presumably to the ladies' locker-room, because they came into the bar—separately—about five minutes later.'

'You say separately. Who arrived first?'

'Debbie Hall.'

'And how long after her did Mary Hartford appear?'

'About two minutes.' Again no hesitation. Lambert fancied the Secretary was shrewd enough to appreciate the implications. It seemed each of the women had had enough time alone to commit the killing. But then to come to the bar and behave normally amidst the innocent?

'You will understand that I have to ask you the kind of question I now put to you. Indeed, I shall ask it of others in relation to you. Now, would you say from your previous knowledge that both of these ladies were behaving normally in that short period in the bar?'

For the first time in this series of questions there was a pause. Quite an interval; long enough for Hook to look up from his notes and join Lambert in his study of Parsons's long, lined face.

'My knowledge of the female psyche isn't extensive enough to be confident about what would be normal.' The little joke didn't come off, the nervous giggle fell false into the intense seriousness of the room. 'Perhaps Debbie Hall was a little more talkative than usual. But then Debbie's always . . . lively.' His searching for the word made it sound an insult.

'And Mary Hartford?' prompted Lambert. Again the interlocutors waited unhelpfully, far too experienced to relieve embarrassment with reassuring small-talk: a man might reveal more about himself as well as others if this kind of stress was maintained.

'She was quiet. Very quiet, I suppose. Just said yes or no if anyone spoke to her. But you can't think she . . .' The voice faltered away into silence as his listeners assessed him and his thoughts.

'We certainly shan't be forming any conclusions at the moment.' Lambert spoke only when it was apparent that Parsons was not going to go on without prompting. 'What about the rest of the Committee?'

Parsons looked like a man back on ground he had prepared. 'Michael Taylor and Bill Birch picked up their papers and left as soon as we had finished,' he said. 'Whether they went to the Gents' or the bar I wouldn't know, but they were in the bar by the time I arrived, because as Captain and Vice-Captain they were talking about first team matches.' Lambert nodded and looked down at his list. Needlessly, for he knew perfectly well that only Parsons himself had not been covered, but he wanted to give the Secretary time to volunteer any further, unprompted thoughts on Taylor and Birch. None came.

'And you?' he asked softly.

'I checked through my notes of the meeting to make sure I had everything needed for the minutes—I don't take shorthand. Then I went to the bar.'

'How long was that after the end of the meeting?'

'It's difficult to be precise. Three minutes. Four at the outside.' Pretty precise, thought Lambert, for a man who had no idea then that precise timing would be important. But Parsons had spent thirty years of military life developing habits of precision.

'What about the deceased?' he asked heavily.

'The Chairman went and opened the wall-safe and seemed to be checking some papers in there. He was still at the safe when I left.'

'You had no conversation with him?'

'No, nothing.'

Parsons's reply came just too quickly, was just too clipped and insistent, to tone with his previous responses. Suddenly he was defensive, obstinate rather than helpful as he had been thus far. Neither of them had referred to James Shepherd by name. Lambert had lapsed into the quasi-legal 'the deceased' and Parsons had retreated behind 'the Chairman'. Shepherd's heavy, dominating personality was being diminished to anonymity. Or perhaps both were concealing a dislike which could no longer be expressed with decency. Parsons must have felt this sudden shift in atmosphere as they arrived at his own relationship with the Chairman. Even as Lambert wrote 'Probably disliked Shepherd' as his first note beneath the Secretary's

name, Parsons felt compelled to fill the uneasy pause
with a confession.

'The Chairman and I didn't get on so well. He appointed
me four years ago and I think he was satisfied with my
work. But we didn't talk much, except about the business
of the Club of course . . .' He petered out lamely, as if aware
of the danger of moving from saying too little to saying too
much. 'You appear, then, to have been the last person to
see James Shepherd alive,' said Lambert. He enunciated it
like a formal charge, allowing the implications to sink into
the context of Parsons's expressed dislike for his Chairman.
On this occasion he won no trick in the macabre little game
of cat and mouse. Perhaps Parsons had been awaiting the
expression of this thought.

'Apart of course from his murderer!' he said evenly.

Lambert afforded him a grim little smile, as if acknowledging his nerve. 'The murder weapon,' he went on. 'Had
you seen it before?'

'What was the murder weapon?' asked the Secretary
steadily. Lambert realized that he could not have seen the
knife used to kill Shepherd—unless of course he had used
it himself. 'Sorry, David, that wasn't supposed to be a trap.
It was, in the pathologist's description, "a heavy knife,
probably military in origin", and it had a seven-inch blade.'

'That would be Mr Shepherd's own instrument. He
always had it laid out before him at our main Committee
and other meetings, along with pen and paper. As a paper-
knife, I suppose.'

'But he wouldn't need a paper-knife during meetings.'

'He didn't need the other things either. The Secretary
takes the minutes. My impression was that he used these
things when he chaired his Company meetings, and thought
them part of a Chairman's equipment. Susan or I always
laid them out ready for him when there was a meeting of
the full Committee.'

'Where was the knife kept, then?'

'In the drawer beneath the table with the pen and ink
stand.'

Lambert took Parsons through the rest of his movements after the meeting. After they had all met up for drinks in the bar, he had gone briefly back to his office, provided some statistics for Michael Taylor, and left the club at the same time as the Captain. He thought Bill Birch, who had seen him leave his office, would vouch for this.

Lambert explained that he would be checking out this account with the recollections of the other Committee members. 'But you would understand that,' he said, leaning back with the air of one about to conclude a routine working exchange. 'You must have had some experience of courts martial yourself in your army years, so you will appreciate the need for meticulous cross-checking of evidence.'

It was merely a means of returning to the area he had decided to probe earlier in the interview. It produced a reaction that was quite unexpected. Parsons's eyes blazed wide and astonished; the tight, thin-lipped mouth lurched briefly open. Lambert was already watching his man, but Bert Hook and even the stenographer at the other end of the room looked up involuntarily as they caught the Secretary's sharp intake of breath.

'What do you mean?' said Parsons. His voice was harsh, forced through lips which quivered with excitement and fear. Across the big table, questioner and witness stared at each other for a moment with open hostility. Lambert was surprised by the strength of his own reaction to the enmity blazing suddenly opposite him.

'I merely meant, Colonel Parsons—' how far away seemed the 'David' he had used successfully earlier—'that you must almost certainly have appeared as a witness, perhaps even as defending or prosecuting officer, in at least one and probably several military trials. As the procedures used for gathering and presenting evidence are similar to those used by the civil police, you might be expected to be familiar with those procedures, and to understand the kind of evidence we have to gather.' It was heavy-handed, even pompous, but intentionally so, as an attempt to sting Parsons into revelation.

The Secretary glared at him for a moment as if challenging his honesty, then dropped his eyes to the table. There was something here; Lambert moved in quickly. 'What did you think I meant?' he challenged.

Parsons said nothing. He stared at the table in front of him for what seemed a long time. The watchers saw that the hands which met in front of him gripped each other very hard, for the knuckles were a glossy white. Lambert thought, 'Come on, you poor sod. There's no way we're going to make it easy for you. You're going to speak first,' and tried not to enjoy the sickly excitement of the tension.

Parsons eventually raised his eyes and tried to look steadily at the Superintendent. His eyes flickered briefly to the impassive but equally implacable Hook, then back to the table. He had to make two attempts to speak, for the words stuck in a dry throat the first time.

'Nothing,' he said dully. 'I misunderstood you for a moment, that's all.' There was another pause. Far away in the men's bar, a clock chimed, faint but regular.

'Then I think you should tell us what you thought I meant,' said Lambert quietly. Parsons shook his head. The thin lips were pale, but they stuck out in a surly pout; the grey eyes stared straight ahead. But for his breathing, which was still not quite controlled, the Secretary might have become a statue. Lambert, studying him closely, recognized the sullen obstinacy usually met only in the very young and the very old. At this moment, the most reasoned argument was going to batter in vain against a closed mind. It was a response to stress he had met before. He would return again to the raw nerve he had touched, but at this moment he would get nothing.

He looked at his watch. 10.50. He had arranged to see Mary Hartford at eleven, during a break in her hospital duties. 'Well, David, we'll certainly need to talk further,' he said.

Whether or not it was meant as a dismissal, Parsons was only too ready to take it as one. His chair squealed back on the parquet floor and he was on his feet before he spoke.

'I'll be here,' was all he said. His attempt at a smile as he went through the door was not a success.

'Not like you to let him away at that point,' Bert Hook said accusingly when they were alone. He had caught the scent of secrets as strongly as his chief.

'He wasn't for telling us any more, even if it had been in his own interests. And I have to see Mary Hartford,' said Lambert, getting up.

'And military records are easily available to a Super, pursuing a murder inquiry,' said Hook.

'Precisely. Put a call through to Army Records on my behalf and ask for his dossier. Must dash now.'

He was preparing to face the oven heat of his own car when Hook came running into the car park, a sight which would have arrested even a less perceptive man than his Superintendent.

'Call from CID section,' panted the Sergeant. 'Len Jackson, your Greens Committee Chairman. He wasn't at the hotel in Nottingham where he said he'd be last night. And he hasn't arrived at the firm he was supposed to visit this morning. Len Jackson has disappeared.'

CHAPTER 6

If Lambert felt a little nervous as he pulled up at Mary Hartford's gate, it was not professional indecision. It was merely the wholly proper trepidation induced in the breast of any ordinary golfer about to interview a woman visited with the title of Lady Captain.

Cherry Cottage was as trim and well presented as its owner. The flowering cherry at the gate which gave it its name was at the end of its spring glory, so that pink blossom lay as thickly upon the ground as upon its branches. Nothing else in the front garden was more than four feet high, save for the roses and clematis that climbed about the mellow brick of the cottage itself. Lambert's swift but expert survey could nowhere find a weed, and the small lawns were so neatly edged that they might have been cut with scissors.

The subject of his visit was waiting for him under the tiled porch, watching his appreciation of her garden with amused pride. 'It's not always like that,' she called, tactfully announcing her presence to a trained eye that had in fact already noted it. 'Old Fred was here yesterday. Nowadays I only tend the things I like. I thought we'd have coffee in the garden. It's such a glorious morning and I shall be indoors for the rest of the day. And we shall be quite private enough for you to grill me unmercifully.'

She led the way to a table dappled with the shade of an old apple tree in the rear garden, where a coffee pot and cups were already set. Perhaps she was used to having to put people at their ease. Only golfers might be intimidated by her Captaincy, but everyone tended to be in awe of Matron. Or Chief Nursing Officer, as he must now remember to call her.

'Well, this is nice,' he said conventionally, as he settled into his seat and watched her pour. It was.

'But it's taken an event like last night's to bring you here,' she said shrewdly, reminding him where he did not need reminding of the serious purpose of this meeting.

Mary Hartford was not a woman to be caught off guard. Her hand was rock-steady as she handed him the china cup and saucer. Her soft dark hair was unflecked by grey; Lambert, a novice in such matters, thought it was not dyed. Not for the first time when interviewing a woman, he wished he could have his wife's shrewd, reluctant, unprofessional opinion of what appearances might suggest.

The Secretary's list had told him Mary Hartford was forty-nine: she looked several years younger as she sat quiet and confident in the scented seclusion she had so carefully created. She wore no hospital dress, but the crisp white blouse and grey skirt would have been in place anywhere. There was enough lace about the blouse, enough colour about the deep ruby of the brooch at her breast, to suggest femininity. The lightly tanned face had a very little make-up, perhaps applied with care to suggest its absence. The figure was trim enough to suggest the county tennis player she had once been, the features sharply attractive enough to make a chauvinist Superintendent wonder how she had managed to remain single. She was, he decided, one of the very few women who contrived to preserve elegance within the sensible shoes dictated by hospital routine.

Lambert, striving to assess her state of mind whilst he took sugar and stirred his coffee with elaborate care, wondered uncomfortably how much she was aware of his scrutiny. 'Well, fire away!' she said, and sipped calmly at her own unsugared cup: she looked far more at home with the flowered china in her small, manicured fingers than he felt as he grasped the cup with his too large ones. The dark brown eyes looked into his with enough amusement to convince him that if he did not assert his role she would conduct the interview for him. In a different context, she must be as practised at questioning people as he was.

'Would you start by telling me your movements at the end of the Committee meeting last night, please?' he said. In reaching for his notebook and pad, he felt a relief which took him over twenty years back to his detective-constable days.

'Certainly. I gathered up my papers and put them in my document case. The men rushed to empty straining bladders, the women to repair the ravages of a humid evening.' Lambert was mildly shocked by this directness in a woman of her years, then remembered her medical background: this trim, attractive woman dealt in her small hospital with a steady stream of prostates and hysterectomies, no doubt in a cheerful and businesslike way.

'The women in this case being you and Debbie Hall. You went to the ladies' locker-room together?' It sounded vaguely like an improper suggestion and he sensed a little amusement in her affirmative. 'And where from there?' he went on.

'To the bar.'

'But you didn't arrive there together.' It was a statement, and one which showed that he had questioned at least one other person about her movements. A quick intake of breath showed him she had appreciated the fact, but this time he did not look up into her face.

'We didn't quite leave the locker-room together either.' He detected a tiny note of disapproval, but the voice was as steady as ever. 'I went into the ladies' lounge to check on the pairings for our medal competition on Tuesday. I must have arrived in the bar a couple of minutes after Debbie.'

'Did anyone see you or speak to you in those two minutes?'

For the first time, there was a pause before she answered. 'You mean did I have access to James Shepherd without any witnesses?'

Lambert smiled ruefully at her. It was exactly what he had been probing, but he was dismayed to find her following his train of thought so quickly. 'If you like,' he said.

'I don't, but I understand it's necessary,' came the precise reply. 'I didn't go back into the Committee Room or see Shepherd again alive.'

'Or dead?' said Lambert, instinctively and brutally. Perhaps he was nettled by her previous control. Now, for the first time, she was ruffled.

'Of course not,' she said; her voice had dropped a full octave and her eyes no longer looked into his.

Somewhere behind Lambert, a thrush poured out its full-throated, irrelevant song. Whilst she was thrown off balance, he decided to throw in the one other small fact Parsons had released about her. 'You will appreciate, Mary, that I will be questioning all the people at that meeting about their own behaviour and that of others. If that seems impertinent, you must remember that this is a murder inquiry. I have been told that you were very quiet in the bar after the meeting.' He pretended to cull his memory, and produced a phrase as if it were the quotation it certainly was not. ' "Monosyllabic and preoccupied", I believe.'

Now he did look at Mary Hartford, but she did not return

his glance. She put her coffee cup back on the table with a steady hand, but he felt a great effort had gone into the movement. When she spoke, her voice was level, but he had the impression of the same determination and concentration; to his surprise, he felt admiration rising within him for the very control which was frustrating him.

'It may well have been so,' she said quietly. 'I'd had a full day at the hospital, a quick sandwich, and a long evening meeting at the Golf Club. I didn't feel exactly chirpy. But I didn't kill James Shepherd.'

'Nor has anyone accused you of killing him,' said Lambert, just as quietly. 'What can you tell me about the movements of the other people involved?' She shook her head dumbly. 'One of them is a murderer, Mary,' he reminded her. This time she nodded, but it was a few seconds before she trusted her voice again. When it came, her tone was as even as ever—too even, perhaps, because the words came almost in a monotone, which told its own tale of tension.

'Debbie and I you know about. After I had been to check on the Medal competition I told you about, I passed the door of the Committee Room again. It was open, but I couldn't see inside. I heard David Parsons saying something about finance. I suppose Shepherd was in there too, because he wasn't in the bar when I got there. I didn't hear him.'

She had not once retreated behind 'the Chairman' in her references to the dead man. Now her blunt, unadorned use of his surname under stress suggested unmistakably that she had had no great love for him. Lambert closed his notebook, waited for the relaxation he hoped this gesture might bring, and then asked simply, 'Did you like James Shepherd?'

'No.' The uncompromising monosyllable came much more promptly than he had expected. It was followed by a long pause, during which he waited with an impassivity he could not feel. He wished the robin at the edge of his vision would not hop so persistently nearer: it was within two feet of his large black shoe.

'But I wasn't alone in that. And I didn't kill him.' For the first time in minutes, the brown eyes looked full into his; they were full now of entreaty, not amusement. At this moment when he least wanted it, there came into his mind the pathologist's words when he had asked about knowledge of armed combat in relation to Shepherd's mortal wound, '. . . a bit of medical knowledge would do as well or better.' He looked again at those clean, efficient, beautifully manicured hands.

'When did you leave?' he said after another long pause. His own voice sounded to him more unnatural than the suspect's.

'I couldn't be precise about the time, but it must have been soon after ten, because the bar had shut. We had one drink and left.'

'"We" being?'

'Debbie Hall, Michael Taylor, Bill Birch, David Parsons and myself. David Parsons left first, I think: when I came out, his car had gone. His reserved space is next to the Lady Captain's, so I noticed.'

'Did the rest of you leave all together?' asked Lambert hopefully.

'Almost, but not quite. I don't think any of us had our Committee files in the bar, so we went our separate ways to collect them. I went back to the ladies' lounge and made a note of the prizewinners in our spring competition, because I've to present the prizes on our next ladies' day. I may have been, oh, perhaps five minutes.'

Was she striving deliberately to be casual? She must realize the possibilities of those five minutes. Lambert stretched the moment with an elaborate note. 'Were you last away from the car park then?' he asked.

'I really couldn't say. It didn't seem important at the time, of course.'

He was sure now that she was striving to be matter-of-fact. 'Think, Mary. It could be crucial.' To you. To someone else, perhaps. She hesitated, and from brisk Mary Hartford the hesitation was an admission that there was something more.

At length she said, 'A car roared away noisily as I came out. I couldn't see it, but I'm almost sure it was Michael Taylor's sports car. But there was someone still in the car park,' she said, looking at the cups between them. The robin had hopped to the biscuit beneath the table.

'Who?'

'It was Bill Birch. It was almost dark but we called good night to each other.' The silence hung like a tangible thing between them, investing this simple fact with more weight than it should have carried.

'Were you two last away?'

'I think so.' It was scarcely audible. Two sharp minds on opposite sides of the garden table were busy with the implications and possibilities.

Lambert put away his notebook. 'There has been one other unusual incident since the murder,' he said. 'You will know Mr Shepherd's car?'

'The maroon Rolls-Royce,' she said quietly. She was looking at the table again now, but for an instant the cool brown eyes had widened with what might have been fear.

'It was broken into by someone this morning. It could of course be unconnected with the murder, but that would be a remarkable coincidence—'

'In broad daylight?'

'Yes. At about half past nine this morning.'

'Did they have a key?'

This woman should have been a detective: these were the first aspects of the affair that had struck Lambert. 'It seems so, unless the car was left open. There's no evidence of the door being forced.'

'He never left it unlocked. Whoever did it had a key.' For a moment she was following her own train of thought. He watched her curiously, until she saw him and came back to him with a little start. With a grim smile she said, 'At least I have an alibi for that. I was on my ward rounds from nine to ten: about fifty people could vouch for me.'

'That would seem to be quite enough,' smiled Lambert.

It was silly, but it should be much easier to eliminate his suspects from the car entry than the murder. And if the two were connected . . .

He rose to go. 'There isn't anything else I should know, is there?' he said. 'I need hardly tell you that in a murder inquiry it would be foolish to try to protect your friends. The most effective way to safeguard the innocent in these cases is to reveal the guilty.' Pompous, obvious, but he would have to say something similar to all of them.

'I understand that,' she said. She had the air of someone who had assessed all this before she saw him. She had said all she was going to say, he knew. The two professionals stood facing each other across the coffee cups in that most English of settings. They liked each other, these two physical opposites: she trim, attractive, demure, but all steel within; he tall, reassuring, becoming dishevelled as the day's humidity rose steadily.

She followed him down to the low wooden gate. 'I'll no doubt need to come back to you when I've seen the others,' he said. If the prospect worried her, she gave no sign of it to Lambert.

'Of course,' she said with a smile. 'You know where to find me.' She gestured towards the hospital; he could just see its red roof, not more than a hundred and fifty yards away. At the very last, he suddenly stepped outside routine and played a card instinctively.

'One strange thing. Len Jackson seems to have disappeared. He's on the Committee, though he'd given prior notice that he would not be at your meeting last night. I don't suppose you—'

'Len Jackson isn't your murderer,' she interrupted decisively. He waited, but she said nothing further. She was animated now, anxious even, but not with fear for herself.

'Why do you say that, Mary?' She was thinking hard about the question before he had the words out. She shook her head, colouring a little for the first time in the interview.

'Ask Debbie Hall,' she said.

CHAPTER 7

It was less than two miles back to the golf club and the murder room. Lambert wished it was further, for he needed time to organize his thoughts. He had narrowed the field of possible killers, seen two of his five suspects, collected some other important facts. It was fair progress with still a little of his first morning left. Yet he had an uncomfortable feeling that he was further from an arrest than he had been when he started.

He drove through a village busy with its own concerns. The heat had kept things quieter than usual, but there were the usual quota of women pushing heavily laden trolleys from the area's only supermarket, the usual two cars on the yellow lines outside Barclay's Bank. A toddler waved a messily ravaged orange at him from her push-chair, and he wondered as usual that a world of such obvious innocence could surround the evil which was his concern.

There was nothing at the club to lighten his gloom. Members were gathered in quiet little groups at the other end of the car park, discussing the sensational news. They acknowledged his wave of recognition but made no attempt to inquire about his progress; murder could still the most curious of tongues for a while. Within the building, Detective-Sergeant North was waiting for him with a face which offered no prospect of relief. He had been directed to enter the dead man's house and search it for revealing papers or other items.

North didn't wait to be asked for his report. His news was brief, disgustingly so from his point of view, and he wanted it out. 'Nothing,' he said lugubriously. 'I've been carefully through his bureau. Nothing but business papers, and precious few of those.'

'Photographs?'

'Three of his dead wife, framed and obvious to all. An album from his youth. Nothing faintly revealing.'

'Relatives?'

'His wife died many years ago. No children. There's an older sister in Torquay.'

'Have you made contact?'

'By phone this morning.' North permitted a flicker of self-satisfaction to cross his sallow features. 'They weren't close. The locals had already been in to break the news before I spoke to her, of course. She seemed shocked, but not heartbroken.' It was a fair summary of everyone's reaction so far. 'The locals are going back to her this afternoon when she's had time to compose herself. They'll probe, of course, to find if she can name anyone she thinks might have had reason to kill him. I'll be surprised if they come up with anything: she seemed to know very little about his life here, and not to want to know much. I gather she liked her sister-in-law rather better than her brother.'

'Come on, Jim. Think about that house. Smell it out. Didn't it say *anything* to you about Shepherd?' North looked hard at the Superintendent and tried not to be thrown by the unexpected use of his Christian name. He hadn't worked with Lambert before: as a young, recently installed DS, he wanted to come up with something if he could.

'Not much,' he said slowly. 'In fact, the strongest impression about it was how little it said about its owner. It's a rich man's house, opulent without being showy. Everything of the best: a well-filled drinks cabinet, Bang and Olufsen electronics and so on. But somehow nothing seemed *used*. It was all too neat and clinical for a man living alone. Of course, he has a daily woman two mornings a week who keeps it like that, and a gardener five hours a week. I'm seeing both of them this afternoon but I don't think they'll add much. They didn't see much of Shepherd; as you'd expect, he paid them regularly and handsomely.' So they might even be the first people to be upset by this death, thought Lambert bitterly.

'Answer-phone?' he said.

'Sorry,' said North. 'One call on it last night from his
personal secretary to tell him about a changed appointment
today. He must have wiped everything else before he went
to the Committee meeting last night.' Before he rang me,
thought Lambert. He wondered for the tenth futile time
what Shepherd had meant to tell him in the meeting which
had never taken place: he must have had some inkling of
danger.

'Stay with him,' said Lambert, trying to impart an enthusiasm he could not feel. 'Try his bank, his solicitor, his
work. The personal secretary might come up with something.'

'Already arranged.' This time DS North smiled openly,
glad of the chance to emphasize his efficiency.

'You said you'd spoken to the secretary on the phone.
What's she like?'

'A formidable, efficient dragon of sixty, with four grown-
up children and a husband a solicitor.' He grinned wryly,
because he knew the Superintendent's thought had been
the same as his own. A nubile Girl Friday might have
undertaken an affair with her boss; pillow talk intimacies
could offer invaluable leads to a man's hopes and fears.
Lambert felt yet another door clanging shut on James
Shepherd, murder victim. Yet he was not anonymous:
both the subjects questioned had confessed a dislike,
which he fancied was in fact something much stronger
than that.

Bert Hook had stood stolid but attentive through all this:
North was a fellow-Sergeant, even though fifteen years his
junior. Just when forgotten, he made one of his surprising
interventions. 'Did you try his dustbin?'

'It's the American influence,' explained a smiling Lambert to North. 'Young Sergeants like Bert are always alert
for the latest ideas. In this throwaway age, transatlantic
tycoons reveal themselves through the contents of their
dustbins—'

'Trashcans,' said Hook imperturbably.

'Now there's a lovely attitude,' said his Superintendent.

'The dustbin bags were collected at nine this morning,' said North smoothly, anxious to cut short a double act which threatened to exclude him.

'So much for the sociological approach,' said Lambert. 'Now, Bert, go and see Vic Edwards in the bar and order us some of the Club's best sandwiches. If you amend your ways and cut out these transatlantic expletives, I might even run to a couple of halves of bitter.'

'That will need to be after you've seen Michael Taylor.'

'You got him to come here?' said Lambert. He liked the notion of interviewing Taylor where the crime had taken place.

'Easily,' said Hook. 'He said that as Captain he'd planned to pop into the Club anyway to see the Secretary and discuss the situation, so it was quite convenient. He's due here in two minutes.' Hook went off to order lunch and North departed to continue his unrewarding research into the private life of James Shepherd, OBE, Captain of Industry, Golf Club Chairman, and murder victim.

In the midday sun, the panelled Committee Room was hot and airless. Lambert stood on a chair and managed to open the single high window above the frosted glass of the bay. As he did so, Michael Taylor drove into the Captain's space in the car park with a noisy flourish. In the passenger seat of his gleaming red sports car, the blonde girl looked as though she had been installed to complete the décor for a TV commercial, so that he half-expected Taylor to spring from the car and extol the virtues of some male toiletry. Instead, he spoke to the girl in low tones, gestured towards the Club, and extracted a putter and balls from the boot of the car; from his perch, Lambert saw a small bald spot on the crown of his head that he had never noticed before.

The girl was directed towards the putting green, evidently with the suggestion that she should occupy herself there until Taylor was finished with Lambert. It was a proposition for which she evinced no obvious enthusiasm, but she did not look as though enthusiasm was her strong suit. Lambert, striving to accommodate himself to the habits of a new

generation, had not yet attuned himself to attractive girls
chewing gum. She was young, slight, less ample in every
curve and gesture than the delicious Debbie Hall whom
Lambert and Hook had lately appreciated from that same
putting green. Taylor seemed to find her satisfactory
enough; he despatched her with a final friendly tap on her
right buttock, a gesture recorded by the Superintendent
with professional detachment.

When Lambert met him at the door of the Club, he was
watching the tightly stretched denim on the girl's rear as it
disappeared from sight. 'Got to keep the secretary bird
happy!' he said breezily, but with a hint of apology; Lambert
dismissed unworthy queries about typing and shorthand
speeds from his mind as being irrelevant to this inquiry.
'Mind if I pop in first to see David Parsons?' said Taylor.
'I've a couple of queries to sort out about men's invitation
day and—'

'I'd prefer that we got our interview over first,' said
Lambert, more curtly than he had intended. 'I've a tight
schedule if I'm to see everyone involved today.' It was true,
but the real reason was that he wanted to prevent any
possible collusion between his witnesses before the coming
interview. If Taylor divined that, well and good. He wasn't
averse to a little increase in tension at this point. To that
end, he gave the Captain a quick tour of his club, ostensibly
to let him see what the police were doing about what Hook
called 'the nuts and bolts' of the inquiry.

Two detective constables were checking painstakingly
through every room in the club for any scrap of material
which might be significant; they had reached the lounge.
The larger of the two, who were on the floor in their shirt
sleeves, was placing a hairpin he had just retrieved with
tweezers on to a plate which already held several similar
trophies. He moved with elaborate care, too immersed in
his task by now to see any incongruity in the picture he
presented. Michael Taylor hastened to assure them that he
was Club Captain, with the capital letters evident in his
diction, but the constable addressed his report directly to

Lambert. 'Nearly finished in here, sir. We did the Secretary's office whilst he was in with you, as you said. We've done the little room next door, too—the girl says it's the Treasurer's office. There's a locked filing cabinet in there, but you said to leave all documents to you in any case. We've got the front bar, the snooker-room and the ladies' lounge to do yet. The forensic boys will be going over all the carpets with fibre-optic lamps this afternoon. We'll get into the changing-rooms and the showers then. You did say we could keep the whole of the club closed all day? People keep trying to get in there.'

'Please do, please do.' Michael Taylor, anxious to assert his Captain's predominance, rushed in, but it was Lambert's nod that the policemen waited for. As they made their way back towards the Committee Room, Taylor maintained a barrage of breezy small talk designed to preserve the normal relationship on this ground of Captain and club member. Lambert grunted monosyllables, wrapped himself within his profession, and waited.

Possibly it was Taylor's attitude that suggested the move he made when they reached what was now the Murder Room. Whilst Taylor went in as bidden, he called Bert Hook for a moment into the corridor. 'I don't know our Captain very well, Bert,' said Lambert in low tones, 'but rumour has it that he has a difficult wife. I pass it on for what it's worth, which may be absolutely nothing. Usual technique in the interview—come in without invitation from me as and when you think it useful.'

The Committee Room seemed dark and oppressive after the brilliance of the day outside. Michael Taylor plainly felt this, for he had been silenced by his return to this room, with its sinister chalk outline in the lightest part and the stenographer waiting impersonal and expectant in the nimbus of his desk-light at the darkest extreme of oak panelling. He had to be asked to sit down opposite Lambert and Hook; when he did so, he could not take his eyes off the murder weapon. Hook had followed his Chief's suggestion and placed the heavy knife with its long blade exactly midway on the six feet of table between Taylor and Lambert. It was a cheap dramatic trick, but effective. The Captain stared with gruesome intensity at the knife; Lambert shuffled his papers and did not hurry his first question.

Despite Taylor's rather ineffective efforts to assert his position as Captain in his own club, there was no doubt now who controlled the situation. The transformation of the imposing Committee Room into a Murder Room, the heavy presence in a professional setting of the Superintendent he had previously known only as an unassuming member, the macabre artefact on the table before him, all had their effects on Michael Taylor. There was a nervous eagerness about his replies as Lambert took him unhurriedly through the routine opening questions about his movements on the previous night.

'I left the room as soon as the meeting was over. I went to the bar with Bill Birch. We were talking about first team matches and selecting teams—'

'Straight to the bar?'

'Yes, I think so. We'd arranged to talk before the meeting.'

'Who was in the room when you left?'

'Well, Debbie Hall and Mary Hartford left with us, though they didn't go straight to the bar. That left behind David Parsons—he was looking up some financial figures and I was only too glad to leave him to it. And the Chairman of course, poor devil!'

It was the first time anyone had expressed sympathy for the late James Shepherd. Even now, it came only as the last, brittle breeziness of an assumed confidence. Taylor was trying to deal in the clichés of the persona he strove to fit, and the attempt was becoming more desperate as he failed to draw a response from Lambert and Hook which would put him at his ease.

'We had just one drink before the bar closed, then left.' Taylor had continued his evidence unprompted, like a man anxious to conclude an unpleasant experience as quickly as possible. Or a man who had rehearsed his story and wanted to deliver it before he forgot his lines.

'But you didn't leave directly.' Lambert was chancing his arm: neither of his previous witnesses had said this, but neither had mentioned seeing Taylor go straight from the bar to his car, and Mary Hartford was almost certain she had seen Taylor's car leaving after an interval of five minutes or so. The Captain's eyes widened.

'I can't remember,' he said sullenly. Then, more aggressively, 'None of us thought at the time we were going to have to account for—'

'One of you did. At least one.' Lambert's words stopped Taylor as abruptly as if he had switched off a radio. 'James Shepherd was brutally murdered in the twenty minutes which followed the end of your meeting. The Secretary tells me that you left this room immediately after the meeting: if Bill Birch confirms your movements up to the time when you all met up in the bar, we have accounted for perhaps the first ten of those twenty minutes. Can you now detail to me your movements in the next five? Think carefully for as long as you like. It may be important to others as well as to yourself.'

Taylor was shaken by this blunt approach, as Lambert had intended him to be. The detectives studied him closely, watching his surface confidence ooze away as he obeyed the injunction to think hard before speaking. He was blond, fresh-faced, handsome in an obvious way. His present discomfort was the more noticeable because he obviously paid great attention to the detail of his appearance. He was expensively dressed in fashionably casual clothes, his informality being a striking contrast to the old-fashioned decorum of Parsons, who had sat in the same chair two hours earlier. His fawn trousers and crisp green shirt had not yet been affected by the heat of the day and his cravat had been arranged with meticulous care to its every fold. Lambert wondered if he had changed specially into this golf club uniform before he left work to come here. This was a man to whom clothes were important: he noted the fact with relish, for he had a well-researched theory that men who paid great attention to their dress were weak under pressure.

Taylor looked like an ageing juvenile lead in a bad play, about to say, 'By Jove, I could use a drink!' Probably he could: Lambert congratulated himself on the quite accidental placing of the Captain at this point in the day's programme. The Club's bar might be due to open, but the Superintendent had ambushed his man before he could patronize it.

'I went to the Gents',' said Taylor dully. 'After the bar, I mean. Then out to my car and away.'

'Did anyone see you?'

'No. I don't think so.' The answer was a little too quick for a man for whom witnesses meant an alibi.

'How long did this take?'

'I don't know. Perhaps three or four minutes. How long does it take? I had a pee, washed my hands, combed my hair.' Lambert realized suddenly that the large and regular waves of blond hair which Taylor now stroked automatically were probably the contours of a permanent wave.

'No doubt Bill Birch will be able to confirm the first part of your story.' Lambert stressed 'first' just strongly enough to add an ominous note to the obvious query about the rest. He wrote carefully upon his pad. He thought to himself, 'Careful, you're disliking this spurious sod more and more.' There came back to him across twenty years and more a maxim promulgated to him by his Aberdonian CID chief when he was a new detective-constable: 'Detectives who indulge in personal preferences among witnesses will find they inhibit thorough investigation.' Curious how the stresses of an investigation revived memories long dead. He could even hear the careful Caledonian enunciation of the syllables, though he had not thought about his mentor for years.

'I doubt whether anyone saw me after I left the bar.' Taylor licked dry lips; his self-control, brittle from the outset, was slipping away under their steady but gentle pressure. The Bond-type figure who had roared in with his girl in the red sports car, more a piece of self-deception than an established image with others, had already almost gone.

He had drained away through pin-pricks of self-doubt rather than any great emotional outburst: shaken, not stirred, thought Lambert, a whimsicality he wished he could visit upon the stolid Hook.

'There was no one in the locker-room when I was there. I didn't see anyone in the car park when I went out. Damn it all, there's no reason why I should have! We're talking about five minutes altogether.'

'Quite,' said Lambert quietly. 'And the minimum time for someone to re-enter the Committee Room, kill Mr Shepherd with a weapon conveniently at hand, and shut the door carefully as he left is no more than one of those minutes. In two, he could empty the wall-safe as well.'

Taylor's eyes, riveted on the knife between them for so long, flicked up over Lambert's shoulder, to where the wall-safe gaped still half open as it had been found after the murder. The Superintendent did not move at all; when Taylor's eyes came back to his face, he found the same unblinking scrutiny. Eventually, Lambert looked down and made a note on his pad to check with all club members. Someone might have been in or around the car park in the twilight; golfers walked their dogs, even on summer evenings their wives, as well as using the course. They could have seen Taylor without his noticing them: no reason why an innocent man should be searching for witnesses at that time. Laborious telephone and leg work for some young DC over the next few days.

Secretly, he was irritated. If Taylor was not his killer, he would like to have cleared him of the killing at this point. If Taylor was telling the truth, Bill Birch would be able to confirm his movements up to the time when he met the others in the bar. That still left five minutes unaccounted for afterwards: not long, but as long as anyone was likely to have had in this case. So far he had not been able to eliminate one of the three Committee members he had seen from suspicion. Parsons, Taylor, even Mary Hartford— why that 'even'?—could all conceivably have plunged seven inches of steel into the left ventricle of James Shepherd.

Even a man not at the meeting, Len Jackson, had added himself to the list by his mysterious disappearance. He told himself he was lucky to have a limited field; the search for the Yorkshire Ripper had ranged over half a million.

He must turn to motive, and to whatever facts and opinions Taylor could contribute about his fellow Committee members. He had little doubt that this vain, surprisingly ineffective man, surrounded with the obvious trappings of success, was a considerable womanizer. Always a fruitful line of inquiry: in well over half of successful murder investigations, sex figured as a full or partial motive; in domestic killings, the proportion was higher still.

He looked up again at the Captain, and caught him licking his lips and relaxing just a little; perhaps he thought the interview was over and he was about to be dismissed. Had he not been so obviously rattled, that might well have been so; Lambert was anxious to get the evidence of all members of the Committee about last night's fateful twenty minutes as quickly as possible. When he had put the different accounts together, he would come back with more questions. But Michael Taylor was disconcerted, and thus vulnerable.

'Did you like James Shepherd?' Lambert asked suddenly. Taylor's fresh face changed abruptly: his dismay showed as clearly as fear on the face of a child. This was certainly not a man who should plan murder. But thankfully for detection and the crime figures, murderers did not always come from the ranks of those best equipped for the task.

'What's that to you?' A flash of temper. Good.

'It has nothing to do with me personally. It has everything to do with me as the agent of a murder inquiry. Yesterday, I couldn't have cared less about your private life or your relationship with the deceased. Today, I am interested in anything which might give me the smallest help in finding a violent killer.'

It was a risk: he had spoken vigorously, even with distaste. His Chief Constable would certainly have disapproved of his tone. A different man from Taylor might have turned surly and uncommunicative. But he was not that sort of man. He plucked nervously at the gold watch upon his wrist; the colour drained from his too-revealing face; he looked suddenly older as he gazed down at the table; Lambert could see again the incipient bald patch he had never noticed before today.

'I didn't like him,' Taylor said dully, 'and he didn't like me. I don't know why he couldn't have treated me better—' He looked up: for an instant, his blue child's eyes met Lambert's with a hurt appeal against injustice. Then he remembered where he was and his voice trickled away into silence as he stared dully at the table. He was a schoolboy who had owned up to a minor crime and who now waited to be lectured and dismissed.

This had to be explored, but he was not going to say much more without further prompting. 'If in doubt, make 'em sweat,' thought Lambert unkindly; he began the elaborate ritual of lighting his pipe. He set matches, pipe, pouch and ramming tool on the table in front of him, and began to fill and tamp the bowl of the briar with exaggerated thoroughness. Pure ham: Hook looked hard at his notes lest his face should reveal the thought, and Lambert was glad that Christine could not see him now. No one could demolish pretension like a wife. But it had worked before, and suddenly Taylor was watching the Superintendent with the fascination of a dog waiting upon its master. Towards the end of Lambert's performance, he invited Taylor to play a minor role, and the Captain fumbled in his pocket and produced a gold cigarette case. He extracted and lit a French cigarette with the exaggerated care of a man trying to control his movements and conduct his own answering ritual, but his hands shook a lot, and the flickering flame of his lighter etched his nervousness upon the air.

'Why didn't he like you?' Lambert reopened the conversation with studied casualness, apparently giving all his attention to the final mysteries of his pipe. He tried not to think about what Christine would say about his performance; schoolteachers lived in a healthy, open world, where such deceits could be reserved for amateur dramatics. Or so he chose to think. Under the weight of her puritan disapproval, he hardly produced his pipe at all at home now. His wife would have been aghast at the elaborate rite he made out of his performance here—and perhaps even pleased when it failed to work. Taylor was uncomfortable still, but on his guard. He drew upon his cigarette and affected a shrug which was just too theatrical to be convincing. He did not trust his voice enough to support the gesture with speech.

Lambert puffed his pipe, hoping the man opposite him could not divine the indecision behind the smoke. It was not likely he would: the vain, shallow man before him smoked nervously, trying to keep his hands still and look calm. It would not take a lot to break him down completely, but he was the kind of man who would demand his solicitor and wrap himself in all the protective armour his money offered him. Lambert would take this on if he had to, but he was anxious to introduce nothing that would slow the pace of the inquiry.

It was Hook who solved his dilemma. Either he sensed his chief's indecision or he took this silence as his cue. He played his one possible trump card with uncompromising directness. 'What is your relationship with your wife?' he said. The question came harshly, with a hint of impatience, from a quarter whence Taylor had least expected it, and it had an immediate effect. The fresh face flushed suddenly to the roots of the carefully coiffured yellow hair and the pale blue eyes widened with fear as well as anger. He stuttered into a 'What the devil—' but his voice was too shaken for him to trust it further and he trailed away into silence. There was a desperate air about him now, but he could turn stubborn and uncooperative: Lambert judged that it was the moment for the official clichés that might lure him into disclosures.

'I'll be quite frank with you. Sergeant Hook was given . . . an indication, that we should question you about this area. You must understand that in a murder inquiry all

suggestions of this sort must be painstakingly checked out.'
Pompous. And deceitful. Hook had been doing no more
than operating on his chief's intuition. But the Captain's
reputation was a badly kept secret anyway. If Taylor in
turn gave him any pointers about other suspects, he would
protect him in the same way: nine-tenths of information of
this kind proved irrelevant to the case, and there would be
enough difficulties left behind in the club without enduring
breaches among its Committee.

Taylor looked at once furious and pathetic; the colour
which had so lately flamed through his features was draining
away. He looked full into the Superintendent's face now,
and Lambert prompted the pale, uncertain figure. 'Let me
give you a word of advice, Michael, about the way we
proceed. We shall have to question the five members of the
Committee present last night not only about themselves
and their own affairs but about their fellow Committee-
members. If we do not make an arrest within forty-eight
hours, we shall question a much wider range of people at
one further remove from the murder—people such as golf
club members and the working associates of the five people
at the centre of the investigation. There is not the slightest
chance that you will be able to conceal large areas of your
private life. Certainly it will make my work easier if you talk
to me frankly now; I suggest to you that it will also be much
easier for you.'

'How far would it go?' Taylor's voice had a nervous
hoarseness which made the listeners strain for his words
even in that quiet room. The fish was hooked; Lambert
tried not to sound eager as he worked patiently to land it.

'I can make no promises about what will eventually be
seen as relevant to the case. What I can say is that all
statements or portions of statements which are not required
for an eventual court case will be destroyed. If you are
totally honest with me now, there should be only a minimal
need for cross-checking your statements against the views
of other people. If you withhold anything which might have
a bearing on the crime—and you must see that until we

have more information all personal secrets among the five people I have mentioned are of interest to me—we shall be bound to pursue it with others.'

It was his longest speech of a busy morning. He knew from twenty years' experience that it was genuinely good advice, but he was using his reassuring tone as much as the logic of what he said to coax the wavering Taylor into the revelation of a private life he already guessed at. Having finished his counsel, he puffed at his pipe and studied his victim—for that is what the Captain now appeared—with an impassivity which was assured rather than felt. There was pity within him for the increasingly wretched man who fidgeted before him. He also felt and deplored in himself the excitement he always experienced when a witness seemed about to talk about areas he had tried to conceal. Perhaps it was no more than the excitement of the angler about to net a well-played fish; more likely, he thought sourly, it was the curiosity of the repellent urchin who turned over damp stones to see what lay beneath.

Michael Taylor spoke without warning and without look-ing up from his cigarette. His tones were drained of emotion, heavy with the weary resignation of a man who finds himself in a corner and is not a natural fighter. For a wild moment, Lambert hoped he was listening to the beginning of a murderer's confession.

'You know my wife is a de Volke.' It was a statement not a question. Lambert had not known. He had seen Taylor's wife only once, at the Golf Club's formal dinner-dance. He remembered her as severe, slightly older than her extrovert husband, glittering with what to him seemed an excess of costume jewellery. With a policeman's shock, he realized now that the jewellery had been genuine and that the small, severe woman had sparkled under many thousands of pounds: the de Volkes owned some of the largest diamond deposits in South Africa.

Taylor was going on. 'I married her at nineteen.' A pause, then a drooping of the wide shoulders, a confession of what he refused to confront most of the time himself, 'All this—

comes from her.' He looked round automatically for evidence of 'all this' and found himself without tangible indications of what he meant. The dark, impersonal room enclosed him; his tormentors studied him impassively across the big oak table; the knife lay like an accusation between them. Numbly, he tapped the gold cigarette case he had set down before him. Lambert nodded his understanding and waited expectantly.

'My firm is run on her money. She lets me play with my tinpot advertising agency, she says, as long as I don't step too far out of line. I can have drink, cars, business jaunts, women—so long as I don't actually go to bed with them.' A bitter half-smile, a hint of emotion amidst the enveloping self-abasement. 'Ten years ago, when I was thirty-two, I kicked over the traces and left. In three weeks, I was back. I'd got used to wealth. The wage I got as an unqualified accountant wouldn't have kept me in clothes. My wife took me back and laughed at me. From then on we've both known where we stood.' There was no self-pity, only a contempt for himself so absolute that now it was his listeners who were uncomfortable. Taylor stubbed his cigarette out slowly and watched the thin thread of smoke that rose from the butt. He was emotionally exhausted, unconscious for a moment of his surroundings and the occasion.

It was Lambert now who had to remind him of that occasion. 'And James Shepherd knew of this situation?' he said gently. Taylor seemed to bring his thoughts back from a long way away, to focus with difficulty on Lambert and Hook. Numbed by his self-denigration, he answered without any attempt at the jaunty confidence he had pretended at the outset of their exchanges; he spoke now as if the revelation was a relief. 'That bastard knew everything that went on around here. It was his hobby. He knew my wife; he knew the accounts of my firm; he knew just how much she put in each year to keep it going. He seemed to know just when I was in the office and when I was elsewhere. Once he taunted me that he was going to take over my company and integrate it into his. I don't suppose he would ever have wanted a struggling little advertising agency that made a loss in real terms, but he enjoyed watching me squirm under the threat.'

Again the self-humiliation was so obvious that it was frightening. Taylor was staring fixedly at the spot where Shepherd had last stood. Neither Lambert nor Hook dared to intervene and there was a long pause in the airless room before the Captain eventually looked back to them. Again he seemed to have to force himself back to an awareness of their presence and the circumstances in which he spoke. 'There have been women,' he said without the semblance of a smile. 'Probably you know that.' Lambert gave him the tiniest nod, pushing him forward rather than signifying agreement; a pretended omniscience is part of any detective's stock-in-trade. 'Some of them were in the Golf Club. Two of them were serious. My wife didn't know. Shepherd did. I suppose it was easy for him to find out. When he wanted to be, he could be quite a charmer himself, and no doubt other women were prepared to talk to him. Anyway, whenever he wanted to watch me squirm, he told me how much he liked my wife—and how he was sure she would like to hear about my friendships with women here. On the night I was installed as Captain, he did it in front of other people.'

His voice had trailed away almost to nothing again, and he stopped altogether with the misery of that memory. Lambert recalled the jaunty, beautifully presented image of an extrovert Captain, breezily at home with all men, which Michael Taylor had briefly presented on his arrival today. That was his normal persona with the members, and seeing him but infrequently and in large gatherings, most of them probably accepted it. The image he strove so hard to create was more important to Taylor than it would have been to most people. The destruction of that image in his moment of triumph must have been for him a terrible moment. Had this culmination of years of torment from his Chairman driven him to desperate and violent retribution?

Taylor raised his pale blue eyes and looked the Superintendent full in the face with an effort that was physically apparent. But he had abnegated his self-respect too completely to sustain the effort. His gaze fell back to the murder weapon, and now it seemed to afford him not fear but a grim satisfaction. He turned the gold cigarette case over in his hands, but he was looking still at the knife when he said evenly, 'I didn't kill Shepherd. At this moment, I wish I had.'

CHAPTER 8

Taylor seemed on the point of physical as well as mental exhaustion. They would get little more from him at this point. Lambert made a few notes, anticipating glumly the interview he would need to have with Mrs Taylor if they did not find their killer quickly. When he asked Taylor to consider whether he could offer anything useful about his fellow Committee members, the Captain looked at him without comprehension: he was plainly too immersed in his personal shame and distress to be capable of such reflection. Moreover, as he had just indicated he had no interest at present in helping to unmask a murderer of whom he thoroughly approved. Lambert made an appointment to see him at his office the next day to pursue Taylor's thoughts about his golf club colleagues when he might be more rational. Then he dismissed him thankfully.

It was not until the door closed behind the wretched Taylor that he realized how tense he had become during the interview. Both he and Hook stood up and moved over to the big bay. 'Sometimes I hate this job,' said Lambert heavily. Yet he was expressing what he thought he should feel rather than what he actually did; not far beneath his surface regret was the knowledge that they had broken Taylor down more easily, made him reveal his thoughts more completely, than they could realistically have hoped.

This guilty exultation was tempered by the thought that they were no nearer to finding a murderer.

Bert Hook had not the complication of emotions that beset his chief. 'Personally, I hope it's that miserable little sod and not poor old Parsons,' he said, 'but I can't see him having the guts for murder.' Lambert looked down into his Sergeant's heavy, experienced features with surprise. Plainly Hook shared neither his pity for Taylor nor his compunction about their success. Of course, he had not seen as Lambert had that other Taylor, with his cheery dominance of the first tee and the nineteenth hole on Sunday mornings. But there were other reasons why he dismissed Taylor so readily: his contempt was that of the man who has worked very hard for everything he has achieved, who expects and copes with setbacks. Bert Hook was a Barnardo's boy and proud of it, though he never mentioned it. Taylor was to him one to whom the good things of life had been presented free, but who crumbled as soon as the going became rough. His abject performance in the last hour touched no chord of sympathy in Bert Hook, who saw a man who would treat him and the police with cavalier disdain in a different situation. Probably Hook's vision was the clearer one; certainly it was the more practical one for the investigation. Lambert, who saw in Taylor a limited personality in a situation which had years ago passed beyond him, wondered uncomfortably if he was becoming soft at the core under the weight of rank and age.

'Time for those sandwiches,' he said, suddenly anxious to escape the case for a while. The discreet tap at the door seemed right on cue, but it was not Vic Edwards with lunch as he had hoped, but CID Sergeant Harding with his fingerprint equipment.

'All right to take the Secretary's dabs now, sir?' he asked.

'You might well get the Captain's as well if you're quick,' said Lambert, and led the Sergeant with his trays and powders along the few yards of corridor to Parsons's room. Behind the door there were raised voices: he discerned

Taylor's excited tenor and Parsons's lower, insistent inter-missions, but he could make out no words; he cursed the solid oak doors of this oldest part of the clubhouse. He knocked, entered, and took in the scene at a glance. The bottle of whisky stood open upon the desk, but only a single glass was visible, clasped in both hands by the Captain as he sat at Parsons's desk. The Secretary stood over him as Lambert's entry froze them in a guilty tableau. Taylor, perhaps emboldened by the whisky, flashed him an un-guarded glance in which hate mingled with fear. Parsons deliberately looked at Sergeant Harding behind him rather than at the Superintendent. Though Lambert might never know what they had been discussing, he was sure it was not Golf Club business.

'Ah, good. Two birds with one stone here for you, Sergeant Harding,' he said, He avoided the bad taste of including the word 'kill' in the cliché, but brooked no argument about the fingerprinting. Taylor glanced quickly up at Parsons, then acquiesced along with the Secretary in the process.

When Lambert went back to the murder room, Hook was concluding a phone call. 'Very good, sir . . . Helpful of you to call . . . No, indeed. Er, you do realize that we'll need to check? Yes, thank you again for ringing in. Goodbye, sir.'

'Masterful,' said Lambert. 'Have you thought of becom-ing a receptionist when you get your police pension, Bert?'

'Politeness costs nothing,' said Hook magisterially. 'That was Len Jackson, you'll be pleased to hear.'

'Will I, indeed? Why?'

'Because it may eliminate one loose end from your list.' Hook did not deign to remark his chief's wince at his mangled metaphor. 'He spent last night at his mother's house, outside Nottingham.'

'Scarcely the most convincing witness,' said Lambert automatically.

'I've warned him we'll check it out. It sounds the kind of village where someone will have seen him or his car. Especially as he was brought up there. For what it's worth, I'm pretty sure it will prove genuine enough.'

'Did he say why he was there?'

'Evasive. Bit embarrassed. I didn't press him.'

'Quite right, Bert; we'll have to check out his story anyway. Ah, this time I believe it *is* lunch.' Vic Edwards entered with a large tray which was promisingly full. 'Just leave it anywhere on the table, Vic. We're ready for it.'

The steward set down his burden carefully on the table. 'I see that thing's back!' he said, keeping his tray a wary distance from the murder weapon and regarding the knife with evident distaste.

'Tools of our trade, I'm afraid, Vic,' said Lambert breezily, looking at the thick roast ham with approval and checking that the mustard was present. 'Mr Shepherd will have no further use for it, but it will no doubt become Exhibit A in a court case before too long.'

The steward nodded; his repugnance was scarcely assuaged. 'I don't suppose Mr Parsons will fancy having it back when all this is over.'

'Mr Parsons?' Lambert studied his notepad with determined unconcern. Hook began to take things slowly off the tray.

'Yes. It's his knife, isn't it?' Edwards turned his attention reluctantly back to the heavy, long-bladed dagger.

'Well, there would hardly be two around like that in the same club,' said Lambert inconsequentially.

'No, that's Mr Parsons's old knife all right. Turkish, I think he said when he first came. He bought it when he was abroad somewhere.' Edwards made as if to pick up the knife, then hastily abandoned the idea as its grisly associations came back to him.

Hook's eyes met Lambert's even as the door closed behind the steward. 'Parsons said the knife belonged to Shepherd,' he said needlessly. He was seeking confirmation of his own recollection; he began to riffle back through his notes of the morning's interview. Lambert walked over to the pile of typed sheets the stenographer had left behind and thumbed back to the third sheet. 'True enough,' he said. "Mr Shepherd's own instrument" was our Secretary's rather quaint phrase for seven inches of cold steel. Now, why would he want to deceive us about that?'

'Guilt,' said Hook, but with no great certainty.

'Quite possibly. The trouble is that, as we both know, innocent people often behave guiltily, or at least irrationally, in circumstances like this.'

'Let's go and ask him about it,' said Hook, to whom the simplest methods were normally the best.

'We'd have to prise him away from Michael Taylor. No great harm in that. Any word on Colonel Parsons from military records yet?'

'They're ringing back at four o'clock. I had to lean on them pretty hard to get them to move at all today.'

'In that case, I think we keep our powder dry until we have more information. Let's hit him with everything at once. If, that is, we collect anything else,' he said with grim superstition, as if touching wood lest Parsons's military career should offer them nothing. 'Look, Bert, I've had enough of this room for a while and I expect you have. Follow me.'

Hook locked the door behind them and Lambert, carrying the tray solemnly ahead like a high priest, led his acolyte through the deserted corridors and the big main lounge of the clubhouse. Pressing the security handle of the door beyond the bar, he moved to where a sheltered terrace gave shade from the broiling sun but allowed a view of the peaceful green acres of the course. There they said little else until they were half way through the pile of sandwiches and two modest halves of foaming bitter.

'"A land in which it seemèd always afternoon,"' said Lambert, lying back in his garden chair and surveying the distant oaks through half-closed eyes. 'Tennyson,' he added some twenty seconds later, when Hook's silence seemed to indicate that he had surrendered himself absolutely to that lotus-land of sun-warmed lethargy.

'The Hon. Lionel?' murmured Hook. Bert was more a cricket than a literary historian, having been a fearsome fast bowler in his heyday.

'Lord Alfred,' Lambert informed him.

'Sounds like an opening bat with all day to bugger about,' said his Sergeant. Lambert thought this rather an unfair speculation about a man who could cut a dash when he chose to, but dragged himself reluctantly back to duty. He sat upright and put his notes on the white metal table beside his plate.

'We've interviewed three of our five suspects and gathered some information. I suppose you could say we're gradually getting a fuller picture, but not necessarily a clearer one. James Shepherd was for me rather a faceless figure at eight o'clock this morning, a prosperous businessman and Golf Club Chairman, with the trappings of success in his Rolls-Royce and so on. Now he emerges as a rather unsavoury bully who used his power and knowledge for purposes that were almost sadistic. But we're no nearer to deciding who killed him. We haven't really had the chance to compare notes yet on our three morning suspects. What do you make of Parsons, for a start?'   .

Hook was properly cautious. 'He seems anxious to be as helpful as possible. As far as we know, he produced the information about his Committee and himself promptly and efficiently. Black mark: he deceived us about the murder weapon.'

'Which could be the foolish but not unusual behaviour of an innocent man. It's scarcely unknown for those who had nothing to do with a killing to panic when they find themselves dragged in by ownership of the implement involved. But I think there's also something in his military background that he's concealing from us. We'll reserve judgement on David Parsons until we've talked to him further—hopefully with a few more cards in our hand.' Lambert turned to his next sheet of paper. 'Mary Hartford.'

'I haven't even clapped eyes on her,' said Hook with unseemly satisfaction. 'What did you make of your Lady Captain in your clandestine exchange?'

'Sometimes I wish I'd never taught you words like that. Mary Hartford is a lady.'

'Many a splendid female has been driven to murder by gentlemen like our Mr Shepherd,' Hook asserted smugly.

'She would almost certainly be the first who was also Matron of a hospital and Lady Captain of a golf club,' mused Lambert. 'She had opportunity, like Parsons and Taylor. No motive that we know of as yet: I fancy she detested Shepherd, but it needs something more tangible than that to commit murder.'

He lay back in his chair and looked at the azure sky through eyelids barely open: despite his long professional experience, it still seemed bizarre to be talking of murder in a context like this. Or to be considering that trim, compassionate helper of the sick, Mary Hartford, as a suspect. Reluctantly he forced this last thought into his assessment of the evidence. 'Mary is used to death, has lived with it for years in hospitals. She wouldn't flinch from the thought of a corpse like some of the others . . .'

'And she has the medical knowledge which our eminent pathologist says just might be involved in this murder—to kill anyone with one stab wound is not very common, as we know,' urged Hook with some relish.

Lambert shook his head unhappily, admitting Mary Hartford to his possibles but unable as yet to see her as a murderer. Across the course, at tiny thread of smoke rose straight as a rod into the still, warm air above the tree-tops. He watched a kestrel hover motionless a hundred feet above the rough on the eighteenth, then drop like a stone on to some unseen prey. Shepherd's death had been as swift, as unexpected, as expertly executed as that. And yet old Burgess had said when he admitted the possibility of expert knowledge that it 'could just as easily have been a lucky strike'. That heavy knife, with its seven inches of slightly curved blade, didn't look as though it needed too much luck with a desperate hand behind it.

Hook, who had been writing as they spoke, now pushed his pad across the table to Lambert. The Superintendent was amused as usual by the neat, almost prim handwriting which filled the pages of the CID-issue pad. It was so unexpected from this heavy, rubicund figure that he always wondered what the calligraphers they occasionally consulted in their work would make of it. He suspected that the fact that Hook, like him, had been a small child in the days of post-war austerity, when paper was scarce and precious, had shaped his hand far more than Freudian deprivations. Increasingly in the modern force, as typewriter and word-processor prevailed, Hook's hand stood out by its legibility.

'Michael Taylor,' Lambert read. 'Golf Club Captain. Vain, womanizing, tries to create an image which is probably more important to him than to anyone else. Hated the deceased, who threatened his whole way of life because he might at any time destroy Taylor's standing with his wife. Taylor admits he is completely dependent on his wife's money: he has tried to live a different life without it and failed. Query: has he the "bottle" for a murderer? No. But men driven to desperation often commit one violent act. When put under moderate pressure in our interview, he appeared near to collapse. This reaction again would be typical of the man who, driven beyond endurance, has committed a rash and violent act.'

As Lambert read and pursed his lips, Hook waited a little defensively for his reaction. The Sergeant did not usually crystallize his thoughts into a summary of this kind: written judgements could be made to look very silly by subsequent events, whereas spoken ones were more easily forgotten. Having speculated in writing, he scarcely thought his efforts objective, but he was ready to defend them. But all Lambert said was, 'How desperate does Taylor look to you now, Bert?' as he looked past Hook to the course. The Sergeant turned in his chair. At first he saw only the plume of smoke beyond the tree-tops, now thicker and blacker but rising straight as ever into the motionless air. Then, focusing his eyes on things nearer and lower, he saw the Captain and the Secretary strolling by the woods on the eighteenth, Taylor now hands in pockets, Parsons as erect as ever and still wearing his jacket in the sweltering heat. Certainly the

Captain had recovered his poise, even if after watching him half an hour ago they could only regard it as an image rather than reality. The two were in animated discussion, presumably about the course, for both made gestures which seemed related to their surroundings.

The two detectives watched them curiously while they finished their sandwiches and beer. Reluctantly, Lambert gathered his papers and made ready for the afternoon's activities. He had two people still to see: Debbie Hall and Bill Birch. Hook had already set up the first of these for him, but had not so far been able to contact Bill Birch. Now Vic Edwards appeared to recall him to duty. 'Mr Birch on the phone for you, Superintendent,' he said a little self-consciously: it was the first time he had ever addressed Lambert by his professional title.

'John?' It was a relief to Lambert to hear his first name again after so much formality with people he knew. 'Terrible business last night.' Lambert was listening for a trace of grief in the still recognizably Northern tones; Birch had been in the Home Counties now for twenty years, but scorned to disguise his Lancashire origins. There was no grief; rather did Lambert detect a note of elation as Birch went on, 'As they used to say in Hollywood, "He had it coming to him," though I'm sure that's in very bad taste and I wouldn't say it to a proper policeman. One I didn't know, I mean.' He trailed away a little on the last note of explanation; he had been waiting for the Superintendent to interrupt with some emollient phrase, but Lambert had been listening acutely for any hint of knowledge. 'I believe our esteemed Boss was stabbed to death. It's thrown things into confusion here, I can tell you. I've been trying to sort out the works all morning.' Lambert had thought at first that Birch was referring to Shepherd's chairmanship of the golf club; in his hectic round of interviews, he had forgotten that Bill Birch worked for Shepherd. Now he grunted just enough non-committal sympathy to encourage Birch forward.

'I suppose this means our match is off this evening?' said

the Vice-Captain. Again Lambert was lost for a moment. Then he remembered what the tumbling events of the day had driven from his mind: Bill Birch and he had arranged to play their second round tie in the summer match-play tournament at 4.30 this very evening. He thought quickly. The decision he came to would have been considered eccentric, even unprofessional, by his Chief Constable.

'No, Bill, let's play. I'll certainly be ready for some fresh air by then, and from what you say, so will you. I must see you some time today anyway, so let's combine work with pleasure. That's if you don't mind answering questions as we stride down the fairways. We can postpone the serious match for a few days if you like and just play a friendly.'

'Suits me, John. Spoken like a golfer. What a shame it would be to waste weather like this. See you at the Club at around four-thirty.'

Lambert felt his spirits lift. There was a golfer lurking still within the policeman, then. Or perhaps, as Christine always said, a schoolboy. At any rate he was reassured by this little surge of humanity, until he remembered that Bill Birch, whom he liked, was today a murder suspect. He had seemed on the phone open, guilt-free, buoyant with the anticipation of sport in the perfect evening. But that was conduct entirely appropriate for the cool and nerveless murderer the case so far seemed to demand. And even more than the others he had seen, Bill Birch had been cheerfully resilient to the death of James Shepherd, OBE, and Chairman of his company.

Through the thick walls of the clubhouse he heard a faint, excited shout. A heavy vehicle swung with a squeal of tyres into the Golf Club's private road and a siren shrieked its urgent note. By the time Lambert got back to the terrace, the cause of the uproar was obvious. That didn't stop a wide-eyed Michael Taylor, carefully waved blond hair now unkempt with agitation, from telling him.

'The greenkeeper's cottage,' he gasped, 'in the woods by the seventeenth. It's burning like paper!'

Over the trees, the thick plume of smoke had become an ugly black column. As they watched, it spread outwards in oily clouds. Even at this distance, there fell upon their ears the sharp crackle of flaming timber.

CHAPTER 9

With the clubhouse closed, there were not many people about to witness the drama. Hook wished his eight-year-old son could have been here to watch. The gleaming red fire-engine raced crazily across the green acres of Burnham Cross golf course. As their conveyance careered across the fairway, the helmeted firemen stood erect and impassive as toy soldiers. But at the gap where they disappeared between two tall beeches into the practice ground, the earth was rutted from the passage of the greenkeeper's tractor. Here the fire-engine rocked crazily, and its passengers had to cling on like sailors on a storm-tossed trawler.

Taylor, McBrain the Club professional, the learner whose lesson had been disrupted, and the few golfers in this area of the course ran in a ragged procession behind this scarlet vanguard. Parsons moved almost as swiftly behind them without essaying more than a swift march, mysteriously combining speed with dignity even in a crisis, a magisterial shepherd behind his unlikely flock. At a further remove, Lambert and Hook followed with the aldermanic gait appropriate to policemen of rank and experience; it was no more than four hundred yards, and they might need to arrive unruffled amid whatever destruction awaited them.

The old greenkeeper's cottage was a tiny but solid stone-built building, approached by a wide but overgrown track. In the days of the private estate which had stood here for a century before the golf course, it had been a labourer's cottage. The Club had modernized and furnished the dwelling some years previously. The Head Greenkeeper was now accommodated in a new house near the clubhouse, but a

succession of his assistants had occupied the little cottage
in the woods over the years. For the last six months it had
been empty, the current green staff being generally young
men still living at home with their parents. This quiet haven
in the woods, where even the wildest slice rarely penetrated,
was largely forgotten, except when older golfers reminisced
about the course in days of yore.

The end of the cottage adjacent to its single door was well
ablaze and the flames were crackling hungrily around the
tinder-dry leaves in the surrounding undergrowth. Fortunately, the fire-engine had been able to push its way down
the overgrown track to the edge of the little clearing that
still surrounded the old building. As Lambert and Hook
arrived upon the noisy scene, the first hose began to play
upon the blaze.

There was a fierce hiss of steam from the undergrowth.
Fortunately, the trees in their proud new growth were full
of sap; only a few bushes and saplings at the base of larger
trees would perish. From the tiny building, there was a
sudden belch of steam and smoke, as if a dragon had been
trapped within it; Hook thought again of his son. Long after
all flames had died, the firemen continued to play their
hoses upon the cottage, moving cautiously nearer until
eventually they crouched beneath the low, collapsed doorway and peered into the smoking darkness. It was a single-
storey building; the roof had perished at this end but
remained intact elsewhere.

'Good thing we were called so promptly,' said the Fire
Officer when he had finally given the order to douse the
hoses. 'No loss of life certainly, and not much real damage,
I fancy.'

'The building is presently disused,' said David Parsons.
Lambert could think of no one but Parsons who would have
used the word 'disused', which seemed to belong to written
English. Perhaps he was quoting one of his own reports on
the club's assets. A black fragment settled softly upon
the forearm of the Secretary's suit and he removed it
fastidiously. Secretary and Captain cautiously circled the

smouldering hovel; their members watched the firemen reassembling their implements upon the engine.

There was an acrid smell of burnt plaster and decayed wallpaper mingling with the damp smoke. For a nightmare moment, Lambert was back in the blitz, waking as an infant with his grandmother's dead arm across his chest, and fire, water and this same smell all about him. If Hell existed, he had known since that moment that it would smell like this. He steeled himself to go if necessary through that black opening into the smoking hovel: a Superintendent could not indulge in the fears of childhood.

It was the Fire Officer who revived interest in an incident that seemed to have run its course. He spoke in a low voice to Lambert, but the tall trees which surrounded the tiny clearing seemed to confine the sound, so that the words were audible to most of the cluster of people who surrounded the little ruined building. 'It's arson, I think, Superintendent,' said the fireman. His words were almost apologetic, as if he hated to disturb the peace his men had so recently restored to this sylvan scene. 'There were oily rags just through the porch in the main room, and the ends of the timber that had been built in a pyramid over them. Probably just kids. Anyone bent on real destruction would have built his pyre more centrally: the back room's hardly damaged.'

He spoke almost apologetically, as if wishing to play down the sensation of his announcement. For him, this was a minor incident, with no danger to life and no serious damage; there was satisfaction in the fact that his team had responded quickly and efficiently to the alarm. The deliberate nature of the fire was an irritation, but almost certainly stemmed from the minor vandalism with which they perpetually contended nowadays: there could surely be no motive of insurance or revenge in firing this quiet little dwelling in the woods. And now that he had reported it to this senior police officer who was so usefully present, it need be no further concern of his. He had no knowledge, of course, that the rather drawn Superintendent and his more rubicund Sergeant were busy with a concern greater than petty crime.

The circle of watchers, which had been on the point of breaking up, moved forward at the Fire Officer's words. For these golfers, curiosity and the possibility of spicing their eye-witness accounts with an element of drama were stronger even than the desire to resume play on the course. As the firemen fell back, the dozen spectators crowded round the dark rectangle that was all that remained of the doorway to the small stone building. The last wisps of black smoke billowed softly from the jagged aperture the flames had carved in the old roof.

'Stand back, please. This could be a police matter. Though no doubt our friend is right that this was started by kids or yobbos.' It was David Parsons who had spoken, effortlessly donning the mantle of command which nowa-days stemmed only from his post of Club Secretary. For a moment Lambert was ridiculously grateful to him for accepting the opprobrium such seemingly officious conduct must surely bring. And for dragging him back from his private childhood nightmare.

The watchers shrugged and turned away with no more than the odd murmur of disappointment. By the time the fire-engine had eased its way off the scene, reversing cau-tiously down the overgrown track which it had recently covered so speedily, there were only four figures by the blackened stones. The smoke had ceased to rise. Secretary and Captain looked at Superintendent and Sergeant, uncer-tain whether the rights of property took precedence over police procedure in this situation.

'Lead on, Macduff,' said Lambert, forcing a grim little smile. Parsons and Taylor stooped under the smouldering lintel and moved gingerly into the ruin. Hook mused upon the possibilities of literary learning, grimaced, and followed his chief into the darkness.

At first they could see very little. The smoke had black-ened windows already grimy with disuse. As his eyes gradu-ally adjusted, Hook saw how the flames had devoured the exposed beams of what must once have been a tiny parlour, entered directly by the front door which had just ceased to exist. The hole in the roof which gave him the light to see this was directly above the point where the fire had been started and had roared to its destructive peak. A few charred sticks remained in a tell-tale circle around the source of the fire; the firemen's hoses had scattered shreds of rag beyond the sticks. Had the fire raged for another ten minutes unchecked, the source would probably never have been evident. As it was, Hook agreed with the Fire Officer's diagnosis: almost certainly mischievous kids. Or mindless young vandals: the distinction was not sometimes as obvious as the public thought.

The other three now moved through a charred but largely undamaged door to what must long ago have been the single bedroom of the original labourer's cottage. Hook followed them—and stopped as they had done in astonishment. The place not only had been but *was* a bedroom. The double bed against the far wall occupied half the small floor space. Its linen and blankets were crisp and clean apart from the smuts of fire-damage. The musty carpet had been charred and the paint blistered around the door by the flames and smoke. There was a single broken pane in the window, and water on the floor and walls from the firemen's hoses. Otherwise the room might have been in current use. Hook's gaze followed Lambert's to the quartz clock on the bedside table. The second hand crawled slowly around its small white face. The time it showed was three minutes to two. Hook, glancing automatically at his police issue watch, confirmed what he already knew, that this was exactly right.

There was a strange, inappropriate odour mingling with the acrid smells of burnt wood and wet fabric that hung in the room. Hook sniffed and remained puzzled. It was Michael Taylor, more practised in the scents of the boudoir, who placed it for him. 'It's perfume!' he said in astonishment. He picked up the photograph which stood in its neat silver frame on the single windowsill of the tiny room. Hook heard the mutters of astonishment as the three men in front of him bent over the photograph and held it in the light from the tiny window.

Then, for the first time in five minutes, he heard his chief's voice, firm, authoritative, but tinged nevertheless with shock. 'We'd better get out. This place will need to be investigated with proper lights.' The Secretary and Captain moved meekly outside, only too glad to be clear of a room which now filled them with unease. It was Taylor who used the term 'love-nest' and confirmed to Hook's dawning senses the purpose for which the room must have been used.

In the clear summer light outside, Lambert passed the photograph to Hook. A man and a woman, arms affectionately around each other's waists, smiled conventionally at the camera. It was only when Lambert saw Hook's blank incomprehension that he realized that his Sergeant had seen neither of the subjects before. He pointed to the man. 'James Shepherd, deceased,' he said tersely. It was not a very recent photograph, despite the new frame; Shepherd looked perhaps ten years younger.

The woman in the picture was younger also, but her features had altered little over the intervening years. Hook looked from the picture to his Superintendent's face. Lambert's voice, which might have been triumphant, was troubled, even distressed.

'It's Mary Hartford,' he said.

CHAPTER 10

Lambert strode away like a man in a fury. Hook, struggling in his wake, gave up the attempt to match his chief's pace and marched at the military medium he thought appropriate to a veteran cricketer. Behind him, the Captain and Secretary of Burnham Cross Golf Club formed a third and distinct rank in this straggling procession to their club-house.

The Superintendent was already on the phone when
Hook arrived in the murder room, sweating and breathless.
'Unavailable?' Lambert repeated the word into the instrument as though it were an obscenity. 'This is Superintendent
Lambert, CID. I'm in charge of a murder investigation.
You had better tell me exactly where Miss Hartford is at
this moment.' Lambert very rarely pulled rank to secure co-
operation. When he did, experienced men read it as a danger
signal. Bert Hook was very experienced: he snatched his
pad and pencil, sank into a chair, and gave his total concentration to securing a low profile.

There was a pause. Lambert regarded the telephone with
extreme distaste and Hook found his notes on their interview
with Michael Taylor utterly absorbing. Then the cool voice
on the other end of the line resumed. 'Miss Hartford has
just gone into theatre.' So sucks to you, Superintendent: the
voice resumed the air of cool superiority it had briefly
forsaken.

'Into theatre? Surely that isn't usual for a Matron?'
Lambert, shaken by his findings in the fire-damaged cottage,
looked more uncertain than Hook had ever seen him.

'We are a small, rather informal hospital, Superintendent.' The hospital administrator, provided with an impec-
cable and impenetrable placing for his Senior Nursing
Officer, was beginning to enjoy the situation. 'Miss Hartford, unlike some of her colleagues in larger hospitals, has
always been anxious to maintain direct contact with the
work we do here. Whenever possible, she undertakes a
session as theatre sister. I'm afraid it would be quite impossible for us to disturb her there.' Even Hook, on the other
side of the room, caught the triumphant rectitude of this
last statement.

'Of course not. Even insensitive policemen wouldn't want
that,' said Lambert drily. 'You won't know of course when
the theatre session will finish. Perhaps you would make sure
she contacts us here as soon as she is available. Burnham
Cross 4210; the phone will be manned even if I am not here
myself.'

'It is, as you say, quite impossible to say when Miss Hartford will be finished in theatre. Three operations are scheduled and one can't forecast exact timings.' The officious voice, secure of its ground, was not to be deprived of its moment of bureaucratic patronage. 'Miss Hartford will of course be very tired. Theatre sessions are taxing affairs and come on top of her other duties. I'll give her your message but—'

'Just make sure she knows I want her to get in touch. She'll ring,' said Lambert tersely. He put down the phone and stared at it before he said 'Damn!' Very quietly, but with real feeling, thought Bert Hook, studying his pad with intensity and trying to look like one of the room's 'thirties fittings. He had a sudden disturbing image of this woman he had never seen, poised with bloodsoaked hands over an anaesthetized body on the operating table. Now she was an angel of mercy; had she last night crouched in this very room with hands more guiltily red, over another body? He stole an involuntary glance at the chalk outline beyond the big table and was glad he was not normally so inconveniently imaginative.

Lambert caught the movement and looked at his Sergeant for the first time since they had stared together at the faded photograph of Mary Hartford with James Shepherd. 'All right, Bert, you can surface again,' he said with the briefest of smiles. 'We can't see Mary Hartford for three or four hours. What do we do in the meantime?'

Hook ignored the question, sensing where Lambert's mind really was. 'Did she do it?' he asked simply. It was so much an amateur's question, so much the voice of Joe Public, that Lambert had to laugh.

'I don't know, Bert. If you're asking if I *feel* she did it, I'd say no. But she's highly intelligent, highly competent, and on her own admission she didn't like Shepherd. Now there's this photograph, found in what appears to be a lovers' meeting-place. At best she has withheld information; at worst she has deliberately tried to deceive me.'

'At best, there may be a perfectly innocent explanation,'

said Hook dutifully. Lambert wondered if his prejudices were showing so obviously these days. Some part of him obstinately refused to consider Mary Hartford a serious suspect, whilst the rest of him followed thirty years' training in straining for objectivity in assessment. Bert Hook had read the situation too easily for his comfort; probably, as often before, he had merely underestimated the insights of his florid, stolid subordinate. He shrugged, deliberately trying to free mind and body of the tensions he felt about the case. 'We shall have to see her again, obviously. Until then, there's no point in speculation.'

Hook liked that 'we': however modest and unambitious the front he presented, it was nice to be involved as an equal; however incurious he sometimes chose to appear, he was eager to meet this trim, efficient, female mandarin, whom his chief so patently hoped was not guilty.

'What next?' he said, as he saw Lambert checking times on the sheet before him.

'What would you like?' said the Superintendent, with a determined return to his normal manner.

'To visit Debbie Hall,' said Hook without hesitation.

'Your wishes shall be answered. You cynical sergeants should note how responsive the senior officer of the 'eighties is to your slightest preference. We are due to call upon the fair creature in twenty minutes.'

'Yes. I arranged it this morning,' said Hook. Lambert flashed a baleful look at the top of his Sergeant's head; Hook had suddenly found his notes irresistible again.

'Alert DC Spencer to the manning of the phone and the needs of the murder room in our absence. DI Rushton should be here shortly to take over.'

Whilst Hook went to instruct his young colleague, Lambert climbed upon a chair to try to open the high leaded windows to their maximum. With a struggle, he managed to open the reluctant section another inch, a concession it had not made for many years. From his unintended vantage point, he found himself looking down on a subdued Michael Taylor, not six yards away at the wheel of the red Porsche. He was talking quietly to the vapid blonde girl; she chewed still, looking at the Captain with neither curiosity nor affection. Lambert wondered where she had been during the traumas of Taylor's interview and the excitements of the fire. She seemed to have no great capacity for excitement.

Suddenly, Lambert felt very sorry for Taylor. He looked smaller and paler than when he had arrived, despite his physical re-establishment within the trappings of success. As he started the powerful engine, he looked up at the club he supposedly commanded, and was suddenly staring into the Superintendent's elevated face. Lambert, his bulk precariously balanced on the leather chair, felt like an inefficient spy; he had to resist a ridiculous urge to call out and explain that he was only opening the window. Taylor had been attempting a return to panache, with his arm on the back of the seat behind the girl as he prepared to reverse. This was now destroyed: the car lurched back unevenly. Despite the throaty roar of its engine, the Porsche departed from the club without any of the flamboyance of its arrival two hours earlier.

'All set, sir.' Hook had materialized behind his chief on silent size eleven feet.

'Right,' said Lambert, descending with a brave attempt at athleticism from the chair, but knowing that his impassive Sergeant had heard the cracking of his knees. 'Now to the face that launched a thousand ships.'

'Regatta Queen as well as golfer, is she?' said Hook as he gathered his papers.

'. . . "And burnt the topless towers of Ilium,"' added the Superintendent firmly.

'Hmm. Statistically, arson is not a crime which commonly links with murder,' Hook asserted relentlessly, as they passed a bewildered DC Spencer in the corridor.

'But in this case it could be, as we've just seen.' Lambert, if he had not scored a victory, felt he had terminated a surrealist exchange with an unexpected neatness.

In his office near the front door, David Parsons was

sturdily resisting the probings of the press. George Williams, retired Fleet Street sports hack who now ran a golf page in the local weekly, was rejuvenated by the scent of a scoop. He was a member of the Club; this, more than his seventy-three years and venerable head of white hair, meant that the Secretary had at least to see him.

'At least tell me who found the body,' George pleaded with Parsons. 'Were there female hysterics?'

'No comment, George,' said David Parsons. There was a hint of desperation breaking through his patient denials: plainly this was only the latest of many.

'I can't say "A spokesman refused to comment" for everything, David. Give us a break. The big boys will be down soon; you're better in my gentle old hands, as the actress said to—'

'I found the body, George.' The old Welshman turned eagerly to discover who this publicity-hungry ingenue could be—and found himself looking into the amused, experienced eyes of Superintendent Lambert. 'No further news for you yet. You can say the police are treating the case as one of murder.'

'Hardly surprising when a man is found with a large knife in his chest,' said Williams drily. So he knew that much. Inevitable really, once more than one or two people knew. Lambert was glad Michael Taylor had left without seeing Williams. Or had he? There was no knowing how long the innocent-looking old Welshman had been here. Still, the attentions of the press were inescapable: George Williams would be on to the nationals as soon as he left here, if he hadn't already contacted them.

'Foul play is definitely suspected,' said Williams with relish as he scribbled. 'What other clichés can you offer me? Are you close to an arrest?'

'Nothing further for you yet, George. Keep it low-key now and you'll be the first to know when we have any news.'

'Now where have I heard that before?' Williams scratched his Celtic locks in mock-puzzlement.

The CID men turned away from him. There was no ill-

humour on either side. Each knew the rules of this game
from long practice: within the limits of those rules, they
trusted each other. Lambert had his hand on the handle
of the door when he heard the veteran behind him say
plaintively, 'Can't you even tell me what he was going to
talk to me about today?'

Whether the question was addressed to the Secretary or
as a last, despairing appeal for information to himself,
Lambert could not tell. As he turned, a little too quickly to
conceal his excitement, he took in the little scene behind
him. Williams was grinning, as he divined that the last
small card he had been able to play might yet turn out to
be a trump. Parsons's eyes, which had been turned on
Williams with all the distaste he felt for the trade he plied,
were now despite himself wide with interest. Or excitement?
Or fear? It was impossible to tell.

'You had arranged to see him this morning?' said
Lambert. He spoke quietly, but the sudden silence in the
entrance hall of the club gave his words more weight than
he would have wished.

'No. *He* arranged to meet me!' Williams's bright old eyes
twinkled blue and alert. He was going to enjoy this moment.
Suddenly his thoughts were in demand; it was a change
from being held off.

'What about?' said Lambert. If there was anything in
this, he would move Williams quickly away from the Secretary; for the moment, he was content to observe Parsons's
reactions from the corner of his eye.

'No idea,' said Williams reluctantly. Did Parsons relax?
It could just as easily have been disappointment which
made his shoulders drop a little.

'Didn't he give you any inkling why he wanted to see
you?' said Lambert. 'Can you remember his exact words?
It could be important.'

Williams thought carefully: he felt his brief moment at
the centre of the investigation passing from him, and all his
journalist's training made him want to cling to it.

'He said he had something to tell me which I would

find interesting, that's all. I took it he meant some new development at the club.'

Lambert looked directly at Parsons now. 'Are there any building plans or the like that the Chairman might have wanted to reveal to the local press, David?'

Parsons shook his head. 'Nothing. We've just agreed to have a pro-am here next year. It might—'

'Shepherd never told me anything about golfing affairs,' said Williams decisively. 'He always left me to collect such details from our esteemed Secretary.'

'Can you think what it might have been, David?'

Parsons shook his head. 'Not for the life of me, I'm afraid.'

'Did the Chairman often ask to speak to you like this?' Lambert asked Williams.

'Never,' said Williams portentously. He was torn between disappointment in admitting that he was not a habitual confidant of the Chairman and his desire to give extra significance to this moment of mystery in which he was the central figure. His dramatic instincts won.

'Perhaps he wished to tell me something about one of the luminaries of the club,' he said, relishing the notion as his mind developed it.

'It's possible, I suppose,' said Lambert, as drily as he could, 'but we shouldn't—'

'Perhaps about the murderer!' said Williams. His blue Celtic eyes twinkled as fervently as a Welsh preacher's; headlines pranced through his mind as he became the central figure in a melodrama. 'Golf Club Chairman Died in Bloodbath Before He Could Speak!' he intoned. Hook winced in mock horror, Parsons's mouth dropped open in genuine outrage. Pleased with his effects, Williams fixed his eye upon the middle distance and tried, 'What did Murdered Tycoon Wish to Tell Ace Investigative Crime Reporter George Williams?'

Lambert intervened before the scandalized Secretary could speak. 'Keep things quiet for the present, George. I promise you the full story as soon as we have an arrest.

With enough gory detail to give you an "exclusive" tag if I can.' He was uncomfortably aware that beneath his banter the shrewd old newshawk was probably right: if Shepherd indeed planned revelations about someone, that mysterious someone might have silenced him for ever last night. The murderer had chosen a moment when there were at least four others around as alternative subjects, and covered his or her tracks with coolness and skill, but the killing still had the marks of a ruthless improvization from someone driven to action in a hurry.

'When did Mr Shepherd ring you?'

'About six o'clock,' said Williams.

'Where from?'

The old Welshman thought carefully. He would have liked to maintain his position as a key witness, but he had to shake his head reluctantly. 'He didn't say.'

'No background noises to give you a clue?'

'No. It was quiet.'

It was no more than one would have expected. If Shepherd's call was as significant as it now appeared, he would hardly have rung from a public place. The timing of the call to Williams suggested that Shepherd's request for a meeting with Lambert had been connected with it. Probably the late-night rendezvous at the golf club which he had tried to arrange had been designed to secure him some kind of police protection against the revelations he proposed to make. The little silver-framed photograph of Mary Hartford with her arm round Shepherd's waist hung obstinately in Lambert's mind's eye. Others, he told himself stubbornly, might have secrets as yet still hidden.

'This could be evidence, George, in due course. Keep it strictly to yourself for the moment. It would be a terrible deprivation for us all if you became the next victim!' He tried hard to keep his face straight as Williams searched it in sudden anxiety. Hook supported him with a nod of impressive gravity, while the Secretary plainly found the thought of violence turned upon a journalist a sudden consolation in this time of trial.

The detectives left Parsons to stonewall further questions from Williams and went into the car park. Lambert had left the Vauxhall in the only patch of shade he could find when he returned from his meeting with Mary Hartford, but the sun had moved on to it now; when he opened the door the heat was that of an oven. He said, 'You drive, Bert, I'll navigate. I've got the address of Debbie's office.' They were nerving themselves to enter the car when there was a shout from the other end of the car park.

Detective-Inspector Rushton hurried towards them, a man pleasantly aware of his own importance. A man, perhaps, with new evidence to offer, thought Bert Hook, who had seen Rushton, ten years his junior, move from raw young DC to DI, still young for the rank, still keen. 'We've done the car, sir,' Rushton called when he was still ten yards from them. 'There were a few prints, which will need to be checked out against the ones from your Committee members.' Lambert wished his colleagues wouldn't put that 'your' in with such satisfaction; it made him feel this baffling case was being treated as a training exercise he had organized for his juniors. In truth he had forgotten for the moment the mysterious break-in to Shepherd's maroon Rolls-Royce.

'Anything else?' he asked. It was the role expected of him: Rushton, sharp-suited, sharp-featured, keen as mustard, plainly had more to offer yet. Lambert felt a little stab of indignation at a DI without s single grey hair, then a spurt of irritation with himself for the thought.

'There's this, sir,' said Rushton, producing an object he had half-concealed behind his person; like an amateur conjuror, thought Hook sourly. Lambert had seen this mien often before in officers with news to impart to the man in charge of an investigation. It strove for a becoming modesty, but failed before the sense of achievement deriving from some important discovery. 'It was under the front passenger seat. Of course, it may mean nothing at all, sir. It depends who it belongs to.'

Rushton held towards them a small handbag. It was of

grey leather, simply styled; practical enough to hold several items, elegant enough to accompany the most sophisticated outfit. Superintendent Lambert stared at it for a moment without speaking. He could not get out of his head the absurd idea that the bag was exactly the shade of grey he had seen once before that day.

The grey of the skirt that had seemed so cool against the spring blossom in the garden of Mary Hartford.

CHAPTER 11

As the car moved from the narrow golf club lane to the wider road outside, Hook eased the speed up over forty and there was a welcome rush of air through the fully lowered front windows.

Neither of the men spoke. Hook was anticipating the coming interview with Debbie Hall; Lambert was reviewing the retrospect of a day when every incident, every new finding, every interview, seemed to cloud rather than clarify the picture. He knew a lot more than he had known at eight o'clock that morning. They had virtually eliminated those people like Len Jackson who were peripheral possibilities in the inquiry. They had established both the ownership of the murder weapon and the fact that the owner had lied about it. The mysterious violation of Shepherd's Rolls-Royce was almost certainly connected with the murder. But how? The fire in the greenkeeper's cottage in the woods might well be connected, in view of the old photograph of Shepherd with Mary Hartford which it had revealed. Already there was an urgent need for him to talk again to both David Parsons and Mary Hartford. Probably indeed, to Michael Taylor as well when he had more information from elsewhere, for the shaken Captain of Burnham Cross Golf was plainly a frightened man.

All this underlined the fact that he had not yet eliminated any of the three major suspects he had seen from the inquiry,

he thought gloomily. And he still had two more, Debbie
Hall and Bill Birch, to interview. For different reasons, he
hoped neither of them was guilty. But then, not one of the
five struck him as a murderer, and yet he was now convinced
that one of them must be.

He was startled from this reverie by the shrill bleat of the
car phone. He was still disturbed by this latest contribution
of technology to modern policing; as far as he was concerned,
it merely meant that he was accessible where he had thought
himself insulated from outside interference. So it proved
now: it was his Chief Constable. Cyril Garner was brisk,
almost accusing. 'I need an update from you, John. As you
haven't had time to contact me.'

Lambert grimaced at the phone, while Hook gave the
road ahead his concentrated attention; only his ears were
alert to the delicious diversion of a little spat between
his superiors. 'We've had rather a full morning, sir,' said
Lambert, in measured tones which held no hint of apology.
He listed the day's happenings and summarized his interviews with the precision which Hook unfailingly admired:
he was not to know that on this occasion his Superintendent
had been organizing the evidence in his own mind at the
very moment when the car phone had interrupted him.

'How close are you to an arrest?' Garner might or might
not have assimilated the complex array of information with
which Lambert had presented him, but he came up with
the one question which really concerned him. Lambert
smiled at his use of a phrase which seemed to come straight
from a press release: the media were the bane of Cyril
Garner's life.

'It's difficult to say, sir. We still have two of our famous
five to interview. By the end of the day, I hope we shall
have a clearer picture.'

'Hope won't get people off my back, John. Jim Shepherd
was a big man locally. And Chairman of the Golf Club. It's
the sort of label these damned newshounds love to fasten
on. Why haven't you gone straight in for this Hartford
woman?'

'She's in theatre at the hospital at the moment, sir. I'll see her later today.' Lambert was careful not to sound defensive; if the Matron proved to be his killer, it wouldn't do to sound anything but objective now. He allowed himself a rueful private smile: if Mary Hartford was his murderer, the press boys would have plenty of lively copy. 'Lady Captain Kills Golf Club Captain in Love Tiff' was a juicy enough opening to stimulate their wilder imaginings.

'We need progress, John, and quickly. Two of the nationals were on to me this morning. And ITV have just rung. They're threatening us with a camera crew.' Television was Garner's particular bête noir; he had been made to look very foolish a year ago when stung to a moment of pique by an aggressive young questioner at a press conference about a bank robbery.

'Did you head them off, sir?' Lambert was less concerned with media attention than his Chief Constable, but the presence of a huge television van and a camera crew in the car park at the golf club would be a major irritation. He realized for the first time how photogenic the backdrop to this murder was. The green acres of Burnham Cross in late spring, the clubhouse redolent with privilege and the trappings of an earlier era, the Chairman's silent, accusing Rolls-Royce, the woodland cottage damaged by the mysterious fire. He could see the pictures now as the cameras panned round, hear the voice-over filling in the sensational background to these quiet scenes, hinting at scandals lurking beneath the surface of this shrine of respectability. All true, he thought suddenly. Whatever the eventual solution to this enigma, there were certain to be some sensational disclosures for the fourth estate to exploit.

'I've promised them a conference with full disclosures on our progress tomorrow,' said Garner. It was his usual delaying tactic to give himself breathing space. Often it worked; this time Lambert doubted if the reporters would hold off completely with such promising material already available. 'I shall need you there with me,' said Garner, making it sound like a punishment. 'Unless of course we have our murderer under lock and key by then!'

Lambert thought, 'In which case you'll gather every pressman and media man you can and take the credit alone, as part of your push for an OBE.' He had no need to reply to the Chief Constable's last sally, as Garner had rung off abruptly. He pictured him behind the big desk at headquarters, relaxing in the thought of a rebuke administered to his Superintendent. 'Must keep the workers on the ball!' He had heard him say it before, when he had sat by that desk and listened to Garner talking to other staff. Sometimes the retirement not too far ahead seemed quite attractive.

Not for the first time on this case, he was struck by the contrast between their work and its setting. The fresh emerald of new leaf and the pinks and creams of spring blossom flew past in an agreeable confusion. The scents of young growth and mown lawns drove through the open windows of the car. They were on their way to see an attractive woman. But their business was to question her about a brutal murder; indeed, their first priority would be to establish whether this charming creature could be the one who had thrust seven inches of cold steel into the defenceless chest of James Shepherd. Perhaps, thought Lambert with alarm, there was a gutter pressman lurking within him: for he had divined within himself a certain relish at the prospect.

Soon they were on the outskirts of Mersham, and he directed Hook to a street within two hundred yards of the ancient narrow centre of the town. Mersham Office Services Bureau was in an old house of mellow stone. The Georgian windows had been enlarged and replaced, in a style which was not quite in keeping with the original, but the effect within was bright and cheerful. A girl who could be little more than twenty sat behind a word-processor at the reception desk. She looked as cool and comfortable in her sleeveless blouse as the policemen were hot and sticky in suits. Not for the first time in this early heat wave, Lambert wondered why female clothing was supposed by men to be frivolous and impractical: to him, women seemed to adapt effortlessly to the erratic British seasons, whilst men's formal attire was basically the same in winter and summer.

'Is Miss Hall available? She's expecting us,' he said to the girl. He was trying to be discreet, but in what seemed to be an all-female world the two tall men in worsted must shout 'policemen' to anyone who cared to speculate upon their occupations.

The girl nodded. 'Please come through to her room. She's interviewing an applicant for a post but she'll be with you in just a moment.' She led them down a short corridor to a door marked 'Deborah Hall, Manager'. Lambert wondered whether the present vogue for Christian names would ever penetrate the police force; he could not imagine the Chief Constable putting 'Cyril Garner' on his door to still the apprehension in the breasts of young constables.

The room was at the back of the building. There was a small yard outside the window, with plants in barrels, and beyond the stone wall the tops of full-grown oaks against the sky-line. Through the open window, they could just hear shrill childish voices through the still air; the oaks must be the boundary of the local park. Lambert had not known that Debbie Hall was in charge of this prosperous little business. She had told him she worked there, nothing more.

The room had a large desk, with a desk diary and a small silver bowl of roses as its only relief. There were windows in two of the walls; geraniums flowered on the one which looked towards the park. On the other, north-facing sill, African violets flowered luxuriantly enough to make Lambert envious; he had attempted them with only intermittent success for ten years.

There was one good-quality print on the long wall, a small bronze horse on the top of the single filing cabinet. But the room was not bare and functional. The flowers ensured that; moreover, the fine blue fitted carpet was relieved by three elegant armchairs, light in design but able to accommodate comfortably even Bert Hook's sturdy posterior. 'How the other half lives,' the Sergeant murmured appreciatively, as he sank thankfully into the seat and thought of police-stations, with desks which were never tidy, chairs which were never comfortable and cups which never had saucers. Within seconds he sprang upright, starting guiltily like one discovered in illicit hedonism.

Lambert, staring through the window towards the park, knew from the sudden wave of perfume upon the heavy air that Debbie Hall had arrived. She motioned them to the armchairs and he was aware that, receiving them upon her own ground, she and not he controlled the preliminaries of the interview. He half-expected her to sit above them at the desk, in the obvious position of dominance; instead, she ordered tea on the intercom and disposed herself comfortably on the third armchair. Hook had waited for her to sit: now he backed two paces behind her like a faithful retainer and circled her chair on silent, footman's feet to seat himself respectfully in the chair beside his Superintendent. Debbie crossed her ankles quietly, and riveted the Sergeant's attention upon her nyloned calves. Lambert, assembling his papers on his knees whilst he collected his thoughts, coughed irritably. It was difficult enough trying to preserve the formalities of an investigation with people one knew, without one's general factotum suddenly behaving like a moonsick calf.

He framed a slight, official opening smile—and found himself looking full into the most dazzling blue eyes he had ever seen. He had known Debbie Hall for about three years: he understood now her effect upon the relatively unprepared Bert Hook. With almost thirty years of police work behind him, the grizzled Sergeant was unmoved by the charms of girls like the one Michael Taylor had brought to the club in his Porsche. Debbie Hall's warmth was natural, uncalculated, freely given, not a tool to exact the behaviour she wished to produce. As a consequence, it was the more devastating for those unfamiliar with it. Naturally outgoing, used to being the centre of attention, she was yet unaffected and generous. Lambert did not know her well, but no one

in any gathering which contained her could be unaware of
her presence. He had watched her before in social contexts,
telling himself his interest in her effects was professional but
wondering the while if it was the simple pleasure men take
in watching an attractive and vivacious woman. He had not
cared to discuss with Christine which of the two it might
be: wives notoriously lacked objectivity in such matters.

Now for the first time he was himself exposed to the direct
and concentrated effect of those wide blue eyes, at once
uncomplicated and enigmatic, and the unconscious sensu-
ality of the wide lips below. She had changed since her
lesson at the golf club to a soft blue skirt and a sleeveless
cream cotton blouse. This accentuated the corn-gold of her
hair and the honeyed smoothness of her arms and neck.
She was very lightly but quite carefully made up, so that
Lambert wondered if this was the reason for her slight delay
in joining them. As if in immediate rebuke of his cynicism,
a small car started in the yard below the window and drove
carefully through the gates: presumably the girl Debbie had
just interviewed. She looked at him with the slightest of
smiles, so that he had to work hard to banish the idea that
she read his thoughts and was amused.

There was nothing stunning about her features: he concentrated for a moment upon her nose, which was flattish
and insignificant. But those remarkable eyes seemed to
make everything else unimportant; when they were turned
full upon whoever had her attention, it was difficult to dwell
on anything else.

'It was good of you to come to see me here,' she said.
Lambert, mumbling his conventional line about wishing to
disrupt people's working patterns as little as possible, felt
that she understood immediately his desire to see her in an
environment away from the golf club. 'I saw Michael Taylor
driving in to be grilled as I left this morning,' she said, 'and
I knew you'd already questioned David Parsons. I thought
perhaps we would all be summoned there, to ensure that
the murderer returned to the scene of his crime.'

'Or her crime,' returned Lambert drily, with what he

hoped was an answering half-smile. He was aware that Debbie, without any apparent intention to do so, could soon begin to control an interview he should guide himself.

'You think it could have been Mary Hartford or me.' The full lips pursed, the proposition was weighed. 'I suppose it's possible, if either of us was silly enough or desperate enough. From your position, I suppose it looks almost as likely as anything else.'

If it was a prepared performance, it was a very skilled one. The two men were studying her intently; she was no doubt conscious of this, but she gave no sign of strain. It was true that there was something faintly brittle in her manner, and perhaps she talked to fill in a silence she felt uncomfortable, but that was behaviour one might expect of the innocent. Lambert was aware that Hook's eyes had flickered briefly to him with the mention of Mary Hartford, wondering whether he would choose to reveal what they had learned about the Club's Lady Captain. He should know better by now, his Superintendent thought fretfully.

'I didn't do it. But that sort of assurance is no use to you, is it? The other four would all tell you the same, no doubt. And one of us is lying.' Only the tiny, involuntary shiver on the last thought suggested that she was not as calm as she appeared to be. Her awareness of the thoughts of others, her lack of egotism, were disconcerting as well as unusual. And she had coolly assumed from the start that only the Committee members were suspects, he noted. A shrewd assessment of the situation from the facts she knew? A murderer's knowledge of the exact details of the time and place of the crime? Lambert looked into those candid blue eyes and felt again that far from learning anything he was revealing his own thought processes. He almost twitched when she seemed to be answering his thoughts with her next words.

'I could have done it, I suppose. I left the Committee Room with Mary: we went to the ladies' locker-room. I remember we stood side by side in front of the mirrors.'

Lambert remembered Mary Hartford's early directness,

'. . . The men went to relieve straining bladders, the women to repair the ravages of a humid evening.' He hastened to get his next question in before Debbie could anticipate him again. 'What happened after that?'

'Mary went into the ladies' lounge. I think to check the results of our Spring Meeting.'

'And you went to the bar.' For the first time since they had entered the room, she hesitated. He caught the movement of Bert Hook as he leaned forward in anticipation. Lambert studied Debbie's face intently: it was easy at last because for the first time those eyes had left his. She was staring at the carpet between them. But for the life of him, he couldn't make out whether she was concerned about her own safety or Mary Hartford's; it was quite clear from her cool assessment of the situation thus far that she would be aware that she was removing Mary's alibi as well as her own when she said she had left the Lady Captain alone in the ladies' lounge.

Lambert let the silence hang between them for two or three long seconds, no more. Then he turned the screw of tension a little more. 'You finished the evening with a drink in the bar, I believe. Presumably you went straight there from the locker-room?' Usually, he would have asked her to relate her own movements rather than leading her, but he wanted to remind her that there were other statements as well as hers, even that the key statement would be the one which failed to tally with the others: perhaps he was a little nettled by her composure thus far. By accident, it was the right question: her eyes came straight back to his with what he thought was a little flash of fear. Her answer, though, was direct. And not the one he had expected.

'No. Not directly. I tried to ring Len.'

This time Bert Hook wrote diligently on his pad and did not move a muscle. 'Better, Bert,' thought Lambert with approval; it would never do if stolid Bert Hook began to reveal his excitement during an interview.

'This would be Len Jackson?' said Lambert impassively. He remembered Mary Hartford's sudden assertion at the

end of her interview that Len Jackson could not have killed
Shepherd, and her terse direction when he asked why not
to 'ask Debbie Hall'. Well, they had checked out Len
anyway, and he could not have killed Shepherd. He thought
suddenly, irrelevantly, that if Mary Hartford was a killer it
was strange conduct in a murderer to be so ready to exoner-
ate another suspect. But Debbie was going on.

'Didn't you know about Len and me?' Wide-eyed frank-
ness, a look of genuine surprise, no embarrassment; even a
suggestion of irritation that she should have to go over
ground she had assumed was familiar.

'Len and I have been lovers for three years.' It had the
matter-of-fact, passionless exactitude of a sentence uttered
in court and prepared hours earlier with a lawyer's advice.
'I knew you'd seen Michael Taylor. I thought he would have
told you all about this.' It was dismissive, contemptuous.
Lambert saw no reason to tell her that Taylor had been so
preoccupied with his own miseries that he had not as yet
talked about anyone else.

Debbie Hall seemed to have taken a decision. She looked
at the floor in front of her and kept her eyes there as she
began to speak: Lambert felt rather as if a camera which
looked through his eyes and into his mind had been switched
off. 'I attract men. It has been a fact of life for me since I
was fifteen and I suppose I've learned to cope with it by
now; certainly to live with it, at any rate.' She took a deep
breath and paused to choose her next words, without looking
up. The curves of her breasts beneath the cream blouse
moved gently, as if to reinforce what she was saying.

'Most women would love to be sought as I have been
sought, and still am. In fact, it makes life bloody compli-
cated. The easiest protection is to pretend you are experienced, worldly-wise and as hard as nails. Perhaps you
become all of these things if you go on pretending hard
enough for long enough. I've been pretending for a long
time now. I was married, disastrously, at twenty-one and
divorced at twenty-six. I still don't volunteer that readily,
since every half-baked Casanova in sight thinks you're randy

as hell and dying to tear his trousers off as soon as you can get him in private.' There was a surge of bitterness in the tone and the sardonic smile, but the eyes didn't leave the floor and the matter-of-fact, analytical style was resumed immediately.

'There have been men since then. Two of them were serious. I lived with the first for almost two years before he walked out. The second is Len. I suppose that, if I were as hard as most people think I am and as hard as this self-protective shell I've grown about myself says I should be, I would never have got seriously involved with him. He has a wife and two children; they live half a mile from my flat. That breaks two of the rules to start with: never play with married men and always play away.' She paused, as if wondering again how to phrase the next idea. She stared still at the carpet, like one looking for shapes in a fire. For a moment, her fingers drummed lightly and silently on the arm of her chair as she considered her words, but there were no white knuckles, no sudden clenching of the hands, to betray tension.

'I don't think I was playing from the start: certainly it's been very serious for a long time. A year ago we tried to end the whole thing; I went off to a job in Leicester and Len played happy families. For a month we made no contact: that was the agreement. The argument was that only a clean break would work. I've had a few hairy times in my life, but I think that month was the worst I have known. Of course, I presumed Len was coping whilst I tried to adjust to life without him. After four weeks I arrived home from work one night to find him on my doorstep. From that night onwards we have been committed to each other.

'Len is getting a divorce. He was racked with guilt for a year until he reached the decision; I tried not to pressurize him whilst providing a steady income for some manufacturer of sleeping pills. His marriage was on the rocks when he met me, but I suspect it would merely have stayed there without any divorce if I hadn't arrived. Marriages often do, you know, usually because people offer "for the sake of the children" as a reason for their lack of courage to confront reality. In six months, Len's divorce will be final and we shall marry. Strange how two people who have been severely mauled by the institution are so ready to rush into marriage again. I suppose we both think we're older and wiser. But it will work.'

With this final bold and unexpected sentence, she raised her eyes and fixed them again upon Lambert, with a defiance that was none the less robust for its touch of humour. Neither he nor Hook had spoken for a long time; the lines of the interview had been determined by its subject. Lambert felt that the argument was about to pass into sociological and philosophical areas if he did not arrest it. When he now attempted a gentle nudge back into the central ground of the inquiry, it sounded to him jarringly banal.

'Thank you, Debbie, for filling in the picture. It's much better and less embarrassing for us than having to dig these things out. I have to ask you if you think all this could have a bearing on this inquiry.'

'If I sat where you are it could.' She replied so quickly and decisively that it was clear she had weighed the issue carefully herself before the interview. Lambert said nothing, but as he raised his eyebrows quizzically he leaned forward expectantly. It was a movement that was almost a professional tic, for out of the corner of his right eye he noticed Hook making the same movement in unison. Like two bloody hippos attempting formation dancing, he thought, and knew from Debbie's smile that she had noticed their concerted eagerness to encourage.

He reached into his pocket for his pipe, then left it where it was, lest this alert, underestimated woman should see through his smoker's pantomime of deliberation. 'What was your relationship with the deceased?' he asked; thrown off balance, he hoped the stuffiness with which the question was framed would mask the desperation of ideas from which it sprang.

It was a lucky bull's eye, which probably preserved his reputation for shrewdness with Debbie Hall.

'I was coming to that,' she said. 'Probably you know most of it. If you don't, you will certainly be told, so it might as well be by me.' Lambert grunted a non-committal acknowledgement, content to accept an omniscience he did not possess if it served his purpose. 'James Shepherd was my employer for three years immediately after my divorce.' She paused for so long that the two large, patient men opposite her began to fear that she was closing up on them. Neither attempted to break the heavy silence; a scream of delight from a child on a distant swing rang unnaturally loud through the open window behind them. Debbie Hall, for once immersed in herself, was searching again for precise words in which to express difficult facts; and again she eventually found them.

'For a time I was his personal assistant. I was also almost but not quite his mistress.' Lambert tried to thrust from his mind the salacious speculations this curious phrase evoked, the visions of tumbled couches and what witnesses in court called 'heavy petting'. Fortunately for him, those all-divining blue eyes were no longer trained upon his, so that his unworthy conjectures passed unnoticed as he resolutely regarded the wall beyond those ample and appealing curves.

'Shepherd was quite capable of charm when he wanted to exercise it. It took me a while to realize that it was the charm of a snake before it strikes. If you had asked me which member of that Committee could have knifed someone in cold blood and quietly joined the rest of us for a drink, I would have said James Shepherd. I suspect several others would say the same. I suppose it is because someone hated him as desperately as I did that he was killed.'

This intense statement coincided with the resolution in Lambert's brain of a puzzle that had been nagging there since Debbie Hall joined them. There was some connection with events earlier in this tumbling day that he had not been able to make. Now, in the moment of maximum concentration upon Debbie's uncompromising words, it came to him when he least expected it. It was the distinctive perfume which had announced to them Ms Hall's considerable presence in this room: he had smelt it earlier in the day. Not much more than an hour earlier. When he had been looking at a photograph of Shepherd with his arm round the waist of Mary Hartford. It had been the scent that was stronger than all the odours of fire, damage and decay. In the bedroom of that fire-damaged cottage, the perfume upon those crisp sheets had been that of Debbie Hall.

CHAPTER 12

For the moment, Lambert thrust this stunning new fact to the back of his mind. It would be time enough to weigh all the evidence when he had Debbie Hall's account of last night's events.

She was the fourth person that day to declare a hatred for Shepherd. The others had been victims of emotional outbursts, releasing under the stress of examination what they had planned to conceal. But a cool brain operated beneath the sex-symbol exterior of the woman who spoke now. It had planned in outline the whole of the statement she was now making. There was something eerily inappropriate about the whole performance. Had she been tiresomely juvenile, a creature of heaving bosom, fluttering eyelids and easy tears, Lambert would have dealt easily with her. A touch of hardness from him, a few hints of weary impatience, and any attempt at secrecy would have dropped away with the artificiality of her manner. As it was, she was conducting her own interview, but paradoxically revealing just what he wanted to know.

At least, that appeared to be the case. It occurred to him uncomfortably that the coolness of this approach matched that of the murderer on the previous evening. The maxim that if one wished to lie one should tell the truth wherever possible, concealing the important pimple of dishonesty within a mountain of demonstrable truth, seemed to be appreciated by far too many modern criminals. For the moment, he was out of his depth. Watch, listen, record, digest afterwards, he told himself: the advice he gave to aspiring CID men at training courses. He had not often felt so inadequate as he did now, gripping his ball-pen sweatily and frowning at the pad in front of him with what he hoped was a competent air.

Debbie Hall seemed fortunately unaware of his uncertainty, wrapped as she was in her cocoon of concentration. 'James Shepherd got his pleasure from taunting other people. It took me some time to realize that. He was interesting, attractive even: someone of a type I'd never met before. He had real power, and power always fascinates women, even when they pretend it's something different. Certainly it was flattering to receive the attention of the head of the firm. Not that the reasons matter—I'm just trying to explain to myself how I could ever have found him attractive. Anyway, I eventually backed away when I saw how he delighted in damaging other people. Not just mischief either: if he could wreck whole lives, he then felt satisfied and looked for someone else to harm. Like most women, I felt I could change things, warm away this black ice that was at his centre. Of course, I was wrong. Women don't change anything in a man that's deeply rooted when they get there and they end by getting broken themselves . . .'

She suddenly looked nervously at Lambert and Hook. 'Sorry about the trick-cyclist bit!' With a wan smile, she resumed her concentration upon her feet. She was finding this difficult, but she was perfectly in control of herself. She was totally still and quiet, yet her pose and her voice showed the effort of self-discipline she had determined upon and was now carrying through. 'I made two or three efforts to save unsuspecting people from his malice, saw the savagery of his reaction to me, and backed off quickly. By the time I ended our relationship, he knew all about me. I said that the period after my divorce was a difficult one, and I suppose there was quite a lot to know. When I was attracted to him, I hadn't held back information about myself: it's not my way and I probably needed a confidant anyway. Shepherd was a good listener when he wanted to be; later I realized why. His mind stored information like a computer.'

There was another of those lengthy pauses which they knew better than to interrupt. Somewhere in the far recesses of the building the rattle of a typewriter could be faintly heard. Debbie's hands clenched and unclenched slowly. Lambert, able to study her face at leisure because of her downcast eyes, saw her older than her years, for the first time in his experience. The beginnings of crow's feet around the eyes were noticeable, the full lips now thinner and paler, the hair merely untidy rather than attractively casual. the golden tan on the peaches-and-cream complexion was all at once a less effective disguise for the first signs of wrinkling around the chin and neck. He realized the effort of self-control that had gone into this quiet, straightforward account. When she suddenly grasped the wooden arms of the chair, her knuckles glowed white and that self-control seemed in danger of failing. But when the voice resumed eventually, its tone was as measured as ever, belying the lurid nature of the material.

'When I broke off our affair, he was furious, with a cold anger I had never met before. For a month, he left me alone. Then I found he was beginning to attack two of the men I had told him about. I had slept with both of them and they both worked for the firm. Shepherd set about destroying them both in their careers and in their private lives. And he made it clear to them that it was happening as a result of my revelations to him. I had had no serious attachment to either of the men, and by this time I scarcely saw them. But they were about to suffer because of my careless tongue. Oh, I've no doubt that there was more dirt to dig and that Shepherd dug it; he was an expert at that sort of thing and he had all the machinery to do it. But he let me think their coming downfall was all due to me and I believed him.' Another, shorter pause, then a deep, shuddering breath before she spoke on, in the passionless monotone of one under hypnosis.

'I went to bed with him to protect them. It was useless. You policemen say it's no use trying to buy off a blackmailer, and you're right of course. Anyone standing outside sees the game much more clearly. This game was soon played out. Shepherd knew what I felt for him even as he took me. Curiously enough, he didn't seem to mind much. I suspect sex never gave him much satisfaction anyway. He seemed more pleased to have debased me in this way than to have me genuinely responding to him. He threw me out, sacked the two men, and made sure they had to crawl into lower-level jobs elsewhere. It was no more and no less than he did to people all the time.'

The pause this time had an exhausted relief. This was perhaps the part of her story that had troubled her most in prospect. This time, Lambert seized the opportunity to prompt her.

'People like David Parsons?' he said. Debbie looked at him sharply, then smiled slowly.

'Like Colonel/Major David Parsons,' she agreed. 'David and I poured out our troubles to each other over the gin one night after Shepherd had played cat-and-mouse with us at a meeting of my House and Catering Committee at the Club. And like poor, pathetic, randy Mike Taylor. And of course like Len.'

She was not looking at them: Lambert prayed that Hook's sharp, involuntary intake of breath would pass unnoticed, and was rewarded. Debbie was again sufficiently immersed in her own trauma to be unaware of their reactions.

'I told you that Len and I have been meeting for three years and that we are going to marry after his divorce. We tried to keep our affair away from Shepherd, but of course it was hopeless as it became serious. Len left the firm and got a parallel position elsewhere before Shepherd knew anything. He's too good an engineer not to be in demand.' For a moment, her pride flashed through and she was an adolescent, blushing in the quality of her man. 'Perhaps that alerted Shepherd's suspicions. At any rate, he was on to us immediately afterwards. Len's wife had anonymous notes about us. His old mother got a letter over the faked signature of a family friend asking her to intervene with Len to save his marriage. Even Len's children were approached on the way home from school with tales of their father's sins . . . If his marriage hadn't been already finished Shepherd would have seen it off. I think if he'd been content merely to prise Len and me apart he'd have succeeded; one can only take so much of that sort of thing. But he didn't stop there. When I left Len and took up my new post in Leicester, I found a dossier of smut had arrived on the manager's desk the morning before I walked in.

'It was horrible: all his undoubted talents for organization and a small part of an efficient industrial machine turned against us. I know all about persecution complexes; this was genuine persecution. I had glimpsed it being applied to others when I was close to Shepherd, but I had no idea of its range and its crushing persistence.'

'What about the police?' asked Lambert as she paused again. This elicited a rueful, weary smile and a flash of those azure eyes.

'We tried that. They obviously didn't see neurotic adulterers as a priority for their resources. They made a token investigation, but Shepherd had covered his traces too well. The fact that he's a local bigwig and I'm no doubt a woman with a certain reputation can't have helped. Most of the people he used were well-meaning busybodies who thought they were trying to hold together a family. There was nowhere anything which could be traced back to Shepherd himself.

'Perhaps it warned him off, or perhaps he'd done his damnedest and turned his attentions to someone else. For a long time he confined himself to social insults, to embarrassing us at the golf club and so on. Most people we care about know all about us and our plans, and that in itself has become a sort of insulation.

'A month ago, after a meeting of the Committee, he waved a bundle of my letters in front of my nose and said he was so happy for Len and me. The letters were to Shepherd and others at around the time of our association. He said it was good to know Len and I had no secrets from each other: he proposed to send Len the letters shortly as his wedding present.'

Lambert did not realize how much he had warmed to Debbie Hall during her long and difficult recital. Obliquely to his left, he could see the wide eyes of Bert Hook belying the detachment of his pose and showing that he was aghast. Lambert wondered if they would be extending the same sympathy to a male witness, and hastily dismissed this professional query as egocentric nonsense.

'Wouldn't the simplest solution have been simply to tell Len what to expect and disarm Shepherd that way? You seem to have weathered too much together not to be able to get through this. Not that it's my business of course.' This lame disclaimer sprang from his suspicion that he was beginning to act more like a welfare counsellor than a dispassionate recorder of evidence. He told himself firmly that there was a murder motive here, which he was merely investigating fully and quite properly. His suggestion provoked in Debbie the first quick, animated movement since the interview began. It was a fleeting gesture of impatience: her hand flicked suddenly and her head shook sharply and dismissively.

There followed another long silence; she sat still as a blonde sphinx as she weighed her words once more. 'Len Jackson is a very conventional, very ordinary man in lots of ways. I happen to love him very much and I know I can make him happy, so he's not ordinary to me. I've told him of my previous affairs, of the difficult period after my divorce when I tumbled in and out of bed in search of myself, of my time with Shepherd. At least, I've told him as far as he would let me; he always waves it aside and, while he knows about my past, I know the thought of it disturbs him. The squalid detail would upset him far more than he realizes.

'I don't know what exactly is in those letters. They were written a long time ago when I was mentally and physically disturbed. No doubt they are very frank, very foolish, and viewed in the right light very desperate. They say things about my desires, about my own and other people's bodies, which should be whispered under the sheets, not put on paper. They are the pleadings of a neurotic woman whom I left behind a long time ago, a woman Len does not know. I was going to tell Len what to expect, to prepare him for the bombshell. Probably we should have weathered it as we have other things. But it would have hurt my poor Len almost more than I could bear.'

For the first time the voice cracked, the tears pressed against the back of the throat. In five seconds, she had control of herself and looked Lambert defiantly in the eyes. 'If I had thought I could protect Len from those letters by killing Shepherd, I might well have done it,' she said.

The melodramatic challenge of the statement was wrapped in the cool, steady, carefully weighed delivery she had employed throughout the interview. Only the slight trembling of her fingers as they now relaxed on the arm of the chair betrayed the weight of emotion. Only the perceptible relaxation of her shoulders suggested that her statement was now complete. This time the silence was one that she was not going to break.

Lambert tapped his pen for a few moments on his pad: it was an excuse not to confront those disturbing eyes until he was sure where to go next. 'You realize that from the facts as we know them at the moment, you could have done just that? Killed him last night and removed these letters?' He uttered the last two words with a dismissive, belittling scepticism which implied that they might not even exist, though he felt it unworthy of him even as he did so.

'There will be photo-copies of them in a file somewhere. probably in an envelope addressed to "Mr L. Jackson". You forget I know Shepherd's methods well.' It came too quickly for comfort, and neither of the men could conceal his surprise at her shrewd assessment. 'Oh yes, I'd weighed all that. The thought of killing Shepherd has been a delicious piece of escapism for me for three years. But I didn't do it. The thought of him dead by someone else's hand is a marvellous bonus which I would never have dared to hope for.'

'Even though that hand might have been Mary Hartford's?' It was Hook. Speaking for the first time since the interview began. And by God, you old sod, that's below the belt, thought Lambert. But it worked; it shocked Debbie Hall out of the control she had fought so hard to retain.

'That's rubbish!' she snapped. 'Mary isn't a killer. Besides, she was with me after the meeting—'

'That isn't true, Debbie, as you said at the beginning of this interview,' Lambert said quietly. He realized that Hook thought Mary Hartford was their killer and was anxious to complete the evidence, but he was selfishly grateful to his Sergeant for returning the initiative to him. 'You and Mary went your separate ways for a vital couple of minutes before entering the bar. Mary says she was in the ladies' lounge throughout those minutes. So far we have only her word for that. Now, you say you rang Len during those two or three minutes. Presumably he can confirm that.'

'No. I didn't get through.' There was a flat exhaustion in her voice now, showing how much the earlier, measured revelations about her past had cost her. There was a pause, the knowledge seeping into both their minds that now she too had no alibi for those vital minutes.

'Damn!' thought Lambert. 'Damn! Damn! Damn!' It was quite selfish. He was interviewing his fourth suspect and none of them so far could be eliminated as a killer. The thought of Debbie Hall's perfume in that secret love-nest at the old cottage came confusingly back.

'I tried the code twice,' said Debbie, 'but got the same reply: "All lines to Nottingham are engaged. Please try later."' She tried to mimic the operator's irritatingly cheerful tones, but in her emotional fatigue she could not bring it off.

'Where were you ringing Len?'

'At his mother's house. He'd gone there to tell her we're going to get married. He was dreading it: she's a conventional woman, fond of her grandchildren. I wanted to let him know I was thinking of him.' A little smile flitted across her pallid features: she recognized the adolescent anxiety of the last sentence and its incongruity in a woman approaching middle age.

'So you gave up the phone in disgust. What then?'

She shrugged, happy in the thought that this was nearly over. 'I went straight to the bar.'

'Past the door of the ladies' lounge?'

'Yes.' A sudden gasp, which she was not quite quick enough to suppress; she had seen where his questioning was leading her.

'Which was open?'

'Yes.' Scarcely audible.

'So you saw Mary Hartford in there?'

She looked at the floor in silence for so long that he thought he was going to have to repeat the question. 'No. But I didn't go in to check. She could have been behind the door.'

'But she wasn't where you would have expected her in the main body of the room. You don't believe she was in there at all, do you?'

She shook her head wretchedly, still looking at her feet. When eventually she raised the wide blue eyes to look at him, they were full of misery. 'I called her name but she didn't reply. So I presumed she was already in the bar.'

'But she wasn't.'

She sighed unhappily. 'No. Bill Birch and Michael Taylor were there, and David Parsons arrived just in front of me. Mary Hartford came in just afterwards.'

'Can you do any better than "just afterwards", Debbie?'

A pause for thought, an exhausted shake of the head. 'Not really. Perhaps two minutes, but I wouldn't be able to swear to that in court.'

'Of course not. No one knew minutes would be so important at the time. If it consoles you, that tallies with other people's evidence.' Again she tried to smile, perhaps in acknowledgement of this gentle treatment as she strove to conceal her distress. Lambert wondered afterwards whether

his gentleness had been a deliberate tactic or whether instinct deriving from long experience had led him to set her
up in this way for his next question.

'Did you notice anything about Mary's demeanour?' he
asked quietly. Now those remarkable blue eyes stared into
his again, and misery was replaced by another, more active
emotion. Fear. Whether for herself or for her friend he could
not tell. He saw alarm turning as it will to hostility and
tried to stop her clamming up.

'We need to ask. This is a murder inquiry, Debbie.'

'Why just about Mary?'

'Not just about Mary. We shall come to the others. We've
been told already that Mary didn't seem her usual self.'

'By Mike Taylor, I suppose!' For a moment her dislike
blazed clearly. By now it didn't surprise Lambert, but
he realized that before he began the investigation he had
expected Michael Taylor and Debbie Hall, who had obvious
physical similarities, to exhibit similar traits of character.
At least he had learned something about the personalities
involved in this business, he thought wryly. He did not
confirm or deny her supposition about the Captain. After a
pause, Debbie Hall told him what he wanted.

'Mary was quiet. Preoccupied, I suppose. She obviously
didn't want to talk and eventually we left her to herself.
We weren't there more than another five minutes,' she
concluded defensively.

Lambert made a note and did not comment. 'Now, the
question you yourself almost asked just now. Were there
any departures from the norm in the behaviour of any of
the three men with you in the bar?'

Debbie considered. She looked again at Lambert and a
little flash of amusement passed between them as he read
her mind. Having singled out Mary Hartford, she would
like to have found at least a touch of suspicion in the
behaviour of one of the others. She could not.

'No. Bill Birch tried to tease me a bit but neither of us
was in the mood. David Parsons was courteous and correct
as usual. Mike Taylor was tiresome but harmless.' It was

almost a thumbnail sketch of the three; perhaps it seemed so to her, for she gave a tiny giggle that revealed her tension, then took a hasty sip of her cold tea.

She needed all her concentration to keep the cup steady, to avoid a tell-tale rattle of china as she replaced cup on saucer. Lambert nodded to Hook while she was thus preoccupied, and the Sergeant took the cue for which he had waited so patiently. The case against Mary Hartford was building nicely, he thought. This might be a key moment. With the solemnity due to the importance of this thought, he produced the grey handbag from his briefcase. Debbie Hall stared at it in horror, like a rabbit cornered by a stoat.

'Mr Shepherd's car was in the car park overnight,' said Lambert.

'The maroon Rolls-Royce,' said Debbie, needlessly and well-nigh silently.

'Exactly. Someone—we don't know who—broke into it this morning. Naturally, our team has examined the car in great detail since then. There are some fingerprints, which will probably be identified in due course. Under the front passenger seat was this handbag.' Debbie Hall stared at it in astonishment and alarm, the blue eyes growing yet larger in her apprehension.

Let it not belong to someone quite outside the case, prayed Lambert. Let it be Mary Hartford's, thought Hook more simply. Debbie Hall turned slowly to the Superintendent.

'That bag is mine,' she said.

CHAPTER 13

The two detectives had risen to go. After Debbie Hall's admission, the three stood for a moment in a tableau of surprise. Away beyond the trees, a woman called to her children to be careful and a dog barked excitedly; in the silence of that room, they sounded unnaturally close.

For a moment, shock and alarm transfixed the trio. Then in each mind there followed speculation. It was Hook, standing awkwardly with the small grey handbag still in both his large hands, who voiced the first thought, and re-animated the frozen grouping.

'Have you been in Mr Shepherd's car recently?' he asked.

'No.' The answer came almost before the question had been framed. Hook was too well-versed in his chief's methods to help the shaken woman. The two men waited patiently while the silence seemed to menace her. She said nothing, perhaps more because she could not trust herself to speak than from any caution about her situation.

Hook glanced at Lambert, sensed his timing without any overt sign from the Superintendent, and said very quietly, 'Can you tell us then how your bag came to be in his car?

'No!' Again the monosyllable came quickly, but this time with a tremulous note of panic at the back of the throat. This extrovert mistress of social situations was not far from hysteria, and that would help no one.

Tension had not so far secured any revelations. Hook tried one more question. 'When were you last in Mr Shepherd's car?'

A little frisson of horror touched those perfectly formed shoulders, then became a tremor which ran through the entire voluptuous frame. 'Ages ago. A year, maybe two years, maybe even more.' Her hand flicked impatiently at the wave of golden hair that had fallen unbidden across her right eye. 'Why should you believe me anyway?' The petulant, exhausted tone was a warning: soon she would dissolve into tears or screaming and they would get no more out of her.

Lambert, reading the signs, tried a different, conciliatory tack. 'Why shouldn't we believe you? You were honest, even painfully honest, with us earlier. A handbag isn't a murder weapon: we've already got that.' He smiled at the pallid face a yard from his and was relieved to see gratitude appear briefly in those azure circles. 'When did you last have this handbag?'

Debbie Hall thought hard, and Lambert felt a rush of sympathy for the shaken woman who was striving so hard for control where adolescent collapse might have seemed an easier option. 'A few days, maybe a week ago. Wait a minute, I can tell you exactly.' With the return of normal thought processes came a spurt of confidence, so that she reached for her desk diary with hands that, if they shook still, obeyed the commands of her brain more efficiently than they might have done a moment earlier.

'May 5th. Eight days, then. We had a meeting of the Social and Wines Committee to plan the Captains' Day evening. My bag disappeared after that meeting. At first I thought someone had taken it by mistake, or that I'd left it somewhere in the club and someone would hand it in for me. Eventually I had to accept it had been taken; we've had a lot of petty pilfering around the club recently, as you no doubt know.'

'An unfortunate fact of modern life,' nodded Lambert, still smoothing away tension. 'Was James Shepherd at your meeting?'

'He was.' She had anticipated his question: her mind was ticking efficiently again. 'As you know, John, the Chairman and Secretary have the right to attend meetings of all sub-committees. Shepherd often came to mine. He didn't say much, but sat with a supercilious smile, as if he found my efforts at Chairmanship a perpetual source of amusement.'

'I'm sure you're a very efficient Chairperson.' Lambert meant it, though the clumsy word fell awkwardly from his tongue even after much recent practice. 'Presumably as the meeting was about the joint Captains' Day Michael Taylor and Mary Hartford were also there?' he prompted.

'Yes. And Bill Birch, as Vice-Captain, informing himself for next year.'

'If we assume for a moment that Shepherd took your bag, can you think of any possible reason for him to do so?'

The full lips pursed, the fair forehead frowned in concentration. If this woman was a murderer, the pantomime of being anxious to help was being beautifully played. 'No. But it was the kind of thing he might do. He was always picking up things which might incriminate people. Usually documents or letters, which he would photo-copy and replace.' Perhaps she saw his surprise. 'Don't forget I'm both witness and victim of his methods. I saw him operate at close quarters when I was forced to become his mistress.' She spat the word as distastefully as if it had been sour wine. Then she reached out and took the bag from Hook. She opened it, looked surprised to find it empty, then looked back at the Sergeant with a flash of annoyance.

'We haven't emptied it,' said Lambert hastily. 'But of course we have looked inside. Privacy is one of the first casualties of a murder investigation, as I'm afraid you've already found out, Debbie. The bag was empty when retrieved. The point is really whether anything of interest or value has been removed.'

'I think there was only make-up and perhaps a little perfume in there. And probably a handkerchief. It wasn't a bag I used very much. Too small for the practical business-woman,' she smiled, and this time the little joke nearly came off.

'Would the perfume be the same as that you're wearing today?' asked Lambert.

'I suppose it would, if perfume there was. I haven't used any other for the last few months. Len bought me quite a supply.' Despite her best efforts, she was blushing; Bert Hook thought it a wholly admirable effect.

'Of course, the disappearance of your bag may be totally unconnected with the murder,' said Lambert. 'All the same, if you think of any reason why James Shepherd or anyone else should have taken your bag, I'd be grateful if you would contact me immediately.'

Debbie Hall saw the two large men courteously off the premises, even managed a little pleasantry about it with the girl on the reception desk. Bert Hook watched her go back into the building as he put on his safety belt, and wondered whether her reaction would be one of triumph or alarm. Perhaps simple exhaustion would predominate: he felt pretty drained himself, and he had taken a small part in the exchanges.

He was glad that his Superintendent was silent on the journey back to the golf club. The countryside flew past, but Lambert gazed at it with unseeing eyes. They were within a mile of the club and its murder room before he spoke. Then he said tersely, 'That bag. There are three possibilities.' Hook had more sense than to offer suggestions: Lambert was crystallizing his own thoughts.

'One: Debbie Hall was lying and was in Shepherd's car in the last few days. Two: Shepherd took it for reasons yet unknown. Three: someone else took it; in which case, how did it get into Shepherd's Rolls? And why?'

'I don't think Debbie Hall is lying,' said Hook stoutly.

'Good,' said Lambert with a small smile. 'Would that be on account of her big blue eyes, or certain other outstanding attributes?'

'On account of her obvious honesty in the rest of the interview,' said his Sergeant, unruffled. 'She didn't know we were going to throw that bombshell in at the end, but she was very open with us about her affairs.'

'She's quite a bombshell herself. Are you sure you'd be giving a bald, ugly man the same benefit of the doubt as the pneumatic Miss Hall?'

'She hasn't offered to buy me off with her favours,' Bert Hook reminded him with dignity. 'More's the pity. I'm at least as objective about Miss Hall as you are about your angel of mercy, Miss Hartford.'

'In that case, you are a pillar of investigational rectitude, Sergeant Hook, and I congratulate you. We must, as you indicate, strive for objectivity. Which in human terms means we must treat David Parsons, Michael Taylor and Bill Birch in exactly the same way as the women. Oh, maybe it's nothing to do with sex. I'm pretty confident, for instance, that you'll like Bill Birch much more than Michael Taylor, whom you disliked immediately on your own admission. I just think that, whoever our murderer is, he or she has learned the first rule, that you tell the truth whenever possible. If you analyse it, Debbie Hall told us a whole lot of stuff about her private life which we'd have dug out eventually, if we'd have had to.'

'Maybe. I still can't see her as a murderer. Look how she defended her relationship with Len Jackson—how open she was. Look how quickly she admitted that handbag. She's too honest.'

'"If she be false, then Heaven mocks itself,"' said Lambert, amused at his Sergeant's uncharacteristic chivalry, possibly because it voiced what he secretly felt himself. He wondered if Hook had identified Debbie Hall's perfume and made the connection with the heavy scent in the fire-damaged cottage; presumably not. 'Who then is favourite in your book for the homicidal role? Michael Taylor, I suppose.'

'I said I hoped it was him, rather than believed it was him,' said the Sergeant with dignity. 'Taylor had opportunity, motive and the kind of desperation that could lead to violent murder. Whether he has the bottle to plan and execute a killing like this I wouldn't know. The facts I exhorted DC Spencer to gather only this morning point to Mary Hartford. But I haven't even seen her so far.'

If he was hoping for a reaction from his leader, he was disappointed. Lambert did not respond directly. 'Of course, we're assuming it was pre-planned and executed with cool nerve. If Taylor, or anyone else for that matter, was suddenly presented with some crisis by Shepherd, he might have stabbed him impetuously with the nearest implement to hand. The meeting Shepherd had arranged with George Williams might well have been just such a crisis. The fact that there are four other people around without alibis may be no more than good luck. Just as my arrival to meet Shepherd through an arrangement which presumably none of them knew about was a slice of bad luck. The body wouldn't have been found until this morning without that, and we could have been nothing like so precise about the time of death and the elimination of other suspects.'

'We haven't cleared the Captain, the Lady Captain or even the Secretary of your golf club yet,' said Bert Hook, listing these august offices with the satisfaction of a non-member of this privileged circle. 'Colonel Parsons had as good an opportunity as anyone else. Perhaps better, since he stayed behind in the Committee Room with Shepherd for a moment or two after the others left. And he owned the murder weapon—if that's important.'

'The fact that he denied his ownership could be. It's certainly curious. And there's his army record to be investigated; Debbie Hall seemed to confirm there was something strange there when she was talking about them pouring out their troubles to each other over a drink.'

'I still don't see him as this sort of murderer,' said Hook. 'It was both risky—someone could have heard Shepherd call out—and messy. Parsons is too precise.'

'Hmm. There's considerable precision in planning and execution, if we assume it was a planned rather than a spontaneous crime. And David Parsons would certainly have the bottle you so eloquently deny to Michael Taylor, our noble Captain. Anyway, who does strike you as a murderer among our suspects?'

Hook shrugged his shoulders in recognition of the hopelessness of the proposition. He turned the big Vauxhall carefully into the narrow lane leading to the golf club, then said, 'Of course, I haven't even seen this Bill Birch. Why do you think I'll like him?'

'Because he seems an open, winning chap like yourself, Sergeant Hook. Non-smoker, drinks his couple of pints without causing trouble, not a conspicuous womanizer. The backbone of our island nation, like yourself, Bert.'

'But as toffee-nosed as the rest of your golf club hierarchy no doubt!'

'You really must avoid these preconceptions, Bert. Do you really consider Debbie Hall toffee-nosed?'

'*Male* hierarchy,' amended Hook instantly and firmly as he parked the car.

'I doubt whether you'll find Bill Birch toffee-nosed. Any more than I am myself!' Lambert went on hastily before comment could intervene, 'He was a better opening bat than most, I think, and a useful left-arm seamer, if not quite in the Bert Hook class. He's certainly a better golfer than I shall ever be. Anyway, you'll see him shortly; he must be due to arrive at any minute.'

'Vice-Captain,' said Hook. He stood and regarded the reserved car space, wondering whether such an office could really house a reasonable chap like himself. Inconceivable that a good cricketer could be a cold-blooded murderer, but he supposed one should keep an open mind even in the face of such ludicrous suggestions. And even if their man should be only the Vice-Captain of the Golf Club, it would still be a juicy local sensation; on that more satisfying thought, he followed his Superintendent through the heavy wooden doors and into the club.

Detective-Inspector Rushton was in the murder room when they arrived. He could scarcely contain his excitement within the formalities of police address. 'Good news, sir,' he said to Lambert, growing a little taller with the importance it gave him. 'The print boys have been on. There's a good thumbprint on the end of the murder knife. They've got the prints of all our suspects now. It's more than we could have dared to hope for.'

He was prolonging the moment of his news as long as he could, but Lambert was too elated by the windfall to be annoyed. All he said was 'Whose?'

'Miss Hartford's.'

Bert Hook, standing in the dark doorway of the panelled room, just managed to avoid saying, 'I told you so,' to a Superintendent.

CHAPTER 14

Lambert slumped heavily into his chair and glared at the vast expanse of oak table in front of him. When added to the other bits of evidence he had, the print on the handle seemed conclusive. Why then was he uneasy rather than elated?

He tried to analyse his own feelings. It was the first time he had ever had a case where in various degrees he knew all the possible culprits. Was this what was upsetting him? Would he have felt as unwilling to accept the guilt of any of the five suspects? He had found himself defending even the wretched Michael Taylor, a man with whom he felt he had absolutely nothing in common, when Hook had voiced his dislike. He had a gut feeling that something was wrong with the solution which this thumbprint offered them on a plate. But was the feeling based realistically on two decades of experience, or on no more than a liking for Mary Hartford —perhaps even on a respect for the work she did rather than the woman herself? He shook his head angrily, as if he might thus clear it of these confusions.

As if triggered by this movement, the phone rang.

'Have you arrested the Hartford woman yet?' It was Cyril Garner. Even as he put the phone to his ear, Lambert saw Rushton's note on his pad: 'Chief Constable rang at 2.40.'

'Not yet, sir,' he said wearily.

'Surely this thumbprint is conclusive!' said Garner impatiently. 'I was hoping to tell the local radio people we had made an arrest this afternoon.'

'That might be a little premature, sir,' said Lambert. He was clipped and tight-lipped. Hook immersed himself in his notes of the interview with Debbie Hall; Rushton read the signs, but was too full of the importance of the moment and his own part in it to sit down or move away. Lambert looked up at him with distaste: he could imagine Rushton's eager transmission of the news of the thumbprint to the Chief Constable, as if the arrival of the news in the Superintendent's absence underlined the alertness and efficiency of DI Rushton.

'Chief Nursing Officer Hartford is in theatre at the hospital at the moment, sir,' said Lambert.

'Chief Nursing Officer?'

'Matron to you and me, sir. They don't use that title any more, I understand.'

'I see.' Lambert, who in his mind's eye could see Garner weighing the rank in his complex PR weightings, allowed himself a sour smile. But there was enough policeman still in the Chief Constable for him to come back to the evidence and find it damning enough to outweigh other considerations. 'But you will need to confront her with our findings.' Strange how they become 'our' findings as soon as there is progress, thought Lambert; this morning, with no solution in sight, everything was 'your' work. Cyril Garner had the makings of a good golf caddie, but it was not the moment to toy with this delicious image.

'I've left a message for her at the hospital, sir. She will contact me when the theatre schedule is complete and I'll confront her with our findings then.'

Perhaps he should not have picked up and echoed the Chief Constable's ponderous phrase. He could hear the annoyance in Garner's peremptory, 'Do that. We need a confession. And quickly. You've got the picture of her with Shepherd, the handbag, now the thumbprint.' Don't teach granny to suck eggs, you pompous twit, thought Lambert. Then, as he bit back any reply, he suddenly recalled Garner years ago as a Chief Inspector, a hard, efficient team leader who had won loyalty from all his juniors. Unimaginative in some respects, but fair, thorough and industrious. A good example to aspiring CID men. And, at a time when there had been whiffs of corruption in many places, as straight as they came. There were worse men to make Chief Constables. He saw Cyril Garner floundering but honest in a job for which his experience had not prepared him. No wonder he was looking forward to his pension, no wonder a smooth passage with the various media seemed the limit of his ambition. The Peter Principle had promoted him beyond the work he had done efficiently at different levels for twenty years.

'Mary Hartford won't run away, sir. And if she's our murderer, I don't think I'll have much difficulty in getting a confession.'

'I hope so, John. If so, you'll have solved the case within a day. Well done!' In his relief, he was conciliatory, as if he in turn saw Lambert's position anew, and realized he had been riding a Superintendent who had rarely failed over many years. He had assumed now that Mary Hartford was their murderer, Lambert noted. Well, let that pass. The evidence, if not yet overwhelming, pointed strongly in that direction, and it was not the moment to split hairs.

'I'll ring you as soon as I have any news, sir. Incidentally, the handbag isn't hers.' He looked up into the mortified eyes of DI Rushton, who must have passed on the news of the handbag along with the thumbprint in his anxiety to impress the Chief Constable. Rushton hadn't known until this moment, of course, that Debbie Hall had claimed the handbag. Lambert, putting the phone carefully back into its cradle, smiled at him grimly.

Before there could be any exchange between his superiors, Sergeant Hook said, 'Mr Birch arrived whilst you were speaking to the Chief Constable.' A moment later, the Vice-Captain stood awkwardly in the doorway of the room where he had attended the ill-fated Committee meeting on the previous evening.

Waiting for three minutes outside, he had been unable to escape the large red letters on the white card which announced the change in usage to MURDER ROOM. Now as he entered his eye was caught and held immediately, as had been those of the Captain and Secretary before him, by the stark chalk outline between table and wall which marked the place where his Chairman had fallen dead. He was a strong man physically, the strongest they had seen among their suspects, but he swallowed hard, and turned a little paler at the sight of that twisted, evocative caricature upon the parquet floor.

Birch was tall, with dark, closely curled hair, which had only the beginnings of grey at the temples. Hook checked his copy of the Secretary's list of his Committee to confirm that the Vice-Captain was only thirty-nine. He looked a little older than this, but very fit. There were more lines around eyes and forehead than would be normal for someone on the right side of forty, and Hook thought he detected already the first traces of the stoop which bedevils so many tall men as the years advance. He was dressed in a well-cut grey suit, but formal clothes did not sit easily on him; either he had scant use for fashion or he felt happy in more casual apparel. But his brown shoes were highly polished: this and the neat, small knot in his tie gave him a slightly old-fashioned air, as if, determined on rectitude, he had donned a few extra years with this correct attire.

'I came straight from work,' he said. 'Am I the last of your suspects, John?' Rushton and Hook noted the Christian name, as in their world of ranks and protocol they could not fail to do. But it was free and unforced in Birch, not an attempt to assert the privilege of friendship where it might give some small advantage. Bert Hook remembered his Superintendent's passing remark that he would like Birch much more than Michael Taylor, and determined to be objective.

'Are you still game for a few holes, Bill?' said Lambert.

'If you are,' said Birch, looking uncertainly at the two other men in the room. 'It hardly seems the place to be cross-examined, but—'

'Barristers cross-examine. We never do anything so vigorous,' smiled Lambert. 'Yes, no doubt it's highly irregular, but I need to blow a few cobwebs away. I've been interviewing people, here or elsewhere, for the last six hours, with one small break for lunch.' And on the course, he thought ruefully, I shall watch him like a hawk to see if he casts any glances towards the burnt-out cottage in the woods. Murder more than other crimes made one a truant to friendship. Or was he just rationalizing his desertion of the murder room?

Before his resolve could weaken, he led Birch towards the men's locker-room, studiously failing to notice both Rushton's disapproval and Hook's disappointment. 'Of course, we shall probably need you to make and sign a formal statement later,' was all the mollification he floated back to his juniors from the corridor.

When Birch and he presently stood in cotton trousers and short-sleeved shirts on the first tee, he congratulated himself anew upon his decision. Besides them, the rhododendrons were in full pink glory and the thrushes sang a full-throated welcome. A deserted first fairway opened its wide green bosom; the yellow flag on the green hung limp and distant in the heat. And there was a strategy in his actions that was not wholly selfish.

He knew Bill Birch better than any other of his suspects. They had served together on the Greens Committee for three years now, and played both against each other and as partners in club competitions. If it was not yet a close friendship, each respected the other and was willing to make it closer than it was. Lambert knew enough of his Vice-Captain to think him a private man, who would unbend more easily—and thus be more forthcoming—in a situation as confidential and informal as the unusual circumstances would allow.

Birch was a 6-handicapper against Lambert's 12: the Superintendent would need to concentrate if he was to provide a reasonable game for a powerful opponent, despite the advantage his handicap would give him. He was relieved to get a good drive away from the first tee, bouncing straight and long past the fairway bunker which always threatened to gather in his slice. He did not hit the green with his second, but he was only just off on the right. Whilst Birch was playing his second, Lambert looked back at the club-house and took in the scene of peace and privilege. The stream glinted bright under the high sun as it skirted the clubhouse and the eighteenth green. The mellow russet tiles of the pleasantly asymmetrical roof blended perfectly with the lush green of new growth on beech and oak. Massive candelabras of chestnut flower stretched away to the left of the clubhouse. To the right, the trio of weeping willows the club had planted by the bridge over the stream arched gracefully against the backdrop of a massive copper beech, planted by some yeoman of the ancient estate a century before anyone thought of playing golf here.

Incomparable late spring in fertile England, nature burgeoning yet controlled, even in places manicured: very Home Counties! Only two details suggested that in this quiet place there had been unnatural death. One was the club flag, hanging motionless and green halfway up the gleaming white pole at the edge of the practice putting green, in memory of the late Chairman. The other was Bert Hook, standing beneath the verandah of the clubhouse with a large mug of tea and staring in recrimination after his eccentric Superintendent, who had snatched this last of the suspects from his Sergeant's searching gaze, to be interviewed in private on those green acres. Lambert grinned back a little guiltily at Hook's static, accusing presence. In stressing the need for individuality and initiative in senior officers, he always counselled the necessity to say 'Bugger you!' to normal procedures when circumstances called for an individual response. He waved loftily to the stolid figure, whose expression was too far away for him to read. 'Bugger you!' he muttered with relish, and turned to watch his opponent's ball descend in a graceful parabola to finish ten feet from the hole.

Lambert chipped on to the green quite well and holed a tricky five-footer for his four. It gave him a half. It was his last success, however. From the second tee onwards, he began to play more and more raggedly. Bill Birch, on the other hand, showed all his normal consistency, even though Lambert did not open the real business of the meeting until they had played two full holes, testing his opponent for the nervousness he expected in one about to be questioned about a murder. The Vice-Captain was almost ten years younger than him, and, Lambert decided ruefully, at least that decade more supple. He was a left-hander, whose slight natural fade on the longer shots was suited to the course, which had a number of dog-leg holes. His swing was easy and uncomplicated, his iron shots in particular having a crisp accuracy that would have been the envy of better players than John Lambert.

They were halfway up the third fairway, out of sight of the clubhouse, and indeed of any human eye, when he broached this most informal of interviews. 'Well, Bill,' he said. 'You know how James Shepherd died?' Birch nodded, almost eagerly, as if relieved at last to come to grips with the real reason for their meeting.

'It's thrown the factory into some confusion, I can tell you.'

For a moment Lambert was puzzled; then he remembered that Birch worked for Shepherd, in some senior capacity. 'For a start, Bill, can you tell me exactly what the business is and what you do there?'

It was just to fill in background and get Birch talking, but it threw the Vice-Captain a little: he had been waiting all day to talk about murder and last night's meeting. 'Small engineering of various kinds. Originally, we were a tool-making company, and that's still the basis of the business. We have a plastic mouldings plant, and we like to think we're pretty versatile. We've had to be over the last few years,' he said ruefully.

'And your role in all this, Bill?'

'Works Manager,' said Birch, just failing to keep the pride out of his voice.

'And that involves . . .?' Pride could make a man as vulnerable as envy; Lambert followed up instinctively into an area he had not intended to probe.

'Just about everything in a small company. Of course, Shepherd had other irons in the fire as well as our factory: he was a very rich man, especially from his financial services business. That's been one of the few growth areas over the

last few years and Shepherd was an expert.' In his voice
there was the contempt of the man who makes things for
those who make money simply by moving money around.
More significantly, Lambert noted the terse use of
Shepherd's surname where he would have expected 'Mr
Shepherd' or 'James', depending on the degree of formality
in this particular working relationship. He glanced sharply
sideways at Birch, but the Vice-Captain seemed unconscious of anything irregular. He swung a 4-iron away with
a long, enviably slow swing. Lambert watched the white
ball soar against the azure sky, plummet to the edge of the
third green, and roll gently to within five feet of the hole.
His own riposte was savagely topped; it skidded in a low,
ugly curve to the right and found with precision the middle
of the bunker it had been destined for from the moment of
leaving the club.

'And your job is concerned with what?' he said, trying
not to sound aggressive as he banged the offending club
back into his bag.

'Almost everything on the factory floor. Work schedules,
order deadlines, labour relations. We've brought in a lot of
modern technology in the last five years, despite the
recession in engineering generally. With nothing other than
a few voluntary redundancies. We haven't had a strike, or
even a serious labour dispute, since I took over this job
seven years ago.' This time he gave up any attempt to keep
the pride out of his voice. Lambert got his ball out of the
bunker reasonably close to the flag, but Birch holed his
five-footer with total security and they sauntered to the next
tee.

The heat in this sheltered spot beat on them relentlessly,
so that they were glad to get their drives away and move
down the fairway, where the gentlest of breezes gave them
a little relief. Birch, looking at the tree-tops high to their
left, sniffed the air and said, 'It may sound silly without a
cloud in sight, but I think a change is on the way before
long.' The topmost branches of the beeches rustled a little
quite suddenly, as if they had heard and were agreeing.

Despite his northern accent, Birch was a farmer's son; he looked a countryman now as he eyed sky and woods.

When presently they stood by the side of the fifth green, out of sight of the clubhouse and any human presence, Lambert had begun to concentrate his questions on the previous night's events. Birch's account of the meeting and its ending tallied with those of the other Committee members who had been present. So far Lambert felt no need for the notebook he had forsaken to conduct the interview in this unorthodox setting, though he missed Bert Hook's observant presence at his side.

'Can you recall as exactly as possible your movements immediately after the meeting?' Birch looked at him with the faintest trace of a smile, which manifested itself in the dark brown eyes rather than in any movement of the broad, mobile mouth. Then he addressed his ball calmly, concentrated for two seconds, and stroked a long, downhill putt from the edge of the green to within five inches of the hole, as if demonstrating the steady nerve allowed him by a free conscience.

As they moved towards the next tee, he said, 'Look, John, I'm finding this as bizarre as I hope you are. I'm grateful I'm not being grilled in a police station, or even your murder room at the club. If anyone has to "help the police with their inquiries", I can recommend this setting.' He paused and looked down the deserted, tree-fringed sixth fairway. 'But I don't think I can really play golf and concentrate on your questions. Any more than you can play golf and frame them!'

Lambert grinned ruefully. 'If that's a comment on my play over the last five holes, I accept the excuse gratefully, as most golfers would. I'm afraid I can play as badly as that with nothing on my mind, so we'll never know. But you're right, of course. It was ridiculous to think we could have a serious exchange while playing golf. What say we leave our trolleys and stroll ahead without them? I'm still reluctant to move indoors and leave this weather outside, especially if you think it may not last.'

Birch looked at him a little curiously, as if he suspected an ulterior motive. Then he grinned, the wide, conspiratorial grin which retains in some men the schoolboy they thought had disappeared. They set off together without their clubs, towards the spot where a green woodpecker tapped its insistent tattoo in the woods.

'At the end of the meeting we all gathered up our papers. I left almost immediately. So did most of the others. Mary Hartford and Debbie Hall went off together, presumably to the ladies' locker-room. Michael Taylor and I went straight through to the men's locker-room and the toilets. With some relief, I may tell you, since we'd had a pint before the meeting.'

Lambert neither checked his stride nor altered his expression. He looked straight ahead as he said, 'You're quite sure of this, Bill?'

The Vice-Captain took his time before answering steadily, 'About those few facts, yes. Of course, it's surmise about the two women.'

'It's what you say about Michael Taylor that interests me. It doesn't quite tally with his recollection of the order of events.'

'Michael Taylor wouldn't have killed Shepherd. He hasn't the nerve.'

'But Bill Birch might have?' As the Vice-Captain turned towards him, his long, sallow face suddenly flushed and excited, Lambert hastened to elaborate. 'Be thankful, Bill, that investigations don't revolve round such presumptions about character. My experience is that anyone has the nerve for murder if pushed to emotional extremes. I've already had the view that David Parsons is much too nice a chap and Debbie Hall too compassionate a lady to have committed murder. For what it's worth—which is precisely nothing— none of you looks a murderer to me. But one of the five of you almost certainly is.' Birch nodded as he recognized the logic, but his face looked set and sullen. He was not going to find it easy to talk about the other suspects. He was a very different man from Michael Taylor. Where the Captain had collapsed under steady interviewing pressure from Lambert and Hook, his Vice-Captain was likely to prove reserved and uncommunicative. Lambert was finding it difficult to play this fish, finding the pressure of previous friendship interfering with the interview strategy more than with any of the previous four. He decided on a degree of confidence most of his colleagues would have regarded as unprofessional, in an attempt to keep the atmosphere he wanted.

'Look, Bill, it may be something or it may be nothing. Michael Taylor told us he went straight to the bar after the meeting. That he went to the locker-room after, not before, you'd had a drink and been joined by the ladies.'

'No.' Birch's voice was steady, even reluctant, but definite. 'We went after the meeting. I told you, we were a bit desperate.'

'That makes sense,' said Lambert with a grim little smile. He thought of the words from Mary Hartford which had mildly shocked him: 'The men rushed to empty straining bladders, the women to repair the ravages of a humid evening.' For whatever reason, it seemed Michael Taylor had lied when he said he did not go to the locker-room until after the group in the bar broke up.

Beside him, Bill Birch ran a hand through his thick, curly hair as Lambert watched him from the corner of his eye, Had he been sweating earlier? It was possible: the day was as hot as ever. But Lambert was not imagining the strain he saw in the profile beside him. Birch had had a broken nose many years earlier; Lambert wondered inconsequentially why he had never noticed it before, for despite competent repair it was clearly visible from this angle. The draining of the blood from Birch's face had etched the tension on his features; the skin was tightly drawn over the high cheek bones and determined chin.

They walked another forty yards in silence before the Vice-Captain said, 'It might be no more than a mistake on Mike's part.'

'Indeed. But it would be a curious one. Few things are

more imperative than men's bladders at the end of a longish meeting, as you indicated yourself, Bill.'

'But why would he deceive you? The fact that he was with me gives him a clear alibi right up to the end of drinks, when we left, surely?' A pause. Then, with a dawning horror scarcely muted by the nervous giggle which followed it, he said slowly, 'If you believe me, of course.'

Somewhere behind them, a jay peeled off its harsh descending cackle, as if in mocking parody of Birch's involuntary giggle of tension. He said, 'Shouldn't you say something like "It's my job to disbelieve everybody at this stage, sir," like a detective in a play?'

Lambert, who had met the idea often enough before, smiled at him. 'I rather think I prefer to believe everyone until some other piece of evidence suggests otherwise,' he said, as if genuinely curious about his own methods. 'You're right of course about Michael Taylor. It's curious he should leave himself without an alibi for the time he was with you. But it seems he didn't leave the club immediately after you all left the bar. Mary Hartford thinks she heard his car leave the car park a little while later.' As he spoke, Lambert wondered for the first time how much reliance could be placed on the evidence of a woman whose prints were on the murder weapon. Fortunately, the man beside him could not know that.

'That's true,' said Birch slowly. 'I saw him go as I came out. Or saw his tail lights and his number plate.'

'So you were there after him. Was anyone else?'

'Mary Hartford. We called good night to each other through the darkness. I think everyone else had gone. David Parsons certainly had—his parking space was empty. The Chairman's Rolls was still there of course.'

'That didn't strike you as odd?' It had troubled Lambert throughout: none of the witnesses seemed surprised that the Chairman should still be around, unseen, in the club.

'No. With any of the others, it probably would have. But Shepherd was a . . . a secretive man.' Lambert noted the search for the diplomatic word, but said nothing. 'He was always in a corner somewhere with someone. I thought he might be with the Steward, or even alone in the Committee Room. We'd been discussing finance, and that was his field. Especially if anything irregular could be discovered.' The bitterness was unmistakable. Lambert, though he would come back to it, ignored it for the moment.

'We've jumped ahead a little because I told you about Michael Taylor's statement. What happened after you and he had been to the men's locker-room?'

'I went straight to the bar. I left Michael Taylor combing his hair, but he couldn't have been more than two minutes behind me. Debbie Hall and David Parsons arrived together, just after Michael. Mary Hartford came in a couple of minutes later.'

So Birch, like the others, couldn't be eliminated as a suspect. Even on his own admission, he had been on his own for two minutes before the assembly in the bar. Apart from what had happened after they all left the bar; Lambert was increasingly interested in that short period.

'Was there anything unusual in your exchange in the bar?' Lambert was aware of Birch looking sharply into his face, but he stared resolutely ahead and kept walking. After twenty yards in silence, he said, 'The murder was committed either just before or just after you'd all sat round a convivial table in the bar. One of the five of you had either just committed a violent murder or was about to commit it. You can see why I think any abnormality of manner, any behaviour outside the normal personality, could be important. Don't be afraid of anyone being convicted on a chance remark, but you must see that anything which was surprising to you must suggest a line of inquiry to me now.'

It was a long, slightly desperate speech. For he had sensed that something had occurred to Birch which he was reluctant to reveal. They had strolled a long way during all this. Now they emerged through an avenue of majestic chestnuts to a little knoll of ground beside the ninth green, a strategic viewpoint where a stout rustic seat had been placed in memory of a former President of the club. Birch gestured towards this now. 'Let's sit down for a while,' he said hoarsely, and Lambert registered for the first time how white he had gone.

With a whimsical timing that he could not appreciate, the thought crept into his mind that this was a very quiet place to sit down with a murderer. They sat for a full minute in silence. Lambert prompted no more: he knew Birch would not turn back now.

'Most of us seemed normal enough,' he said eventually. 'Mike Taylor and I were talking about fixtures. Debbie Hall and David Parsons talked about the menu and pricing for the evening social on the joint Captains' Day—I remember him making notes. Mary Hartford was very quiet. I spoke to her when she came in and she scarcely answered. When Mike and I had finished, I teased her a bit but she didn't respond. I don't think she even heard. Normally, I get on very well with Mary. She's got a dry, highly developed sense of humour and . . .'

Lambert, looking sharply sideways, realized that Bill Birch, practical man, formidable athlete, rugged survivor of many a sporting tussle, was near to tears. He stared down at the Vice-Captain's well-worn white golf shoes, studying the scuffing on the right toe, and waited. Birch's voice when he went on again after a moment was steady again, but very quiet.

'I thought nothing of it at the time. Just that she had scratched herself, or perhaps collected it at the hospital. But there was a smear of blood on the cuff of Mary Hartford's blouse.'

CHAPTER 15

It was ridiculous, but these two strong men would not look at each other. Each feared what he would see in the other's features. Lambert knew that Birch was distraught, that the revelation of what seemed a damning fact about a woman he liked and respected had severely taxed his self-control. He knew that the Vice-Captain's expression would contain an appeal for reassurance that he could not give. For his part, Birch feared that John Lambert's face would offer only confirmation that this piece of evidence had delivered up his murderer.

'Was it fresh blood?' asked Lambert quietly after a long time. He heard the sharp intake of breath beside him but said no more. Birch must know after his initial revelation that subsidiary questions were inevitable.

'Yes. Bright red. I almost pointed it out so that she could wash it before it dried.' So his mention of blood from her hospital duties hours earlier had never been more than a desperate search for an excuse. Had they not been in that quiet place, his words would have been inaudible. He buried his face in his hands, not with a sudden, dramatic gesture but in slow motion, as if his wretchedness had deprived him of physical energy and coordination. 'I'd rather it had been any of us than Mary. She's been so good to my wife. So thoughtful.'

Lambert was puzzled for a moment. Then he remembered a fact he should never have forgotten. Bill Birch's wife was a cripple. He thought it was multiple sclerosis; certainly it was a degenerative muscular disease which she faced with fortitude, cheerfulness, and rocklike support from her husband. She went into hospital at regular intervals for treatment and the stabilization of her drug intake. He remembered her chatting cheerfully to Mary Hartford at one of the club's social functions.

'If Mary Hartford is arrested, it won't be on your evidence alone, Bill,' was all he could say. He would reveal no detail of the damning case against the Lady Captain that had built up through the events of the day.

'Is that supposed to console me?' said Birch, hopelessly. Low on the horizon, through a gap in the trees behind a distant green, the first grey cloud was impinging upon the universal blue. The farmer's son might yet be right about a change in the weather.

'Not necessarily. But let me assure you that we shall get our murderer, whoever it is. Withholding evidence wouldn't save Mary Hartford, if she killed James Shepherd, though it might delay us and eventually embarrass you.' Lambert had used the words often enough before for them to sound like clichés to him; he reminded himself that they were new to Birch, as to others. 'Now, what happened after you left the bar?'

'We all broke up together, but went in different directions. I went to check how many of the first team had ticked their names for the match on Saturday, and then back to collect my file from the bar.'

'Where did Michael Taylor go?'

'Why do you ask?' Birch was on his guard, but there was relief in his eyes now. The change of questioning away from Mary Hartford had revived hope; the case might not be closed, if Lambert was interested in the movements of other people.

'Because he seems to have told us a lie. He said he went off to the locker-room *after* your drinks in the bar. It appears from what you say that he went elsewhere. I'm naturally curious to know where, since he chose not to tell me himself.'

'I think I can tell you that,' said Birch slowly. There was a tinge of regret in his voice; perhaps he realized that the exoneration of any one of the others threw suspicion back more firmly on to Mary Hartford. 'I went into the Secretary's office to collect a team sheet for Saturday's match. Mike Taylor was coming out as I arrived. He almost cannoned into me in his hurry.'

'Did any conversation pass between you?'

'No, nothing you could call conversation. I said something silly like, "Steady on, Mike, I'll need that foot again!" but he just pushed me aside and rushed off without a word.

'Would you say that was normal behaviour in our Captain?'

This time Birch did look the Superintendent full in the face. The brown eyes were troubled and bewildered, the dark hair for once untidy as his hand brushed it again. His lips trembled a little: this was a much greater strain on the emotions than he had anticipated.

'I don't know,' he said miserably.

But Lambert knew: the normally extrovert Taylor would never have behaved so abruptly unless shocked out of the image he strove to project. But why this panic? Had he come straight from the Committee Room with the murder just accomplished?

He stood up, an indication that their exchange, and the Vice-Captain's ordeal, was nearly over. 'What happened next?'

'That's almost it. David Parsons grinned and said, "The Captain's in a hurry tonight. Perhaps there's a lady waiting somewhere!" He followed Mike out and left. I collected the team sheet I wanted and pulled the door behind me as David had asked. It has a Yale lock.'

'So the Secretary's door was locked by you. What about the Committee Room?'

'That wasn't locked. The door was still slightly ajar: I could see the shaft of light as I left.' Yet someone had locked it. Lambert and the Steward had had to unlock the heavy oak door to discover the body a little while later.

'Think about the order in which people left last night, Bill. It could be very important.'

'When I got into the car park after shutting the Secretary's door I saw Michael Taylor's rear lights shooting away into the darkness as I said. David Parsons's space was already empty. I called good night to Mary and drove away myself. I think we were the last to leave. I can't be absolutely sure about Debbie Hall, because she hasn't a reserved space like the other four of us.'

'Did you actually see Mary Hartford leave?' Birch flashed him a look of open dislike, then looked at the ground by his feet, miserably accepting the necessity for the question.

'She was sitting in her car as I drove out. I'm sure she left right behind me, but of course I can't prove that.'

'You didn't see her lights in your mirror as you went down the lane?'

'I don't reember them. That doesn't mean they weren't there!'

'Of course not.'

But it did mean Mary Hartford might simply have sat in her car until all was quiet, before quietly returning to the scene of her crime to cover her traces, remove Shepherd's keys, and lock the Committee Room door. For that matter, one of the others might have come back after driving away. Had Taylor's flamboyant exit been designed to attract attention deliberately? But the schedule for anyone return-ing had been a tight one: he himself had arrived on the scene within perhaps ten minutes of Birch's leaving. For the first time, he entertained the unpleasant conjecture that the murderer might have been lurking in the shadows last night whilst he walked in the darkness around the outside of the club buildings, watching his every move.

They had used a path through the woods to cut back to their trolleys and golf bags. The two members on the green adjacent to their equipment were the first people they had seen since they had left the clubhouse. 'Tour of inspection of your estate?' called one of them; Lambert realized that their membership of the Greens Committee was a con-venient reason why they should be strolling together down vacant fairways when the evening called out for golf. 'The course is in fine condition, John,' called the other player to the deputy Chairman of his Greens Committee. Lambert shrugged the compliment aside with a reference to the excellent work of the Greenkeeper, but for both of them it was a welcome reminder of a normal world outside the nightmare in which they had been involved for the last half hour.

When they had collected their clubs, they took the direct route back to the clubhouse, past the seventeenth green and down the eighteenth fairway. Lambert walked very slightly behind his man, no more than four or five inches; an observer would have thought of them as side by side. But he watched the Vice-Captain closely. Away in the trees to their left was the Greenkeeper's cottage which had burned so dramatically earlier in the day. He watched for any turn of the head, any glance in that direction, that might reveal that Birch had a hand in that curious happening. He had purposely made no mention of the fire, and the uncomfortable thought now came to him that no one moving in that area would be less likely to be challenged than the Vice-Captain, a member and former Chairman of the Greens Committee, dutifully patrolling the course and inspecting its assets.

If Birch had any involvement in the arson, or even knowledge of it, he gave no sign. Nor did he ostentatiously ignore the burnt-out cottage. When they were almost past, he pointed over the trees to the western sky, where the gathering clouds gave promise of an angry sunset. Lambert reminded himself irritably that his murderer was a very cool customer indeed, quite capable no doubt of simulating total ignorance of a fire he knew all about. As if in response to this thought, Birch now led him directly into his next area of questioning.

'What do you want done about Shepherd's Rolls?' he said, as they approached the clubhouse and the maroon wing of that splendid vehicle crept into view. 'I'll move it if you like. Technically, it's a company asset; I can find safe storage for it at the works until the legalities are sorted out.' Lambert already had a DI at Shepherd's solicitor's, though with this particular crime he expected no help from the details of the will. He ignored Birch's question.

'The Rolls has been fingerprinted and examined. We should have done so in any case after a murder, but there was a curious incident this morning.' Birch stared at him blankly. If he was an actor, he was a very good one: the range from extreme distress at the evidence against Mary Hartford to blank incomprehension now was a considerable one. 'Do you know of any reason why anyone should break into the car?'

'No.' Perhaps a shade too quickly. Check where he was at the time. Look for witnesses. More footwork for someone. If necessary. Mary Hartford might confess tonight.

'The car was opened with a key. Did anyone at the works have a key to the Chairman's Rolls?'

Birch gave a slow, bitter smile. 'You mean did I have a key to the boss's car, John? No, I didn't, and nor did anyone else. Shepherd never employed a chauffeur and I've never seen anyone else drive that Rolls.'

Lambert nodded. This at least was what he had expected, even hoped for. 'Of course, the entry to the car may be totally unconnected with the murder. But it doesn't look like it. Entry was made with a key. James Shepherd's car keys were not in his pockets when the body was found. Someone, presumably the murderer, had removed them. Whoever entered the car was disturbed and we've no idea whether he got what he wanted or not.'

'Or she!' said Birch. And then flushed with annoyance at himself: it had been an involuntary thought. Lambert, who had been about to agree automatically with the qualification he had so often added to his own thoughts, divined just in time that there might be a little more here. He let Birch's embarrassment hang between them for a moment, to show it had been noted, before he said, 'Have you seen anyone who might be connected with this business—no, let's be precise, that means any of your four colleagues who were at last night's meeting—in this car in the last month?'

Birch looked at him sharply. 'What would that prove?'

'Nothing at all. It might give a starting point for a few questions. The innocent will no doubt be only too happy to help.' Lambert was at his blandest; this was a purely professional vein which had nothing to do with the man himself, and for the first time Birch saw him as Superintendent rather than friend. Lambert would have been delighted to know it had taken so long.

They were standing beside the Rolls now. It gleamed blood-red in the western sun; only a tell-tale patch of white powder on the ground beneath the driver's door told the knowledgeable of the work of the fingerprint sergeant. Birch stared at the front passenger seat as he said, 'Mike Taylor was in the car with him.'

'When?'

'Ten days, maybe a fortnight ago. One evening in

Mersham; I was taking my wife for a drink. They were parked near the recreation ground. Talking.'

'Talking?' It was a strange word to use if he had merely glimpsed the pair in passing. Birch looked at him for a moment with what might have been distaste.

'They were still there when we came out of the pub and went home.'

'How long afterwards was this?'

'Three quarters of an hour. Maybe an hour.'

'Thank you, Bill.'

'It may mean absolutely nothing.'

'Just so. Most facts do. But one needs as many as possible before one can see which ones count.'

His feeling, indeed, was that this one added nothing. Michael Taylor had talked about the way Shepherd had taunted and threatened him; it must have happened somewhere. Because Taylor had disintegrated so completely at the end of the morning interview, they had not questioned him about the break-in to the Rolls as they had the others. Now, he had another fact to be followed up in due course. Taylor might well have had reason to retrieve incriminating material of some sort from Shepherd's car this morning. Either he would have his murderer within the next twenty-four hours, or the case would resolve itself into days of patient questioning, much of it in a widening circle of friends and relatives beyond the immediate suspects.

But the Superintendent had discovered one thing he had not known previously. He could scarcely wait to compare Birch's account of the previous night's events with that of the other four. He knew that at least three of his suspects had lied to him; indeed, it was possible that all five had. But it had taken him until now to divine what he thought was the most significant deception.

CHAPTER 16

The two men must have stood by the great maroon car for half a minute, each wrapped in his own thoughts. It was Birch who moved first. 'Is that it for the moment then?' he said. Lambert noted the attempt at a cheerful briskness. The Vice-Captain moved past David Parsons's car to his own reserved space and began to put his clubs and trolley into his car.

'Not quite, Bill, I'm afraid,' said Lambert. He spoke quietly, because they were near the clubhouse, where unseen ears might pick up their private exchanges. Perhaps his low tones sounded menacing to Birch, for the Vice-Captain froze over the boot of his car. For an instant he looked to Lambert as if someone had stopped the videotape which was one of the new instruments of police work. When his head finally turned to look at the Superintendent, there was no friendliness left in the dark, deep-set eyes; exhaustion and fear were plain enough. For the tenth time in the day, Lambert wondered what his relationships would be with these people when the case was over.

'I only want to ask you a few questions about your relationship with the deceased,' he said. It was meant to reassure, but it sounded sinister even to him. He led his reluctant companion through the main entrance, back to where the dark-panelled room shut out the sun and afforded them an uneasy privacy. He answered Bert Hook's interrogative look with a nod: he had shut him out of the investigation for long enough. On the golf course, sitting amidst the peace of those majestic glades of trees, Birch had talked more freely to his friend and sometime golfing partner than he would have done with a third party present. Now it was time to use the possibilities of a more formal setting.

Birch looked at the chalk outline on the floor as nervously as any one before him: Lambert caught the shudder of horror as he turned away from it. With a little spurt of surprise, he realized that Bill Birch, practical engineer, manager of men, and splendid striker of a golf ball, was perhaps the most imaginative of all his suspects.

Birch sat in the chair indicated to him and gazed impatiently at Sergeant Hook, who busied himself with his notes, setting a deliberately laborious heading on a new page. Lambert let silence hang heavily between them for a moment. In truth, he was wondering how to begin again with Birch in this changed atmosphere. Hostility could be used in interrogation: often he found it more useful than empathy. But he was himself uneasy with a friend, as he had not expected to be. There would be no elaborate play with pipe and tobacco this time; he knew he would not be able to work that histrionic trick with Birch.

'Bill, this is a murder investigation. I have to ask you if you know anything about any of your fellow Committee members which might be relevant. I'm grateful for what you've told me already about Mary Hartford and Michael Taylor.' There was a gasp from Birch, a quick glance at Hook, who remained totally impassive over his pad. Birch's eyes had a hunted look as they moved back to Lambert with a gleam of real hostility. 'Judas!' they seemed to say, and Lambert realized he would never have learned what he had on the golf course if he had tackled Birch head-on in here.

'You may not feel it, but what you have revealed is very much in the interests of the people concerned—always providing that they are innocent. The existence of a motive and an opportunity does not make anyone guilty.'

'We all had a motive!' said Birch bitterly. It was almost a snarl, and so unlike his ordinary tones that all three men in the room were shocked. It was while Birch was still wide-eyed at his own reaction that Lambert moved in. 'That's interesting. As you think that, you won't be surprised to hear that in the course of today I have unearthed motives for four of the five of you.' The obvious question hung unasked for a moment, but Birch was far too much on edge to resist it.

'So just one of us is in the clear?' he said reluctantly.

'Oh, by no means. The fifth person is yourself. And you are about to tell me about your motive.'

The Vice-Captain looked at the huge oak table and bit fiercely at his lower lip. It was when he saw bright blood upon that lip that Lambert realized how tense Birch had become. This man had things in him that he had hoped to conceal. The detective in Lambert thrilled with excitement. And the excitement was stronger, much stronger, than the pang of guilt he felt in tricking a friend.

'You said all of you had a motive,' he reminded Birch.

There was a long sigh from the Vice-Captain before he said, 'I meant we all hated James Shepherd.'

'Why?' This was from Hook, and so promptly that Birch was shaken.

'I thought you said you knew all about that,' he said, disconcerted and angry at this question from a new quarter.

'I said we had unearthed motives,' said Lambert shortly. 'Why did you hate him, Bill?'

Birch shifted his tall frame uncomfortably on the heavy oak chair. He looked all round the room, with its thirties décor, its yellowing photographs of Bobby Jones and Henry Cotton on the first tee, its small wall-safe with the door still open and accusing in the corner above the evocative chalk outline.

'He was not a likeable man,' he said lamely.

'So I have discovered. Not all unpopular men are murdered.'

'Unpopular!' Birch's laugh, harsh and bitter, echoed in the still old room. 'You show me anyone who isn't glad he's dead. Anyone.' He wrung his hands together fiercely in a way Lambert had never seen him do before.

'Do I gather he was not a good employer?' The hate on the other side of the table gave the deliberately understated question the ring of irony. Perhaps the implication of disloyalty got through to Birch. Certainly his reaction had the unguarded ferocity Lambert had hoped to provoke.

'Do you think I wouldn't have been away years ago if it

had been possible? Do you think I couldn't have got another job? A better job, even?' For a moment he blazed with the pride of the man who is good at his work and jealous of that excellence; then he looked down at the table and at the fingers of his hands upon the edge of it, aware that he had betrayed himself. He spread his fingers, strong but white with tension, as if undertaking a physical exercise to assert the calm he could not feel.

'Yet you chose not to.' Having made the breach, Lambert fed him the lines like a straight man in a macabre double act. There was a hopeless, caged silence.

'We like it here. Wendy has her friends. It isn't easy for a cripple to move house.' It was not the lameness of this that made him end it with a savage shake of the head: Lambert guessed that self-disgust flooded into Birch with the knowledge that he had tried to use his wife's disability to talk his way free from the net he had closed upon himself. He gave Birch the next platitude, helping him along the path to the revelations they both now recognized as inescapable.

'Bill, my advice as a friend is here exactly the same as my advice as a Superintendent. We shall find the truth eventually. It will come better from you than elsewhere.'

'And what if it has nothing to do with this case?' said Birch hopelessly, aware now that he was merely delaying the inescapable.

'This is a murder case. You must let me be the judge of what is relevant. We shall find out what we have to.'

Birch looked at the safe, at the point where Shepherd had fallen, at Bert Hook's impassive bulk, and finally, with desperate eyes, at the Superintendent. Lambert, stone-faced and inexorable, gave no sign of the inner turmoil he felt. The clash between his suppressed desire to reach out to a friend in torment and the excitement induced by the imminence of some major disclosure led to a sick agitation he could not remember feeling before. He was using the silence in that stifling room like a physical instrument, a rack which would stretch Birch to the breaking-point of emotional revelation. He at once enjoyed his proficiency and despised himself for it. When now he felt his own palms damp, he was not sure whether the sweat came from the stimulation of success or his sympathy with the man opposite him.

'Can you treat what I have to say in confidence?' Birch's tone was leaden and hopeless. Lambert worked to put the compassion he felt into his reply, for both men recognized now that Birch was going to speak out.

'You must know, Bill, that I can't make vague promises of that sort. If it has no bearing on the case, we'll do our very best to make sure that it goes no further than our files: you will know that at some stage I shall need you to sign a statement. If it bears even upon the fringes of the case, some clever counsel, whether retained for defence or prosecution, may well pursue you in court; at that point we have very little control. I'm sorry, but it really is best if you tell us everything now. We shall find out from others if we have to, and other viewpoints may be less sympathetic as well as less well-informed than your own.'

There was a long, despairing sigh but no word from Birch. Lambert's next words were a prompting towards what all three men in the room now recognized as inevitable.

'You said you all had a motive for killing James Shepherd. What was yours?'

'I hated him. I'm not the only one, I know. But he had more on me than the rest.'

'Not necessarily,' said Lambert drily. 'I seem to have spent most of the day learning about the unsavoury side of our Chairman's dealings with people. And I fancy I have more to hear elsewhere once we have finished our talk.' He looked briskly at his watch, a gesture apparently of brusque insensitivity, but one in fact designed to put whatever Birch was about to say into a more matter-of-fact context. Birch's look of startled gratitude showed he had recognized the gesture.

'I killed a man,' he said quietly. It was the pause which followed which gave the simple, appalling statement the weight it warranted. 'Shepherd was the only man alive who knew. He enjoyed that.' Only the last phrase gave an understated hint of passion. Now that Birch had brought himself to the point of revelation, he spoke as calmly as if outlining a schedule for a day's work.

'When was this?' said Bert Hook quietly. Lambert as usual was glad of his intervention; what was needed after all this tension was a simple recital of facts, more likely to be secured by the impersonal questions of a stranger than a friend. Perhaps Hook hoped they were at the beginning of a confession. Lambert could not be so optimistic—or pessimistic: once again he found himself hoping a suspect in this case was not guilty. It was confession of a sort that came from Birch, but not to the murder of Shepherd.

'Five years ago. We were on our way back from a Company meeting in London. It had gone well and we'd had a couple of drinks before we set off back. No more!' Birch looked at both of them with eyes that beseeched them to believe. 'We were in Shepherd's Rolls—the one outside now. It was almost new then. He used to change them every three years but he kept this one. Sometimes I thought it was to taunt me: he used to watch me with that little smile of his whenever I was near it . . .'

'What happened?' said Hook sharply. Birch looked at him in surprise, as if annoyed they did not immediately know all once he had nerved himself to talk about the incident. Then he went on as quietly as before.

'I was driving. Shepherd was in the back. In the front passenger seat was Joe Halliday, our Personnel Manager in those days. He was dying of cancer. We all knew, but none of us spoke of it.' He wiped his face with a handkerchief, but it was a gesture of release rather than strain; there was a kind of relief in confession after all this time. 'On the A40 near Beaconsfield, a soldier suddenly reeled out of the darkness. I swerved across the road, but I couldn't avoid him. Shepherd told me to drive on, but I went back to look.' He gave a little shudder of horror at the recollection, a movement that evoked the terror of that moment in the darkness more vividly than his spare account of it. 'I was pretty sure the man was dead. I rang the hospital on the new car phone. It was the first time I ever used it,' he ended inconsequentially.

Hook, who vaguely recalled the case, looked puzzled. 'But I thought the sick man you mentioned—Halliday—was driving,' he said.

'That's what they cooked up between them. We had just five minutes before the police car and the ambulance arrived together. Joe Halliday thought he was helping me. Shepherd pretended he was. I was still shocked. I don't think I'd ever seen anyone killed before, let alone killed anyone myself. I went along with it.'

'Why, Bill?' said Lambert quietly. It was the first time he had spoken since the Vice-Captain had begun his account of this odd melodrama.

'Wendy.' It was almost a whisper. Hook, to whom the name meant nothing, looked at Lambert and held his peace. 'She's always worried when I'm out in the car. Particularly if there's any drink about. Her father drank himself to death, you see. And since her illness, she's totally dependent on the car and me to get her anywhere. Shepherd said how upset she'd be if I lost my licence, and perhaps my job. Oh, he laid it on thick, did Mr Shepherd.' Birch's bitterness had burst forth anew with the mention of his stricken wife and his self-disgust that he should be invoking her as an explanation of his conduct. The detectives, familiar from past usage with road accidents, could picture the scene clearly enough: the rain sluicing down in the winter darkness; the body lying by the roadside behind the Rolls; the driver, his brain atrophied by shock, a puppet at the disposal of his sinister employer and his well-meaning colleague as they awaited the arrival of the police.

'Joe Halliday said he was the driver. Why I let him, I still don't know. The soldier was blind drunk; that came out at the inquest. I wasn't. I'd had a pint and a half; I'd have been perfectly safe on the breathalyser.'

'What was the inquest verdict?' Hook, who knew, was moving the story along.

'Misadventure. I'd have been perfectly safe, but once I'd told the lie there was no turning back. Once Joe Halliday was dead, Shepherd was the only one who knew. I've never told Wendy. I've often been near to it, but as I'd let the whole thing happen to shield her, it seemed especially pointless to make her suffer with me.'

Birch was the kind of instinctively honest man to whom deception is abhorrent: the very process of concealment must have cost him much over five years, quite apart from Shepherd's exploitation of it. Lambert was quite certain he had told them the absolute truth.

'Anything else?' he said gently.

Birch shook his head, but not quite hopelessly: the very process of confession had been a relief to him after the years of deceit. Lambert, back for a moment in the high dark church of his Catholic childhood, feeling his soul uplifted as he knelt before the altar after the divulgence of his sins to the priest, fancied he could see the lightening of Birch's burden of guilt.

'Think hard for just a little longer, Bill. Is there anything you can tell us about anyone else in the case?'

Birch's face clouded. He was emotionally exhausted, so that it was an effort even to think and frame an answer. 'No. I've told you about Mary Hartford and Mike Taylor. I don't think either of them killed Shepherd.'

'Does that mean that you think David Parsons or Debbie Hall is our murderer?' said Lambert. It was cruel, perhaps unfair at this stage, but he too was tired, physically and emotionally. Birch shook his head helplessly.

'Of course not. I'll tell you one thing, but it won't help you at all. Whoever killed Shepherd has my eternal gratitude!'

'As you say, Bill, that doesn't help. Thank you for being frank. We'll be as discreet as we can. That's genuine, but I can't promise anything more tangible.' Both detectives rose as the Vice-Captain went wearily from the room.

DI Rushton could scarcely wait for Birch to move down the corridor before he knocked and entered, a sheet of paper in his hand and importance gleaming in his every feature.

'Well?' said Lambert sharply. He was too tired to use tact with his subordinates. And Rushton was too full of his news to be offended by his Superintendent's brusqueness. The words tumbled out.

'Sir, we have the report from Army Records about your Secretary, Colonel Parsons. He killed a man in Aden. He was court-martialled for it.'

CHAPTER 17

Lambert took the sheet of paper from Rushton. It had been hastily typed from the tape of the telephone conversation with Army Records. In undramatic prose, it told a short dramatic tale. It was soon digested, even by a brain as saturated as his now felt. The low-key style seemed only to underline the startling nature of the facts on the small sheet before him.

He passed it without a word to Hook and went immediately in search of the Secretary. He found him talking to Bill Birch in the car park. Perhaps Parsons had spotted the Vice-Captain's shaken state: it would not have been difficult. Parsons was talking to him in a low voice of consolation and reassurance. Lambert called, 'David, could you organize a pot of tea for three? And then come and share it with Sergeant Hook and me?'

Parsons showed no sign of discomfort at the summons. Perhaps he thought it was to discuss Bill Birch's evidence, for he must have known how long the Vice-Captain had been with the Superintendent, on the course and in the murder room. 'I'll see you tomorrow then, Bill,' Parsons said. He did not quite put an arm round Birch's shoulder, but he saw him into his car with an avuncular air before turning back to the clubhouse. Lambert, conscious of the creased piece of paper he had left with Hook, found the Secretary's calm surprising, even a little irritating. He was reminded of Birch's view that each of the Committee had good cause to wish Shepherd dead. Even if there was no collusion in this murder, his suspects were all in a sense conspirators, sympathetic towards whichever of their number had removed a powerful enemy.

With the tea came rich fruit cake. He bit into it appreciatively in the two minutes which separated its arrival from that of the Secretary. He closed his eyes and breathed deeply for a moment, restoring energy and concentration with his own highly unorthodox modification of his wife's yoga techniques. Opening one eye, he caught Bert Hook looking at him with the solicitude of an anxious mother; he enjoyed the Sergeant's rosy discomfort. 'We're getting old, Bert: they'll have us out to pasture before long,' he said. But he felt better already; it was the emotional rather than the physical strain of his exchanges with Birch that had upset him. Hook was surprised to see how alert, even eager, he looked, when the Secretary's discreet tap at the door announced his arrival.

'Come and sit down, David,' Lambert said. 'Sorry to have you knocking at doors in your own domain, but the circumstances are hardly usual. Perhaps we shall be back to normal in a day or two.'

'I do hope so. But of course you must use the club premises as you see fit. I shall try to be of assistance.' The Secretary, as precise in gesture as in words, sat carefully and meticulously folded his arms. He seemed very much at ease: in this man, the formal manner was a sign of relaxation rather than nervousness. At the end of his working day, he looked as cool as ever in his lightweight grey jacket, his starched shirt, his red-flecked grey tie with its small, tight knot. If he disapproved of the detectives' shirt sleeves and slackened ties, he gave no sign of it. Lambert, feeling a trickle of sweat beneath his left arm, tried not to resent this lizard-like composure in the airless heat. In the panelled room, scarcely altered since the 'thirties, it was Parsons who looked at home. But his aplomb could scarcely survive this interview.

'I said we should need to return to certain matters,' said Lambert, still carefully affable. 'I think we are now in a

position to do so.' Parsons nodded slowly; he must have
been discomposed, for Lambert had encouraged his illusion
that he was to talk about the evidence of the other members
of the Committee, and Parsons knew that he had now seen
all the other four. But the Secretary merely waited coolly
for his next words. No matter: Lambert had plenty of
material to shake him. Once again, he realized with a spurt
of irritation that he was hoping the man would acquit
himself well. David Parsons, with his meticulous military
ways, was not his type, but he was sympathetic enough to
wish him innocent. A hundred years ago, a great empire
had been built on men such as this.

'The murder weapon,' he said by way of opening. If he
hoped to provoke any revelation, or any further deceit, by
its mere mention, he was disappointed. 'Mr Shepherd's
knife, you said earlier, which we laid out for him at our
Committee meetings.'

Lambert quoted the pathologist's report thoughtfully.
'"A heavy knife, probably military in origin, with a seven-
inch blade."' He looked interrogatively at Parsons, but the
Secretary's grey eyes looked back steadily at him; if the thin
lips tightened a fraction, they made no attempt to frame
words. Suddenly, Lambert was too impatient to fence any
longer.

'We have a witness who says that knife is yours, David.
If you think that witness is lying, you had better say so
now.' There was a silence, but little sign of distress from the
Secretary. Lambert thought he was working out who could
be their informant; he would not of course reveal that it was
Vic Edwards. When all this was over, Secretary and Steward
would have to work closely together again. Always assuming
that Parsons was not his man.

'It was a Turkish army knife, issued at the outset of the
First World War,' said Parsons, his precision not at all
impaired by his discomfort. 'It was in the nature, I suppose,
of a military souvenir. I used it in the office as a paper-
knife, but it was rather heavy for letters. I laid it out ready
for the Chairman for one of our meetings four years ago and

I've done it ever since. It's the only time the knife is used.'

'Why did you say it was Shepherd's property?' Lambert's eyes had not left Parsons's face throughout his explanation.

'In effect it was. I put it away with the ink-stand and pen after each meeting and got them out for the next one a month later. It was the only time the knife was used.' Except for other and more violent purposes; perhaps the thought occurred to both men. Lambert tightened the screw a little.

'David, you are a very well-organized man. I don't think you would have told us the knife was the Chairman's if you hadn't intended to deceive us.'

A pause. Then, 'Dammit, John, I feel I'm being cross-examined already!' In Parsons, the use of the Christian name was the first real sign of discomfort.

Lambert said evenly, 'We are talking about the instrument used in the brutal murder of a defenceless man.' Now Parsons was visibly ruffled. His shrug of the shoulders was theatrical, an attempt at a gesture which did not come naturally to this stiff military figure. But he took his time, and when he spoke again he had almost recovered his calm.

'Just so. I suppose it was because you said it was the murder weapon that I didn't like to admit it was mine. It was foolish, of course. Instinctive, I suppose. But I'm not used to being involved in murder inquiries.' His little nervous laugh was just right for an innocent man, supporting his suggestion of a lie that was natural and of minor importance. He had recovered his composure.

'Not even in your Army days?' Lambert's counter was below the belt, but meant to be so; murder investigations had no Queensbury Rules. The thrust brought its rewards. Parsons swung his face back towards his adversary with the look of a startled animal. For a moment it might have been the face of a murderer, as fear and hate flashed across the unguarded features.

'What do you mean?' was all that Parsons said, but for an instant Lambert had been glad that that heavy Turkish knife was not to hand. He looked calmly at his notes; now he controlled the exchanges and could play them at his pace.

'You were rather foolish not to be more forthcoming this morning, Colonel Parsons.' The Secretary's eyes flashed alarm again at the use of the title, then dropped back to the edge of the huge oak table. 'Army Records are normally secret, but you should have known they would be open to those pursuing a murder inquiry.'

'I didn't kill Shepherd.' The Secretary's tone was dull and hopeless.

'Maybe not. You don't help us to believe that when you try to deceive us elsewhere. It will save time if I tell you that I know you were court-martialled for killing a civilian when you were in the Army.'

In the long pause which followed this, the first breeze to enter this room on this stifling day slid through the high window, ruffling Hook's papers a little on the periphery of the central confrontation. Lambert, knowing Parsons had to speak eventually, was willing to prompt him now. 'In Aden, I believe. I should like you to tell us the circumstances.'

'Oh, I killed him all right! That wasn't in dispute at the court martial.' The blunt words were surprising enough, but it was the tone which was really startling. There was a bitter pride in the Secretary's voice: it was not difficult to see him in another place, in his Colonel's uniform, standing erect and disdainful in a military court as he asserted his guilt defiantly.

'It was a long time ago now, though sometimes in the middle of the night it seems like yesterday. It was at the height of the Aden emergency, when terrorists were assassinating our men and getting away with it. All leave had been stopped and we were only allowed out of camp on duty. One night, on the edge of darkness, we were coming back from a major patrol. We travelled in an armoured truck, with one man to keep watch with a sten gun in the top turret. That man had been my Platoon Sergeant for four years when I was a major. As we passed through a village two miles from camp, he was shot in the back. He fell back into the truck, then died in seconds as I held him.'

He paused. At a nod from Lambert, Bert Hook slid a cup and saucer silently before the Secretary. He sipped the tea, unconscious of what he did. He was staring at the wall behind Lambert, but his terse, low-key account, as sparse and precise as his language about everyday trivia, was a perfect vehicle for the understated melodrama it related. He finished the tea, then looked down into the empty cup as if wondering where it had come from. Then he picked up his account as if he had never paused.

'What the sniper didn't know is that we were only the first of three vehicles returning from the patrol. The lads behind were out of their trucks in a flash and into the house the shots had come from. They were red berets— paratroopers—and they didn't mess about. Three terrorists got away into the fields behind the house: it was dark remember. But we caught five men. Including the one who shot my Sergeant; he had the rifle in his hands.'

'Was that fully established at the inquiry?' This bluntness was from Hook, doing his chief's dirty work for him; the Superintendent might have to live with this man as his golf club Secretary for years after this case was solved.

'Of course it was him!' Parsons's sudden blaze of animation was the more shocking against the low-key control which had so far characterized his account of these events. 'Oh, I know those wogs said afterwards that the man who fired the shot had got away, but they would, wouldn't they? The man who fired those shots was the man I found with the rifle in his hands. Would you have believed his story about picking up the rifle after the sniper fled?' His eyes flashed with challenge, his thin lips curled back with the contempt of the question. Lambert ignored it: he had no intention of getting involved in the passions of terrorism in another place and a previous generation.

When Parsons spoke again, he resumed the simple, under-stated style of his earlier account though his tones now were tinged with a resentment nursed over the years. 'They dragged this ruffian before me as I got out of my truck. My shirt was wet with the warm blood of my Sergeant. The man the paras were holding looked past me at the body and laughed in my face. I took out my service revolver and shot him on the spot. I find it difficult to think that was wrong, even today.'

'But a court martial followed?' Lambert prompted.

'Of course.' Lambert's pride in military justice, even when he might be the victim of it, flashed out. 'It was inevitable. I knew that as soon as I'd shot the vermin. I didn't deny it. The real soldiers were for me: they understood the situation and my reaction. But the civilian pen-pushers felt we were near a political solution in Aden. As usual, they wanted to placate the locals. I was severely reprimanded, reduced to the rank of Major, and sent back home.' He smiled bitterly. 'It was regarded as a light sentence.'

All three of them waited through a heavy silence for the next question. Lambert felt as he asked it as if he were following a well-learned script.

'David, why Colonel Parsons here? You must have left the Army as Major.'

'I applied for the job as Major. Shepherd read my application form, saw that I had been a Colonel, and called me that throughout the interview. I wanted to point out I was now Major, but of course I couldn't do so without revealing to the entire interviewing panel what I've just told you. Which would have meant no job; I'd already lost four other jobs once that tale had come out. When I came here I found that Shepherd had already had our club notepaper and diaries printed with my name on them as Colonel Parsons. So I was stuck with it. It seemed fairly harmless—I thought at first that he was just trying to flatter me.' His drawn face was broken for a moment by a caustic smile at the ludicrous inaccuracy of such a judgement.

'Then I found he knew all about events in Aden and had done it all quite deliberately. At first, I didn't know why. Then I found he had a hold over me . . . He liked having holds over people: as time went on, I found that.'

'Did he threaten you with disclosure?'

'More than that. He threatened to expose me and then dismiss me in disgrace, on account of what he called my "deliberate deception". I like it here. My wife likes it here. We're settled and we have a circle of friends—mostly through the Golf Club. My life would collapse without this job. We've picked the pieces up once. I don't think we could do it again.'

Outside the long leaded window to Lambert's right, the sky had turned to a leaden grey. The air was hot and still as ever, but no bird sang now. David Parsons removed his hands from the table he had gripped during the last minutes of his story. He raised his cool grey eyes to look back into Lambert's and smiled a slow, unexpected smile.

'This morning was the happiest of my life. Whoever killed Shepherd deserves a medal. He was vermin!'

To Lambert, it was becoming a recurrent chorus. And Parsons had used the same term he had employed for that other defenceless man, shot in sudden hatred all those years ago.

CHAPTER 18

Lambert suddenly felt very tired. He stared dully at the table and tried to bully his brain into some degree of agility. When he looked up at the clock, he was surprised to find it was 6.30. He stood up; a minor decision would be a substitute for deep thought.

'Come on, Bert. Let's get home and salvage a few Brownie points whilst we have the chance.' He shuffled his few papers together: he had taken not a single note during their second interview with David Parsons, preferring to leave that to Hook while he watched the Secretary. 'Get home and eat, and see your boys before they go to bed. But I may need you later; don't move far from the phone.'

DI Rushton was delighted to assume sole charge of the

murder room again. Probably he hoped the Chief Constable would ring again whilst the Superintendent was away, thought Lambert sourly. Whereas his own thought as he prepared to leave was that at least Garner wouldn't get through to him here; tired and stale, he did not trust his tongue at this stage of the day.

He drove deliberately slowly, letting the three miles of hawthorn-edged lanes work their own therapy. The scent with the windows down was overpowering, for the air was still and heavy beneath the grey cloud which now filled the whole sky. His small detached house was modest enough, but the garden which was its chief glory was lush with late spring growth. As he turned through the five-barred gate into the gravelled drive, the beech hedge with its bright new leaves seemed as usual to wall in his haven.

Christine was closing the French windows. By the time he got inside, she had the television on and turned at right angles to his armchair. 'They need eighty off the last thirteen overs. Gower's out,' she said. 'But I expect you've been listening to it on your way home.' It was the last of the one-day internationals. He had forgotten it completely: he must be even more tired and disturbed than he was aware of. Christine took one look at him, said, 'Something quick and tasty, I suppose,' and disappeared into the kitchen. She knew better than to ask him for choices about food when he looked like this.

He was glad to watch the flanelled figures flitting busily before the vast, shirt-sleeved crowd on the screen before him, glad to see all this utter seriousness and intense physical endeavour poured into a game. The batsman's flailing smear across a good-length ball connected, the fielder's desperate dive was unavailing, the crowd cheered his failure to prevent the boundary with good-natured excitement. These proper happenings in a sporting context were a reminder of the sensationally inappropriate setting of the crime he was investigating. He settled to watch the cricket and establish a saner background to his world.

When Christine returned with his food, his chin had fallen

forward and the grey hairs on the back of his head seemed more numerous than ever. She remembered her father sleeping like this years ago; when her quiet voice evoked no response, she had to force herself to shake her husband's shoulder. 'Come on, John, grub's up,' she said gently. For no more than a half a second, he looked at her vacantly and didn't know where he was; normally he slept lightly and was instantly awake at any disturbance. It was a moment that brought home to him quite how emotionally draining he had found the day. Although he had twenty-six years' experience of all kinds of police work, this was new ground for him: he had never before had to question acquaintances and friends in a murder inquiry.

He had not thought he was so hungry. The omelette, salad and crisp brown bread had this best of all sauces, so that even the 'No chips then?' with which he acknowledged his wife's switch to a healthier diet for them was no more than a worn-out fragment of comic ritual. He was finishing his first strawberries of the year and Christine was setting the coffee pot upon the table when the phone rang. Her look carried accusation as well as inquiry. 'Probably for me,' he acknowledged. 'It *is* a murder investigation. Christine: I told them to put calls through here.' It would be one of two people. He guessed Cyril Garner, and was wrong.

'John, it's Mary Harford. You want to see me?'

'I *need* to see you, Mary,' he corrected firmly. 'Certain facts have emerged which make it imperative that I see you quickly.'

'This evening? I've only just finished in theatre.'

'This evening, I'm afraid. Shall we say at the Golf Club in an hour's time? Or would you prefer me to come to the hospital?' He could feel the tension at the other end of the line. He wondered if he should have said 'Murder Room' to reinforce the gravity of the meeting: he was dealing with a woman who had apparently concealed an association with the deceased, whose prints had been found on the murder weapon, who had appeared moments after the murder with blood upon the cuff of her blouse, according to Bill Birch.

His Chief Constable would probably feel he should have been waiting at the hospital to arrest her as she emerged from the theatre. Just when he was wondering if she would speak at all, her voice came, low but quite steady.

'No, John, not here. Too many tongues to wag when police question the Chief Nursing Officer. And not at the Golf Club, please. I'd rather not face that room again.' How did she know they were using the Committee Room as their murder room, he wondered. Then he realized she must have rung there as requested before her call to him here. 'May I come to your house?' she said. 'It may be irregular, but I assure you that what I have to say may be said as freely there as anywhere.'

Her words sounded as though they might herald a confession. His spirits should have lifted, but his mouth was dry with despondency. He was being very unprofessional.

'Very well. I'll get Christine to get the coffee going. You remember where we are? See you in quarter of an hour or so, then.'

He put down the phone, thought for a moment, and rang Bert Hook. 'Hope you've managed to eat. Our chief suspect is coming here. Can you be here in ten minutes?' There were limits to his unprofessional procedures; if Mary Hartford was going to confess, or even to deny guilt under his questioning, he wanted a witness and a record.

Christine had poured the coffee. He stirred his thoughtfully, forgetting she had knocked him off sugar. 'Mary Hartford is coming round in a few minutes,' he said.

'Good,' said his wife. 'I like Mary. She's a sparky lady. If more people like her ran the world, it would be a better place.' Lambert looked up startled, searching her face for signs of irony, and finding none. As usual, he had told Christine not the tiniest detail of his working day. How could she know that this modern-day Florence Nightingale seemed the likeliest perpetrator of last night's brutal and calculated murder?

'It's business, Chris. Bert Hook will be arriving as well.'

'Business? Here?' It was an accusation.

'She asked to come here,' he said defensively. 'Anywhere she'll talk will do me,' he added peevishly.

Christine began to clear the table, stacking crockery on a large tray in her quick, efficient way. When the domestic front was tidy, she came and stood behind her husband and began gently massaging his neck. 'This can't be easy for you, John,' she said at length.

'It's more difficult than I expected,' was all he said. The terse understatements were a mark of their understanding.

Christine let Bert Hook in, even asked briefly about his wife and the boys. Hook had married late and happily, so that his children were many years younger than hers. When Mary Hartford's car crunched over the gravel, she was forty yards away at the end of the garden, visible proof that their privacy within the house was assured. Through the big picture window which overlooked the back garden, Lambert and Mary Hartford as they sat opposite each other would catch sight of her at different points in their exchanges. For both of them, she was a reminder of a normal, saner world to set against the Grand Guignol wonderland into which they seemed to have strayed. Their talk of secrets, lies and killing was set against a world where ordinary people watered tomato plants, potted up cuttings and looked to the morrow with hope, not fear.

Mary Hartford looked white and drawn. Hook, who had not seen her before, treated her with exaggerated courtesy, and she was grateful rather than amused. She sank into the armchair opposite Lambert which he had made ready for her, but he noticed she did not relax. Her neck, slender and fragile above her dark green costume, looked longer than he remembered it. She did not put her handbag down beside her chair, but clasped it upon her lap with both hands. The spinsterish pose made him wonder automatically if the bag contained something she wished to conceal. Then he realized as he saw the thin wrists quivering that she was clasping it to still her trembling hands.

'Drink?' he said automatically. 'We have whisky. Or

gin.' He was on his feet, moving awkwardly towards the sideboard.

'No, thank you,' she said, almost primly. From the corner of his eye, Lambert caught Hook's silent sigh of relief: obviously he was thinking of a defence counsel ridiculing a confession extracted in a Superintendent's home from a defendant plied with drink. As if to reassure him, Mary Hartford looked down at her hands and said, 'That coffee you promised would be lovely,' and Hook bustled to serve her.

Lambert had not worked out how to start. Clearly he was going to need to question her: she had not driven here bursting with the need to talk. She looked five years older than she had in the morning; the mouth was thinner, the age-lines around the eyes more visible, the dark patches beneath them more marked.

'I'm sorry to drag you out. You must be very tired after your work in theatre,' he said weakly.

'You didn't: it was I who suggested I came here. And I don't usually look as bad as this, even after theatre, but thanks for the euphemism. What can I do for you?' She took the coffee from Hook and for a moment she might have been composing herself for an interview with a relative of one of her patients. Then her cup rattled in her hand against the saucer and the illusion of calm was gone. She stared at her hands in astonishment, so that Lambert could not believe they had ever let her down like this before. Then she sipped the coffee with determination and forced herself to look straight at him as he spoke.

'I'll be direct with you, Mary. I think you would prefer it. In any case, it will be best.'

'Intriguing,' she said, and the tight lips tried a little smile which they could not hold. 'And ominous.'

'We have not been idle during the day, Mary. I told you of the break-in to Mr Shepherd's car this morning. But you have probably not heard about the fire in the greenkeeper's cottage in the woods by the seventeenth.' In the white face the brown eyes widened, but he thought with surprise, not apprehension. He waited, but she said nothing. He felt in his pocket, found the piece of white card he sought, and tried to produce it as if it were not the Ace of Trumps. 'The cottage is furnished,' he said tersely. 'The bedroom at the back was scarcely touched by the fire. On the mantelpiece we found this.' He passed her the photograph of James Shepherd with his arm round her and those two conventional, innocent smiles at a camera a decade ago, which now seemed overlaid with sinister implications.

He watched her closely as she stared unblinking as a statue at the picture in her hand. At length, her other hand gathered itself into a fist and pushed against her mouth. When she spoke, the nausea at the back of her throat distorted her words.

'I haven't seen this for years.'

'I think you should tell me all about it,' said Lambert. 'In your own time.' The coffee cup, now fortunately empty, shook crazily upon its saucer as she took it up again, and Hook started forward to take it.

There was a long silence before she spoke. Perhaps it was not more than ten seconds: to the two detectives, listening to the slow clicking of the grandfather clock in the hall, it seemed much longer.

'I knew James still had photographs from that time. He reminded me of it when he thought it might embarrass me!' It was exactly the same flash of resentment they had seen in other witnesses: Lambert would have sworn that Michael Taylor and Mary Hartford had nothing in common, but now in her brief, bitter shrug she echoed him. 'I was his mistress for just over a year. Nine, ten years ago now. He could be charming when he wanted, you know. More so in those days. And you can be surprisingly naïve at thirty-nine. I hadn't had many men.' Her eyes stared out through the window at the banks of cloud over the chestnuts; Lambert wanted to tell her that they weren't judging her, then realized that she was trying to explain to herself, not to them, how such a thing could have happened. 'He had power, money, education, most of the usual aphrodisiacs.

He could even make me laugh a little, then. My mother, who was still alive then, thought what a good match it would be. Of course, I saw through him soon enough. It took me months to end it, though. And when I did, how he made me suffer. If you think Hell hath no fury like a woman scorned, you should have seen James Shepherd in action.' She clenched her small fists at the memory, and ground them into her thighs.

It was Hook who broke the silence this time. 'Miss Hartford, can you think of any reason why Mr Shepherd should have kept pictures of you in that old cottage?' he said.

'No. None. None at all.' She seemed near breaking point.

'You didn't go there with him during your association?' asked Lambert gently.

'I didn't even know the place existed then,' she said.

'Can you think of any reason why anyone else should put this photograph there?' said Lambert, and caught Hook's look of surprise behind her chair.

'No. I knew James had photographs, and letters too. He reminded me often enough. I thought from what he said that they were in that wall-safe in the Committee Room in what he called his "black box". But why should anyone else—' She stopped and looked at him, her eyes wide with horror.

'We are dealing with a murderer, Mary. If what you say is true, someone must have put that photograph there. Perhaps to draw our attention to your past relationship with the victim. You may think that "Hell hath no fury" etc. is overrated but we come across it as a motive for violence often enough.'

'Perhaps James wanted to taunt another woman with my picture. It's the kind of thing he would do,' she said; her voice was hollow with shock as she tried to convince herself.

'It's possible, I suppose. If we don't make an arrest within twenty-four hours, we shall have to investigate all kinds of possibilities. Tell me about this "black box" you think was kept in the wall-safe.'

'It was the box in which James kept documents of a particular kind. Letters, photographs, anything which gave him some kind of a hold over people. He used to keep them at home, but after he became Chairman of the Golf Club he kept them in that wall-safe. He had the only key—that safe is no longer used by the Club: there's a bigger and better one in the Secretary's office. James used to smile and nod his head towards the Committee Room when he was threatening us— he liked the feeling that the instrument of torture was near at hand but beyond the reach of any of us.'

'Us? You are aware of this kind of blackmail being used on others?' The brown eyes were steady now, assessing Lambert, wondering how much he already knew. She took a deep, weary breath.

'I was his mistress, John, more's the pity. I know his methods better than anyone. I know all about his hold over Michael Taylor. I can guess from the way in which he said "Colonel Parsons" that there is some query over our Secretary's army rank. I can imagine exactly the way in which he would threaten Debbie Hall and Len Jackson. He has some hold over Bill Birch, though I don't know what . . . Surely all this can't be relevant to your investigation.'

'It may be; you've just listed a nice selection of motives,' said Lambert drily. He nodded to Bert Hook, triggering their pre-arranged direct approach to the next area of questioning. The Sergeant spoke with deliberate formality.

'Miss Hartford, the Superintendent has told you we have been active during the day. As part of the routine, we take the fingerprints of all people known to have been in the vicinity of a serious crime. I understand your prints were taken late this morning, along with those of the other Committee members. We now have the reports of the print and photographic officers who covered the scene of the crime, together with the pathologist's report on the cause and time of death. Now, can you add anything to what you told Superintendent Lambert this morning about your movements after the end of the Committee Meeting last night?'

She did not even turn to look at Hook, though she had listened carefully enough to his words. 'No,' she said. The slender hands were back clasping her handbag; she looked down at the almost girlish fingers as though they belonged to somebody else. Did she suspect already that those fingers had betrayed her?

Lambert's voice when it came was as quiet as hers, but it smashed the surface of the scene beyond repair.

'Did you go back to see Shepherd before or after you had your drink in the bar?' he said. He knew the answer, but he wanted it from her.

The wide brown eyes had only one emotion now as they stared wildly at him: they were small pools of terror. They dominated the face before him until he could see no other feature. He was drawn on inexorably, unwilling to let her flounder into further lies.

'The murder knife has been formally confirmed as the heavy knife you have seen so often in meetings. There was only one print identifiable upon it. It is a thumbprint of yours, Mary.'

They should have been prepared for her reaction. But her previous composure under extreme stress had been such that it caught them by surprise. Mary Hartford, Lady Captain of Burnham Cross Golf Club, Chief Nursing Officer responsible for fifty-two staff, burst into uncontrollable tears.

The sobbing racked the whole of the slender body, so that for a moment it was as if she were subject to some sort of fit. Over the twitching woman, Lambert saw in his Sergeant's face a strange conflict of compassion and triumph. Bert Hook thought they had arrived at their murderer. He was waiting for his Superintendent to charge and caution Mary Hartford about anything she now might wish to say.

Gradually, the sobbing subsided. Neither man offered any physical contact: they had been in similar situations too often to venture that. Lambert waited patiently, watching his wife moving in silhouette against a twilight sky at the bottom of the garden. Eventually, he transferred a man's handkerchief from his pocket to the clutch of those starfish fingers spread across the handbag. When the tears ceased to flow, the small body which now seemed so vulnerable in the big armchair stopped trembling. With a long, shuddering sigh, the moment passed and the brown eyes in the face full of pain looked up again at Lambert.

'What now?' she said hopelessly.

'That's rather up to you, Mary. If you want a lawyer present, you can have one, and of course you don't have to say anything at all if you don't wish to. I should be interested in your account of what happened when you went back to that Committee Room. The true account this time, of course.'

Despite this last thrust, there was a gleam of hope in the now very revealing face opposite him. 'You mean you're still not convinced I did it?' she said wonderingly.

'Whether you did or you didn't, I should obviously be very interested in your story,' said Lambert; his small, sardonic smile was the first one to surface in that quiet lounge for a long time. It seemed to encourage Mary Hartford, who began to speak in measured, low-key tones, as if outlining a nightmare that had happened to someone else.

'I went back to the Committee Room to plead with James about Bill Birch. He'd been particularly cutting to Bill at the end of the meeting. Bill's wife is very ill, probably more ill than even Bill knows. I thought James should know that; surely it would make a difference, even with him. It was— would have been—the first time I'd been alone with him for months. I had to screw myself up to confront him.'

With the recollection, she paused. Lambert tried not to be hypnotized by the sight of his sodden handkerchief twisting into a grey-white rope between those slender, unconscious fingers. The brittle control held. 'When I entered the Committee Room, I thought it was empty at first. Then I saw James's body lying on the other side of the table. My first impulse was to run as far away as possible and pretend I'd never been there. I should be ashamed of that and perhaps I am. I have been a nurse for thirty years now, trained to preserve life. But in this case what should have been instinctive had to be worked out, as a second thought.

'I went round the table to check if James was really dead. He lay on his back with his eyes fully open. No pulse, no heartbeat, no breath. I have seen death many times, John, and I was certain of it here. Perhaps I would have tried the kiss of life, if those eyes I knew so well had not been open. But I knew it was no use.'

The three of them were silent now, weighing that moment of horror when the lips that once had fastened upon Shepherd's in sexual passion had rejected that last, hopeless gesture of mercy. Then Bert Hook said quietly, 'Miss Hartford, why didn't you report the murder at once, as an ordinary innocent citizen should?' He was clutching after the normal procedures he felt being moved away from him; against his better judgement, he felt sympathy suffusing him for this woman he had expected his chief to charge by now.

She looked at him, ravaged, but defiant in her misery. 'I was glad to see him dead!' It would have been shocking if they hadn't heard it so often before. 'I didn't want to see his murderer, male or female, caught. This is what I think now. It wasn't as clear as that then. I checked the body, put my hand on the hilt of the knife, then left it where it was. I thought clearly enough to wipe the handle with my handkerchief, but I must have missed the end if you found a thumbprint. There was nothing in the safe. I went to the lounge. As you say, I was probably fairly quiet over my drink.'

'Others said it, not me, Mary.'

'So why did you ask me whether I went back to the Committee Room before or after the drinks?'

'Mainly to see whether you would tell the truth,' he said shamelessly. 'It wasn't just that you were quiet, you see. That could have been for any number of innocent reasons. But one of your Committee colleagues spotted blood upon your cuff.'

'Bill Birch.' She nodded mirthlessly, whilst Lambert recalled his thought of the morning that this woman should have been a detective. 'Ironic that I should have been trying to protect him when I went back to see James.'

'Probably I shouldn't tell you this, but the information was prised from his reluctant lips. It quite upset him to tell me what a good citizen should,' said Lambert gently. He dared not look at Bert Hook, but if Birch and Hartford were both innocent, they would have to resume a friendship which had been deeper than he had known before this case arose.

Mary Hartford refused more coffee but accepted a very small whisky. She drank it with a wry face, as though it were medicine, then drove shakily but carefully through the five-barred gate and away into the last of the twilight. She had been particularly anxious to avoid Christine. It was the realization of how important the cool, professional front of the hospital matron was to her which brought both men back to that real world they seemed for a time to have forsaken.

They stood by Bert Hook's battered Ford and looked west, to where a vivid purple veined the sky between black clouds. 'Do you believe her?' It was Hook who voiced the banal question which occupied them both.

Lambert continued to look at nature's spectacular chromatic display rather than at his Sergeant as he replied. 'Maybe. Let's set it against what the others say. By this time tomorrow, I think we'll know our murderer.' Hook climbed heavily into his car and started the engine. Still looking at the changed sky, Lambert mused, 'So fair and foul a day I have not seen,' but Hook mercifully did not hear enough to respond.

As Lambert turned back to the house, the first livid fork of lightning rent the sky above the greenhouse and the thunder rumbled ominously up the valley. By the time he reached the door, heavy drops of rain were exploding on the gravel.

CHAPTER 19

The storm raged through most of the night. Christine Lambert slept little, but her exhausted husband was less disturbed.

He woke once to a Wagnerian clamour, with lightning illuminating the room with flashes recurrent enough for an old movie. Later in the night, he cried out with a child's fear, and she knew he was back in the blitz amidst the crash of falling walls and the death of his grandparents. She clasped his arm, soothing the trembling middle-aged man as softly as she would one of the children she taught by day. Soon the trembling ceased; he never woke.

In the early-morning sunlight, the world seemed washed by the storm. The humidity was gone, and the air at the kitchen door was fresh and stimulating; the birds had postponed their dawn chorus until the thunder had rumbled away, so that now the garden was alive with their song. 'No bacon and eggs, I suppose,' Lambert said glumly as he came to the table, but he tackled his muesli and bran with considerable relish.

Even the local paper could not spoil his breakfast. 'Brutal Murder at Local Golf Club,' trumpeted the headline across the front page. There were the ritual comments about Shepherd's pre-eminence in business and golf club affairs. David Parsons had said that his Chairman would be 'much missed', but it would be difficult for a Secretary to say much less. Old George Williams had had to contact one or two former captains to get anything more fulsome about the deceased. Then came, 'The murder investigation is being master-minded by Detective Superintendent John Lambert, himself a long-standing member of the golf club. Superintendent Lambert has headed many successful murder teams and is something of a local celebrity, but at the time of going to press he remained tight-lipped and baffled about this sensational crime.'

Lambert practised his tight-lipped baffled look on the back of his cereal spoon, but the distortion ruined the effect, so he returned to George's deathless prose. 'A shaken Michael Taylor, the current Captain of the Burnham Cross Golf Club, refused to comment and the Lady Captain, Mary Hartford, was occupied with her duties as Senior Nursing Officer at our local hospital. Debbie Hall, the attractive Social Functions Secretary at the Golf Club, said that the killing had come as a complete shock and no one had any idea who could have perpetrated the crime.'

'Pretty dull bricks from precious little straw,' muttered Lambert with satisfaction, and moved to his second cup of tea. Christine, who had watched his perusal of the paper with some apprehension from the kitchen, thought it safe to emerge with fresh toast.

It took Cyril Garner to disturb his calm. The Chief Constable rang as he was finishing his breakfast and said gloomily, 'You've seen the papers?'

'Only the local rag,' said Lambert, with a cheerfulness which was the nearest thing to a licensed insolence which was available to him.

'The nationals have picked it up. They've been on to me already this morning. Wanting to know if we're near an arrest yet and so on. I've stonewalled, but I can't go on for ever.'

It was on the tip of his tongue to tell Garner that he hoped for an arrest before long, but he thought better of it just in time. He didn't want to conduct his tenuous theory through the Chief Constable's maze at this point. He outlined Mary Hartford's story as succinctly as he could. Garner sounded disappointed as he asked, 'Do you believe her?'

'It's possible,' said Lambert evasively. 'She's very well respected as Matron at the Hospital.' He used the out-of-date title as deliberate shorthand, knowing it would impress his socially conscious Chief.

Garner countered with triumphant finality, 'Well, I've arranged a Press Conference for one p.m. at the Golf Club. It will keep these press boys at bay and show them what we're about. You can report to me beforehand; I'll be down at twelve-thirty or so.'

'Damn!' said Lambert, when he was sure his Chief had rung off. But he said it fairly cheerfully: he had been expecting a Press Conference since the case began.

He had reached the garage when Christine called him back for the second, more intriguing phone call. The voice at the other end of the line sounded distraught. 'John? It's Michael Taylor here. I must see you!'

Lambert fell automatically into tones of professional calm. 'Fine, Michael: I need to see you again anyway. I'm off to the murder room at the Golf Club this very minute. Any time this morning would—'

'No! Not there. Not at the clubhouse.' The staccato delivery crackled down the line like gunfire.

'It's where our murder room is, Michael.'

'Near there, then. Not in the clubhouse.'

'All right then. You name the place.

Suddenly Lambert sensed a crisis and willed the frightened voice at the other end of the wire not to cut him off. It had become important that this nervous fish did not escape into the deeper pool beyond his net.

A pause, then the irregular breath of excited distress. 'On the course. Behind the sixth green. It's quiet there. Come alone, in half an hour. I've things to tell you.'

Despite the deliberately controlled reaction of long experience, Lambert felt his own pulse quicken at the prospect. 'Fine. I'll be there, Michael. Can you give me any idea—' But the Captain was gone; Taylor had put the phone down even before the Superintendent accepted the arrangement. Lambert was left staring stupidly at the phone and wondering. A confession? A beguiling thought, but he doubted it. Vital evidence? Much more possible; one of his first tasks today had been to question Taylor about why he had lied about his movements after the Committee Meeting. He

wondered as he drove through the lanes whether what
Taylor had to say would support the case he had begun to
assemble in his own mind. Evidence was what he needed.

Hook was already in the murder room when he arrived,
compiling a more formal account of Mary Hartford's story
from the notes he had made on the previous evening. 'Do
that in the car,' said Lambert. He explained what they were
about as he drove up the narrow unpaved road which led
through the course to the parking-ground by the tenth tee.
This was an alternative starting point used by members
when the course was crowded, as on Saturday and Sunday
mornings. From here, he could cut across to the meeting-
place assigned to him by the Captain: the sixth green was
within two hundred yards of this upper parking-ground.

Hook remained reluctantly in the car as Lambert ob-
served Taylor's repeated instruction to come alone. He had
chosen a quiet place indeed, where no human eye was likely
to observe them at this hour, and Lambert had to quell the
unbidden thought that he might be wandering this verdant
Elysium with a murderer.

After the night's storm, the ground was sodden in a few
places, but the gravelly subsoil would soon absorb the
surface water; among inland courses, this was as dry as any
in England. As the thunder had rolled reluctantly away, the
temperature had risen towards that of the last few days,
though the weather did not seem settled. At a point where
three giant sweet chestnuts formed a huge natural suntrap,
the grass steamed gently under a brilliant sun and the wet
vegetation smelt almost tropical in its warm dampness. The
birds chirruped their shrill approval as they moved to feed
the young in their nests. Otherwise it was almost eerily
quiet. And there was no sign of Michael Taylor.

Lambert stood on the edge of the sixth green and looked
in the direction of the invisible clubhouse. This was the way
the Captain must come, for his car had not been parked on
the upper parking-ground. Lambert had thought he would
be already here, for he had seen the red sports car at the
clubhouse when he called there to collect Hook. He strolled

round the semi-circle behind the green with a proprietorial air, inspecting the eight rhododendrons he had planted with the Greenkeeper at the end of the winter. They had not only taken, but flowered quite well. Now, as he pulled off the dead flowerheads, he saw plenty of light green sprigs of new growth, and indulged in that delicious smugness peculiar to horticultural success.

He looked at his watch. Taylor was ten minutes overdue. Annoying, on a day which would inevitably be crowded without such diversions. He cursed both his dilatory Captain and Cyril Garner's press conference, for they had encroached upon each end of his morning. Reluctantly, he went a further ten yards beyond the rhododendrons to inspect the young copper beech they had planted at the same time.

Initially, it was the sound which puzzled him. A quiet one, which at first he could not place. A murmur of flies. Early in the season for that. Perhaps the damp and the heat upon its heels had brought them out. He moved a step or two further, and the murmur became a more insistent buzzing. Bluebottles. He saw them in a thick column ahead of him as he struggled clumsily through the brambles. Perhaps a stoat had left a half-eaten rabbit here; he moved cautiously.

It was as well he did. For it would never have done for a Superintendent to tread clumsily upon a body. Lambert recognized the expensive sweater Michael Taylor had worn on the previous day. Without it, immediate identification would have been difficult. The Captain lay face downwards. An inch or so of the carefully waved blond hair on the left of the head was undisturbed. The rest of the crown and the whole of the right side of the face were a pulpy mass of blood and bone, where blow after savage blow had been rained upon them.

Lambert stood over what had so recently been a man, paralysed for a moment by shock and revulsion. And the bluebottles resumed their feast upon the shattered skull.

CHAPTER 20

Lambert looked up from the horror before him to the mighty trees above his head. He caught no watching eye, but the disturbing thought persisted that a violent, perhaps an unhinged, killer could not be far away. As he hurried back to his car, he was glad the public could not see one of its senior police representatives so disturbed by this idea.

Bert Hook was immersed in his tabloid newspaper's reaction to the case. 'Golf Club Chief's Violent Murder' barked the headline. A subsidiary heading, above a fuzzy old photograph of Debbie Hall, ran, 'Blonde Dance Secretary Hints at Sex Scandal'. Debbie's refusal to comment had been flexibly interpreted. Lambert wasted a fleeting moment wondering what this organ of enlightenment would make of the scene he had just left.

For the first time ever, he was glad of the car-phone which modern technology had forced upon him. Within minutes, the Serious Crime squad had been alerted. The scene of crime team, the fingerprints officer, the photographer, the five detective constables who would comb the undergrowth around the murder spot, would be here as quickly as the ambulance, whose only function would be to remove in due course the gory mortal remains of Michael Taylor.

Listening to his own voice as it gave the terse commands and the directions which would pinpoint the spot on the course for these professional reinforcements, Lambert thought it that of a stranger. It had the harsh impersonal tone of an automaton. It made him realize how much his discovery behind the sixth green had shaken him. Thirty-six hours earlier, the murder of James Shepherd had removed a man whose passing none so far regretted. The CID could make no distinctions in murder: that was the job of the courts. Lambert would use all his powers to discover Shepherd's murderer, but when that professional task was accomplished he might have sympathy for the killer. The violent dispatch of Michael Taylor was another matter. The late Captain of Burnham Cross Golf Club was flawed, weak, even perhaps pathetic. But his sins were venial: there could be no motive for his brutal despatch other than the desperate need of Shepherd's killer to protect himself. Michael Taylor's nervousness yesterday, his abject collapse under questioning, had not been occasioned by his guilt. He had simply known more than was good for him about the murderer.

Violence bred violence. Once murder was undertaken, the culprit was driven to desperate means to protect himself. Had Lambert heeded the lessons of experience, he might have protected this second victim. Hook, watching his chief sideways, waited for the orders he had not dared to invite during the Superintendent's furious concentration upon the car phone. When Lambert regarded that instrument balefully and muttered, 'Things bad begun make strong themselves by ill,' his Sergeant knew better than to reveal his knowledge that this flawed philosophy was Macbeth's. 'O' levels did not entitle a man to such contributions; quotations were an indulgence best left to Chief Inspectors and above, especially in circumstances such as these.

Lambert said slowly, 'Ring Mary Hartford, Debbie Hall and Bill Birch.' He extracted a golf club diary from the door pocket of the Vauxhall. 'All members' phone numbers are in there. Check what they've been doing in the last hour. Don't mention our second murder, of course.'

Hook looked pained that he should be thought capable of such clumsiness. 'What about David Parsons?' he said.

'Tell the murder room at the clubhouse to alert him. He'll need to guide our colleagues to the exact spot. And I'd better be there to meet them. I'll see Parsons.' Lambert eased his long legs out of the car again, sniffing air that seemed less welcoming than when he had set out for his rendezvous with Taylor half an hour earlier. He came to a small decision. 'Ask those three to come to the murder room before our press conference. Say midday. If we're no further forward, they can hear what Our Leader has to say to the media. Without being sighted by the newshounds, of course.'

Hook was not deceived. 'Do you think we're nearer to an arrest?' he said. Lambert in his chastened mood was serious and communicative. He said quietly, 'I think I know who did it. Proving it may be much more difficult.' He had almost told Hook his murderer. Perhaps the fact that such knowledge had already cost one man his death made him cautious at the point of revelation; or perhaps it was the less worthy consideration that he might be absurdly wrong.

The police cars and the ambulance arrived together, directed by David Parsons, who even in this crisis was careful to select the route where vehicles might least damage his course. The Secretary descended grim-faced from the first of the two police vehicles and stood on one side whilst Lambert organized the disposition of the police teams and led them beneath the trees to their grim work. The column of flies rose and dispersed itself before the CID men, who waved them away distastefully and inched cautiously forward as Lambert called, 'Move carefully—there will be footprints.'

He was relieved to see Dr Burgess coming forward eagerly from the second police car. 'Glad you could come so promptly,' he said, as they moved towards the body together.

'Wouldn't miss it for the world!' said the white-haired man with unconcealed relish. 'You don't provide me with interesting cadavers very often in Burnham Cross.' He stopped without hesitation over the thing that others were treating with revulsion. 'Messy!' was all he said as his venerable, elegant fingers began the preliminary examination of the late Captain of the Golf Club. Lambert watched him for a moment, then turned to supervise the positioning of the tapes which were being strung to cordon off the murder area and mark the limits of the team's detailed investigation of the scene.

The heat was almost back to the level of the previous day, and after the overnight deluge the atmosphere was even more humid. Away to their left, where the sun had just climbed high enough to beat on the edge of the sodden fairway, steam rose, thin and slow, for a few feet above the ground. The growth of lush vegetation seemed almost visible around them, an illusion fostered by the competitive outbursts of birdsong, echoing amidst the tall trees in what seemed an unnatural intensity over the heads of the busy crime squad. Beside him, a shaken voice muttered 'Poor devil! Poor silly devil!' and he turned to see the moist grey eyes of David Parsons staring past him towards the mortal remains of Michael Taylor, now hidden behind the broad backs of policemen.

Lambert said, 'There's no more you can do here, David. Thank you for guiding in the ambulance and our cars.' The Secretary nodded. Despite his pallor and his shaken preoccupation with the body, he was the only man around who looked comfortable in this Turkish bath heat. He wore jacket and tie as usual; as he accepted his dismissal and turned away, he looked down in distaste for two or three seconds at his highly polished brown shoes, whose patina was flecked with the splashes of mud inseparable from this scene. Lambert watched the first fifty yards of his walk back to the clubhouse and the sanctuary of his office. He saw the first signs of age he had noticed in the normally erect military figure. The shoulders drooped a little now, the brisk military march at which he normally moved about his business was diminished to an exhausted trudge. He did not look back.

Burgess knelt by the body on the mat he had brought from his car. His forehead almost touched the ground beside the shattered skull, as if he were taking part in some obscure ceremony of death. He would not disturb the body until it was carried to the path. lab., where thorough investigation could take place. But he knew Lambert would want any preliminary opinions he could offer now. Despite a crustiness that was only half humorous, he felt the pull of teamwork in the face of this most desperate of crimes. When Lambert rejoined him, he was rising stiffly to his feet and wiping his hands automatically on the little towel he carried in his bag.

He glanced sideways at the expectant Superintendent and shrugged.

'You can see most of it,' he said. 'He's been bludgeoned repeatedly with a sharp metal instrument; not more than an hour ago.'

'Murder weapon?'

'Something distinctive, certainly. The skull's been almost sliced away in layers . . . You look as though you have an idea.'

Lambert hadn't wished to prompt, but in the long run it would not matter: the detailed post-mortem would reveal all. 'A golf club?' he said.

Recognition dawned in Burgess, a non-golfer. 'That's it, almost certainly! There are grooves upon the skin at the edges of the wounds. An iron club. If you find the right one, we can confirm it in the lab.'

'So Taylor was beaten to death with a golf club. Presumably by a man, in view of the strength involved?'

'Not quite, and not necessarily are the answers to those two speculations,' said Burgess drily, deftly correcting a layman with his scientist's precision. 'As far as I can see at present, the first blow was struck from directly behind and broke the neck. The rest were rained upon a man lying unconscious on the ground and probably already dead. The mortal blow which severed the spinal cord was a sharply descending blow. Anyone hitting the right spot would have killed a defenceless man. No huge strength is needed with the leverage added by a golf club.'

'And all our suspects are golfers,' said Lambert bitterly. 'But why batter a dead man in that savage way?'

'John, you can't really expect help from me there. Blind anger? Panic? Your territory, not mine, thank God. At least it's made your murder weapon easy to identify.'

'Like Banquo,' said the Superintendent absently. Burgess looked hard at him. He had a busy enough morning, without coping with the references of a literary policeman. Lambert said hurriedly, 'Banquo was struck down with twenty trenchèd gashes on his head. He came back to haunt his murderer in public. Detection was easier in those days!' He thought he knew who would be haunted in the hours of darkness by the nightmare memory of Taylor's shattered skull, but proof was distressingly elusive.

When he returned to his car in the upper car park, Bert Hook was a picture of frustration. Not only had he been kept from the scene of the murder, but his phone calls had been irritatingly inconclusive. 'Not a worthwhile alibi among them,' he said gloomily. He looked at his notes. 'Debbie Hall has gone out to meet a client; her secretary doesn't know who. Bill Birch has been called out to inspect one of their machines at the warehouse in Wycombe. Even David Parsons was out of his office at the time of Taylor's murder. Just in the village collecting some chicken wire for use on the course, according to his Girl Friday. Probably true: he's dropped the wire into the office for the Green-keeper to pick up later in the morning. The only one of the four I've actually spoken to is Miss Hartford. And it took her a hell of a long time to come to the phone.' He brightened a little as a thought struck him. 'I wonder if she was just coming back into the house. She said she'd taken sleeping pills after our interview last night and was still in bed. I suppose it's possible; she's not due in the hospital until this afternoon. Anyway, she's no alibi.' Hook said this with some satisfaction on his rubicund features: she had been his original choice as murderer, and he was reluctant to abandon her yet.

By the time he had completed his report, they were back at the clubhouse. In the murder room, Lambert tried to contact Cyril Garner to tell him of the second murder, but the Chief Constable was addressing a conference for local magistrates. As he put the phone down, there was a discreet knock at the door and DC Spencer entered, ushering in a white-faced but determined Mary Hartford.

'You asked me to come in this morning to sign a statement,' she began. In the excitement of events upon the course, both he and Hook had forgotten. 'Your Sergeant loyally withheld all information when he asked me about my movements, John, but I gather there have been further developments.' Picturing Hook's elephantine evasions in their phone conversation, Lambert could not suppress the ghost of a smile.

'Please sit down, Mary,' he said grimly. 'I'm afraid Michael Taylor's been killed. On the course. And not by accident.' He saw Bert Hook's pained expression behind her, but she would have found out soon enough, anyway. 'Bert, if you see Vic Edwards, the steward, he'll rustle up some coffee for us.' Mary Hartford looked in urgent need of it. She sat bolt upright, staring wide-eyed into the space behind Lambert. For a moment, he thought she was mesmerized by the chalk outline delineating the spot where she had lately crouched over the body of James Shepherd. Then he realized she had not even registered this grim remembrance of her former suitor. She was merely suffering from shock. On her lips and about her wrists there was a tiny, continuous trembling; her neck looked unnaturally thin, like a schoolgirl's half-developed column, an impression reinforced by the blue veins standing out starkly against the white skin.

DI Rushton arrived behind the ample frame of Bert Hook, who carried a coffee tray. In his excitement, he probably did not even see Mary Hartford; had he done so, he would hardly have brandished the evidence he had intended only for the eyes of his Superintendent. By the time he glimpsed the Lady Captain, it was too late. Holding the golf club halfway down its shaft in his handkerchief, he was saying, 'The murder weapon, sir, surely! It was flung into the undergrowth about ten yards from where Taylor fell.'

He had the good grace to look embarrassed and confused when he saw the woman sitting stiff and formal by the table. Curiously, the sight of the club brought a stillness and strength to Mary Hartford. Perhaps the instrument of death summoned to the surface her professional resources. She rose, and looked a query at Lambert. When he nodded, she took the club carefully from Rushton, handling it gingerly at the point of balance as he had.

Lambert watched her carefully as she looked at the club-head. She did not flinch at the russet staining about its sole, although she must have recognized it as dried blood as readily as the three men in the room. She turned the club over and looked at the maker's name on the back of the head. This time she could not keep her voice steady: it rose and fell like a child's when tears threaten.

'This is a lady's club. A "Patti Berg" 5-iron. I think it belongs to Debbie Hall.'

CHAPTER 21

Most policemen are still shocked at the thought of murderous violence from a woman. It would take an ardent feminist to account it sexist in them. DI Rushton and Sergeant Hook looked at each other aghast across the table. It was Lambert who stepped forward and took the club quietly from Mary Hartford, nodding as if he had expected no less. 'I'll ask Miss Hall about it later in the morning,' was all he said, as if he were adding an unimportant footnote to the case.

He ushered Mary Hartford away to the less stressful environment of the ladies' lounge to finish her coffee. On his instructions, she meekly rang her deputy at the hospital and explained that she would be in an hour or so later than the midday she had planned.

The fingerprint experts had already established that the handle of the club had been wiped clean before it was hidden in the brambles. Lambert laid it carefully across the wooden arms of the tall chair which had been the Chairman's place at the Committee table; as he and Hook set about evaluating the situation, it lay like a grim talisman between them. Whilst out on the course the detailed search for evidence continued, the two men sat in the old, quiet room and considered their suspects, now reduced by the Captain's violent departure to four.

'David Parsons, Secretary,' Hook began, following his

neat notes. 'Access to James Shepherd. Could have killed him before the company met for drinks in the bar. If we accept Miss Hartford's story, Shepherd was dead by then. Apparently Parsons left, if not first, then before most of the others. Both Mary Hartford and Mr Birch confirm that his car had gone before they left . . . Is the order of departure significant?'

'It seems to be. Those who remember anything say the Committee Room door was ajar when they last saw it. When I toured the building and found the body it was locked. I think, though I may never be able to test the thought, that the murderer locked the door before he left, probably after he'd watched the other Committee members leave the car park.'

'Why bother?' said Hook. He enjoyed being used as a sounding-board for his chief's ideas, and would have been surprised to know how useful an attribute Lambert found this in his amanuensis.

'Because the murder would not then have been discovered until next day. Vic Edwards checks security each night, but if the door was locked he wouldn't go into the Committee Room. It was only because I searched the premises, knowing Shepherd's car was still outside, that we found the body so quickly. Had we not known of the death until the next day, the range of suspects would have been much wider, even if we had begun with the Committee.'

'So you think our murderer was the last to leave the clubhouse car park that night?'

Lambert shook his head in irritation. 'It's not conclusive, and even as I voice the theory I hear far too many "I thinks" to be convinced. Let's move on to more tangible matters. Parsons killed a man in Aden; brutally and suddenly, in a fit of understandable hatred. He succeeded in concealing the fact from everyone around here except Shepherd, apparently. That gentleman put his lost rank on the club note-paper deliberately to get a hold over him, if we are to believe David Parsons.'

'It tallies with what the others say about Shepherd.'

'Indeed it does. Mary Hartford knew him better than anyone, sensed that Shepherd was taunting Parsons about his rank. And Parsons's violent reaction in Aden has the kind of passionate desperation that lies about our second murder.'

'Facts, sir, not psychology!' Hook was daring enough to remind Lambert of one of the principles he regularly enunciated to his juniors. 'Had Parsons the opportunity to commit this morning's murder? His secretary says he was out in Burnham Cross collecting a roll of wire netting from the suppliers. The wire is in his office now: I've checked.'

'We'll need to check in the village. The wire could have been in the boot of his car for days. There'll be a lot of leg-work for our team if we don't get a confession today.' Hook glanced sharply at his Superintendent: it was the second hint he had given that he was pressing towards a solution. Lambert merely looked down at his own notes and said, 'Debbie Hall.'

'There's evidence against her,' said Bert Hook, stating the obvious with some reluctance, 'but she seemed far too open and honest with us to plot murder.'

Lambert smiled fondly at him—and watched his Sergeant flush right up to his greying temples. '"Beauty is truth; truth beauty", eh?'

'Sir?' Hook recognized the moment to play straight man and used it to cover his embarrassment. He had never quite understood the poem when he had been made to learn it by heart forty years earlier.

But Lambert merely said, 'She wouldn't be the first pneumatic lady with dazzling blue eyes to commit homicide, and you know it, Bert Hook. And her fair locks may beguile you, but you've seen enough of her to know she's no dumb blonde.'

Hook nodded reluctantly and strove to show his objectivity. 'We do know she slept with Shepherd at one time and that he was threatening her marriage to Len Jackson. Her handbag was in the Rolls yesterday morning. And of course Miss Hartford says it's her club which was used to kill Michael Taylor.' Hook became progressively more doleful through this catalogue, producing the last admission like a reluctant witness who sees a fact that cannot be ignored. 'But surely a woman couldn't have . . .'

'Burgess says it is certainly possible. He's sure the first blow with Debbie's 5-iron broke Taylor's neck. The rest was mere embellishment. Perhaps a determination to ensure he really was dead. Perhaps a blind hatred for an accessory who was about to desert. Perhaps even an attempt to convince old-fashioned policemen that it was too vicious a crime for a woman to perpetrate. Who knows? Debbie has no alibi yet.' Lambert realized that he was indulging himself with Bert Hook's discomfort, but he could not leave the subject without reminding his non-golfing Sergeant that, 'The fair Miss Hall swings a powerful 10-handicap iron: you've seen her on the practice area with the pro.'

In happier circumstances, Bert Hook's manly chauvinist eyes would have glowed with lively recollection, but now he looked at his pad and said stubbornly, 'What about your Miss Hartford?'

'*My* Miss Hartford?' said the Superintendent with pretended irritation. 'As far as our Lady Captain goes, much depends on whether you believe her story about how her thumbprint came to be on the knife that killed Shepherd. It's perfectly feasible that someone with her medical background would check the death-wound in the way she described, and look for her letters in the empty safe.'

'But even more feasible that she should have gone back after the Committee Meeting and stabbed Shepherd. She's confessed to a former long-standing relationship with the Chairman, though only when there was no alternative because we'd discovered that photograph in what might once have been a love-nest.'

'That love-nest idea worries me,' said Lambert. 'It's ten years since Shepherd and Mary Hartford were lovers and that photograph could never have been lying in that hut undisturbed for that time. And the perfume used so liberally in there was Debbie Hall's, not Mary Hartford's. Apart from the fact that Mary Hartford denies that they ever even went to that building. Why should they? They weren't particularly secretive about their relationship, according to Mary.'

Hook was startled; he hadn't connected the perfume in the burnt-out cottage with Debbie Hall. '"Hell hath no fury like a woman scorned,"' he said darkly, glad to be able to throw in a quotation of his own for once, and blissfully unaware that it was inaccurate.

'Bill Birch,' said Lambert abruptly, glancing at his watch.

'Plenty of motive, like the others,' said Hook after a pause. 'On his own admission, he hated Shepherd.'

Lambert, to whom Birch's suffering in this room yesterday remained vivid, said, 'Like David Parsons, he has killed a man before. In his case by pure accident and without negligence on his part, if we believe his story—and it tallies with what you remember of the case. But he was guilty of criminal deceit in concealing his part in a fatal accident. Which put him more completely in Shepherd's power than anyone else. He's desperately fond of his crippled wife, and I think he'd do anything to protect her.' Lambert paused. He was thinking of how upset Birch had seemed on the course yesterday when he had thought he was incriminating Mary Hartford. If his emotion had been feigned, he was a consummate actor. But then, as Bert Hook would tiresomely remind him if he passed on his thoughts, all the evidence was that their murderer was just that.

As Hook looked expectantly at his chief, there was an urgent knock at the door, which opened before Lambert could issue the invitation to enter. Rushton, of course. Full of himself. Bursting with his news like an eager child.

'You were right, sir. There were footprints by Taylor's body. Golf shoe prints. One very clear one where our killer had stood over our victim and beaten him with that club. We've photographed it and taken an impression.'

Lambert concealed his excitement and spoke calmly.

'Quite a lot of people keep their golf shoes in the locker-room. It's worth checking.'

'So the Secretary told us, sir. We've inspected them. We found one pair stuffed away behind the lockers, perhaps so that they could be removed later. They're covered with fresh mud which I'm sure match the print we've got. We'll have to check of course, but—'

'Show me!' Lambert's voice was harsh now. He had expected this, but its arrival gave him a sick excitement he could not remember feeling before; more than ever as the climax approached, he wished he did not know the participants in this tight little drama.

Rushton, revelling in the moment, led a little procession of Superintendent, Sergeant Hook and the two detective constables who had followed at his heels. It was no more than twenty yards to the long row of shoes in the locker-room. They could have picked out the ones that mattered without Rushton's eager direction: they were the only ones with thick, fresh mud adhering to their pimpled soles, the only ones laid upside down for their detailed inspection.

'It's the left shoe we're matching,' said Rushton. Lambert nodded and gingerly turned over the right shoe. Under the morning's mud and water, the whiteness had almost disappeared. But the scuffing on the toe of the worn shoe was sickeningly familiar to Lambert. He had seen it only the previous afternoon when he had sat on the seat by the tenth green.

Gazing down at these shoes, and listening to the voice of Bill Birch.

CHAPTER 22

Lambert looked up from the golf shoes to find four policemen staring expectantly at him. Once again, this investigation in which he knew the principals was working its peculiar alchemy. He felt his pulses racing and his irritation rising:

it was a difficult enough case without this unique overlay. Perhaps he should have refused it; but even with that thought came the realization that he would never willingly have done so.

'Where was Birch this morning?' he said gruffly; he tried to invest the surname with the same dispassionate neutrality he would have used in any other case.

'Out of his office. No alibi as yet.' It was Hook, almost apologetically.

'Like the others,' said Lambert moodily.

He went back to the murder room, and this time managed to contact the Chief Constable with the news of the second murder. Cyril Garner was not pleased as Lambert gave him the terse details. He did not interrupt, except with a few disapproving grunts. At the end of the account, he said, 'The press conference will have to go ahead as arranged. You can take the questioning about Taylor's murder.' It sounded like a fretful parent's punishment of a defaulting child. Lambert acquiesced readily enough; he knew the newshounds would be too busy recording the sensational details of the Golf Captain's gory demise for there to be many questions about police action at this stage. And there was still at the back of his mind the wild hope that he might have the solution to offer triumphantly to the media by the time of the conference at one. It was a notion he scarcely dared to entertain himself, still less to communicate to Cyril Garner.

As he put down the phone and stared at it moodily for a moment, Hook appeared in the doorway like the dutiful lieutenant he was.

'Debbie Hall's just arrived,' he said. No appreciation of the lady's ample charms showed now upon his rubicund features. For decent Bert Hook, the golf club which lay still like an accusation across the chair at the head of the table precluded any observation of that sort.

Lambert looked at his watch. 11.45. The morning was flying by. 'Better show her in. And get DI Rushton to intercept Bill Birch as he arrives. Once he's here, we'll have all four of them in here, but I don't want any exchange between them before then.'

'Birch should be here any minute. He's phoned in to the office and they've told him you want him here. Parsons is still in his office and Miss Hartford in the ladies' lounge.'

'Right. Once Bill Birch arrives, wheel them all in here. Come yourself, but I don't want anyone else. I want to try something before the press conference, but without a room full of eager CID beavers. Listen hard and play it by ear. Speak if you feel it useful. Our usual arrangement.' Lambert heard excitement entering his voice as he strove to be matter-of-fact. He could not miss the pleasure Hook tried ineffectively to conceal, as he nodded and turned away to set up this little drama.

In less than thirty seconds, he ushered in Debbie Hall, shut the door quietly behind her, and went away to await the arrival of Birch.

Debbie was demurely attired, in a two-piece suit of olive green and high-heeled shoes of matching leather. The cameo brooch at the throat of her high-necked blouse was the only ornamentation she carried. Her soft blonde curls were more regimented than usual, her lipstick carefully muted, her eyelids without make-up at all. As with many women of good figure, more formal dress seemed only to reinforce her voluptuous attractions, as if the discreet concealment of those splendid curves merely emphasized the amplitude within. Lambert was reminded of a family funeral nearly thirty years ago, when an aunt scarcely five years older than him had inflamed all the hot imaginings of adolescence in her modest navy blue outfit. And nothing could conceal those remarkable eyes of Debbie Hall: wide and blue, they seemed even now to see through to his psyche and be amused. He was glad to be relieved of their examination as he ushered her to a chair.

When he resumed his own, her eyes were fixed upon the object laid across the arms of the late Chairman's seat beside him. They flicked for a moment to his, then back to the golf club—its shaft gleaming dully in the high, oak-panelled room; it was no more than four feet from her.

'Coffee?' said Lambert, as lightly as he could. 'I'm sure we could soon rustle up—'

'No thanks, John. I've had three cups in a pub in Aylesbury. Waiting for the customer who left a message on our answering machine but never turned up for the meeting he'd suggested.' She was looking still at the golf club which had killed Michael Taylor.

She said very quietly, 'That's mine. Why is it here?'

'I'll tell you that in a moment. When did you last handle it?' If she noticed his slight, deliberate searching for the word 'handle' she did not reveal it. She stared at the club a moment longer, until he wondered if she knew the origin of the russet stains about its blade and sole. Then she turned her attention back to him.

'Only a few days ago. I was playing with Mary in a club match. I only found it was missing when I had my lesson here yesterday. I can't think where I lost it. It's easy enough to put a club down whilst you're putting, but usually you remember where. But of course you'd know that. Anyway, someone usually hands them in, but this time that hadn't happened; I asked in the pro's shop.' The torrent of words, too quickly delivered, was postponing the question they both knew had to come. 'Where did you find it?'

'It was found by a detective constable in the undergrowth behind the sixth green. It is almost certainly the instrument which killed Michael Taylor.'

He was watching her carefully. Was the start of horror, the widening of those brilliant blue eyes, a shade theatrical? He was not expert enough to decide. There was nothing histrionic about the low, taut voice in which she said, 'Where? When?'

'Within yards of where your club was found. At around 9.30 this morning.'

'Poor Mike!' It was all she said, but the colour had drained from her features. Her vivacious, attractive face changed in a few seconds to that of a woman sick with shock and fear, a transition which could only be so marked in one of her colouring. Eventually she said, 'What next?' He could not tell from her flat tone whether it was a rhetorical appeal to fate or a question to him about the way he proposed to proceed; he took the opportunity to interpret it as the latter.

'The other three people concerned are coming in for a discussion at twelve.' If she thought the carefully neutral word was a euphemism, she gave no sign. 'Debbie, I need to know where you were between 9 and 9.30 this morning.'

Now the blue eyes might have been made of coloured glass, so striking was the contrast between their lustre and the flat grey-white face in which they were set.

'In my car,' she said. 'Alone. Driving to meet a man I cannot identify, who did not turn up.' She spoke as if each phrase were a nail struck with a hammer.

'Name?' said Lambert.

'Munro. He left a message on the answering machine at 8.55 today. A minute before I arrived.'

'You didn't ring him back?'

'He didn't leave a number. He asked me to meet him in the Brown Cow at Aylesbury. Normally I'd have wanted to discuss preliminary arrangements with him, but he'd mentioned a month's work for four people: it would have been good business for us.'

Lambert rose and made his way quietly to the door. 'I think your colleagues will have arrived by now, Debbie, so we'd better get together. For what it's worth, no one seems to have a clear alibi for this morning. Odd, that.'

As he opened the heavy door, he looked back at her. Her full lips gave him a tight, uncharacteristic smile, in acknowledgement of the small comfort he had just offered her. Then her eyes switched back to the steady contemplation of her golf club, and the blood of Michael Taylor upon its blade.

CHAPTER 23

With Hook as usher, the surviving members of the Burnham Cross Golf Club Committee shuffled silently into the Murder Room. Lambert had seen the same disquiet amongst people enlisted for an identity parade, with the innocent uneasy that the unthinkable might happen and the wrong person be identified for a crime. This time the stakes were much higher. He was sure now of his murderer, but that person gave no helpful hint of demeanour as the chairs scraped noisily over the parquet floor.

He was gambling upon a confession. If necessary, he would take his killer in for prolonged questioning, whilst his team painstakingly assembled more evidence, but if he could secure an admission of guilt now much agony of mind and much police time would be saved. And possibly another life; he blamed himself again for not anticipating the morning's bizarre and desperate despatch of Michael Taylor. The high tension caused by his melodramatic grouping of the suspects might produce useful evidence from the innocent. But above all he hoped the pressure upon the guilty would prove unbearable.

He was deliberately low-key in his introduction. 'Sorry to have to bring you back into here. The Murder Room is almost the only place we can ensure privacy at the moment: you may have seen the preparations in the main lounge for the press conference which will be held at 1 p.m. today. I know you've all been hounded in various ways by the media over the last thirty-six hours. This morning's events will only intensify that. Whatever our progress, whatever we are able to tell the newshounds at one, you will continue to be pursued for quotes: a resolute "No comment" is the best policy, as some of you have already discovered.' Debbie Hall gave him a bleak little smile. But it was Bill Birch who had been looking increasingly puzzled through his introduction.

'John, where is Mike Taylor?' he said now.

All around the huge table, there were gasps. The three other suspects looked sharply at Birch, then down at the grain of the oak before them. In answer to Lambert's glance, Hook shook his head almost imperceptibly. After his restrained opening, the Superintendent was not sorry to have the screw of melodrama turned by someone else.

'Michael Taylor was brutally beaten to death earlier this morning, Bill,' he said quietly. 'With a golf club which belonged to Debbie.' He was glad the instrument had been removed now from its prominent position; the facts were brutal enough, without stage tricks to get in the way of what he planned. The eyes of all four suspects were now upon him, wide and expectant. He wondered how many of them knew about Birch's golf shoes and the imprint of them found by Taylor's body.

'Where were you between 9 and 9.30 this morning?' he said to Birch. The silence in the room made his voice sound heavy with menace. The Vice-Captain was immediately aware of the significance of the question, at the same time as he was beset with the inadequacy of his reply. 'I was on the way to our warehouse in Wycombe,' he said bleakly. 'Alone, of course.'

'Was this arranged yesterday?' asked Lambert.

'No. Someone had phoned this morning. Though who it was, no one seemed to know when I got there.'

There was a long pause whilst everyone in the room weighed the implications of this and Lambert waited for any revealing sign from his murderer. Even a movement of the head would have reassured him, but there was none.

'I want to go back to the murder of James Shepherd in this room,' he said. The little rustle of movement around him marked a transfer, not a release, of the tension. 'I now have a pretty clear idea what happened. The Chairman was killed in the five-minute period before you all met for drinks in the bar.' His murderer's eyes were no wider than anyone else's at these confident assertions. Only Mary Hartford's face showed something like relief: it seemed as though her story might be believed. He acknowledged the look with the tiniest of smiles.

'Miss Hartford in fact discovered the body and checked the death just before she went into the bar.' This time he was sure that everyone's surprise was genuine.

'No wonder you were quiet in the bar,' said Debbie Hall, in a voice which barely carried beyond her neighbour. She moved her hand six inches to grasp Mary Hartford's slim white fist beside her.

'You accept Miss Hartford's story?' It was David Parsons, precise and formal even now.

'Oh yes. She confesses to blood upon her cuff, and Bill Birch noticed it. Of course, it was possible that Miss Hartford had not merely discovered a murder, but actually committed one. Indeed, in checking the death, she inadvertently left a thumbprint upon the handle of the knife in Shepherd's chest.' This time there was an involuntary movement of astonishment from his murderer. 'I am glad our killer did not know that, Mary, when he was trying to implicate you yesterday,' Lambert continued imperturbably.

'Miss Hartford concealed her discovery of the body from me when I saw her. One other person as well as the murderer told me a lie, and that a clumsy one. It was Michael Taylor. He told me he spent some three minutes in the gents' locker-room after, rather than before, you met for drinks. Yet Bill Birch was in the locker-room with him before you all met up in the lounge. Plainly Michael Taylor wanted to account for the time after he had been in the bar. The most obvious deduction would have been that he had committed the murder himself, and I think he realized that eventually. He was killed this morning because he was about to tell me exactly what he did in those vital few minutes after the drinks.' There was absolute silence in the hot room. It was Hook, sturdily concealing his ignorance of his chief's thought-processes, who eventually coughed. In another context, it would have been comic: four intense pairs of eyes flashed across to him, then back to the Superintendent, as if worked by a switch.

'I think the murderer was the last person among you to leave the club,' said Lambert. 'He had already removed Shepherd's "black box" of incriminating material from the wall-safe, but he had to cover his traces and move the keys. The door of this room was unlocked when you came in and found the body, Mary. Probably it was still so when Michael Taylor discovered murderer and body together after the drinks. When I came to the club a little while later, every door around here was locked. The murderer waited to see you all off the premises, checked that no clue was obvious, and shut up everything before leaving with the incriminating documents taken from the safe. The Chairman had arranged to meet me at the club at 10.30. That was bad luck for the murderer. Had I not searched the building with Vic Edwards, the body would almost certainly not have been discovered until next morning.'

Bill Birch had looked increasingly disturbed through all this. Now he burst out, 'But I was last to leave. I told you. I saw Mike Taylor rush off—'

'No, Bill.' It was Mary Hartford, grim but calm. 'You and I were last together. We called to each other in the darkness across the car park. We drove out almost together.'

'But you were not the last to leave,' said Lambert quietly.

'I think we were,' said Birch stubbornly.

'I know you do.' Lambert was implacable, but it was not Birch that he was watching closely. 'You're almost right, but not quite. Miss Hall had gone, and you saw Michael Taylor leave. But what Miss Hartford said was—' he made an elaborate play of consulting his notes, but he knew well enough the exact words he would quote—'"David Parsons left first, I think. When I came out, his car had gone. His reserved space is next to the Lady Captain's, so I noticed."'

Now his murderer was alerted. Now at last David Parsons' eyes blazed with the tell-tale fury he had hoped to bring out. Lambert tried not to betray his own excitement as he went on evenly, 'You assumed because the Secretary's reserved space was empty that he had already left. But David Parsons had not used his space. He was parked in the darkness at the other end of the car park.'

'Proof?' Parsons spat the single word across the table like a missile.

'None, as yet. But then we haven't looked.'

'Merely a theory, then!' Parsons attempted the contemptuous dismissal of an absurd notion, but he was too shaken for it to come off. Lambert pressed on smoothly; now that his man had been disturbed, he must have no time to recover.

'This Committee Room does not have a Yale lock, which anyone could release. It still has its original, heavy key, which is necessary to lock it. That key is held by the Secretary.'

'In his office, where anyone could pick it up!' said Parsons. But his voice cracked, so that a reasonable objection suddenly sounded preposterous.

'Perhaps,' said Lambert. 'Except that you were in your office yourself for as long as the key was there. You put it back after everyone had left. Vic Edwards was able to collect it to open the door for me.' The last part of this was speculation, delivered with the confidence of fact. Parsons's distress convinced him it was true enough, and he pressed on to an even bolder conjecture.

'Now, the break-in to Mr Shepherd's car, in broad daylight. A key was used, so the culprit was probably the murderer, since the Chairman's keys had been removed from his body. It's a little like the Hound of the Baskervilles.'

It was Hook who looked wide-eyed at him now, astonished at the levity of fiction at such a moment. But it was Mary Hartford who said slowly, 'The thing about the hound was that it *didn't* bark at the crucial point, because it knew the murderer.

'Exactly,' said Lambert inexorably. He thought he should have anticipated that this meticulous, shrewd woman would be a devotee of detective fiction: probably only a sense of decorum in this place prevented her from developing the idea through Chesterton's postman. He pressed on hastily to his own exposition: 'It seemed strange that in a large car park, with golfers getting ready for play—don't forget that though the clubhouse was closed the course was open—no one should notice a break-in to the Chairman's Rolls-Royce. Of course, the one person who wouldn't be remarked is the Secretary, whom everyone assumes is going about his normal business. When he had opened the car with the key he had secured the night before, he went back to his office and raised the alarm himself from there.'

'This is ridiculous!' said David Parsons. He articulated the four syllables of the word as carefully as if he were in committee.

'But why break in at all?' said Bill Birch. Lambert was relieved that none of them seemed concerned to defend the Secretary.

'Not to remove anything. That could have been easily accomplished in the darkness after you had left the night before. David already had the press-cuttings about his court-martial in Cyprus: they had been in the wall-safe. The objective was to put something into the car, not take it out. Debbie Hall's grey handbag was planted under the front passenger seat. Perhaps David thought it was Mary Hartford's bag when he acquired it: the two ladies were at the same meeting.' He had caught Parsons's start at the mention of Debbie Hall as the owner of the bag; now the Secretary's sudden look of fury confirmed the thought that had only occurred to him as he spoke.

'The charade of the break-in was only to draw our attention to the presence of the handbag. It was a mistake: we'd have searched the car anyway and found it. It could have been quietly placed there without the brouhaha of a break-in.' Mary Hartford and David Parsons stared wide-eyed at each other, she with dawning horror, he with a blazing defiance; Lambert was glad of the table between them, for he had to stoke these fires further yet.

'Now to the fire in the greenkeeper's cottage. It may have been started with Michael Taylor's connivance: we shall never know, unless David Parsons chooses to tell us. But that doesn't matter. The whole thing was designed to draw attention to Miss Hartford's association some years ago with James Shepherd. It was elaborate, but apparently foolproof: if the fire brigade, called by Michael Taylor, arrived in time to prevent complete destruction, we should find an apparent love-nest, with only Mary Hartford able to deny its existence. If the cottage burnt out completely, it would be an incident unconnected with the death of Shepherd, with our murderer no worse off. The revelation on the same afternoon of Miss Hartford's thumbprint on the handle of the murder knife was a wonderful piece of luck for the murderer. At four o'clock yesterday, there was a pretty damning case against our Lady Captain.' He gave Mary Hartford a grim little smile, reinforcing his use of the past tense. Bert Hook, who had been so keen to arrest that elegant lady on the previous evening, had the good grace to redden slowly in the background.

'It's still a far better case than anything you can trump up against me!' said Parsons. The attempt at bravado sat oddly upon this cold, precise man; the desperate clichés of denial seemed only to confirm his guilt.

Lambert's only acknowledgement of this was to address himself directly to the Secretary. 'But again you were too intricate. Damping the sheets in the cottage with perfume was an imaginative touch. Too imaginative, because you used the wrong perfume. You took it from the handbag you had stolen a week ago, and placed in Shepherd's Rolls this morning. But the perfume you thought was Mary Hartford's was in fact Debbie Hall's. So the perfume and the photograph you placed in that cottage did not tally. Someone was trying to set up our Lady Captain as a murderer. Someone who had been assembling material in the last few days to support such a plan. A handbag, a golf club, could be useful circumstantial evidence when left in the right places. I have no doubt the murderer was weaving a more elaborate web, hoping to enmesh Mary much more deeply, until he heard that Shepherd was planning to tell George Williams about him early this morning. Then he had to improvise and move quickly: hence last night's killing.

'The murderer removed Shepherd's "black box" of incriminating material from the wall-safe. The photograph of Mary Hartford with James Shepherd which he found in that box seemed too good an opportunity to miss. Once we see the intention to frame Mary in subsequent happenings, the murderer has to be someone with the keys to Shepherd's Rolls and easy access to the greenkeeper's cottage.'

'Which could be your friend Bill Birch as easily as me,' said Parsons. 'He was Shepherd's Works Manager and a former Chairman of our Greens Committee.'

For a moment, the boldness of this switch almost disconcerted Lambert. As he thought ahead, he saw the way Parsons's mind had worked, but the swiftness of the switch in his adversary's defences surprised him none the less.

'True. I considered that,' said Lambert harshly. 'What Bill couldn't have committed is your second murder.' Suddenly, he wanted this over. He resented the brutal murder of vain, harmless Michael Taylor far more than that of the unregretted James Shepherd. Perhaps because he felt responsible; he had miscalculated the ruthlessness of Parsons and not thought Taylor in much danger until it was too late.

He had his man now, and had dropped the conjectural tones he had used to the group at large. He was as aggressive as he would have been had he been trying to break Parsons down in an unfurnished interview room at the station. 'Michael Taylor was about to expose you and you guessed it. He had not the temperament for a murderer, or even an accessory. So you beat him to death with Debbie's 5-iron. I presume you simply removed it from a golf bag outside the ladies' locker-room. Probably you thought it was Mary's: Debbie had been playing with her and the bags were together. You had to act quickly to prevent Michael Taylor talking to me, and anything which would throw suspicion on anyone else would have to do.'

'I don't have to listen to this!' said Parsons, and made as

if to rise. Perhaps his legs would not support him, for he did not leave his chair. No one moved to assist him.

Lambert went on without even acknowledging the protest. 'You did what planning you could before you followed Taylor out on to the course, leaving fake messages for Debbie and Bill so as to leave them without alibis. Your own alibi with the chicken wire will be investigated and found wanting. You collected that wire yesterday, not this morning.'

'Conjecture,' said David Parsons flatly, but the panache he tried to summon would not come.

Lambert ignored him. 'The murder weapon was found suspiciously near the crime. If I'd murdered someone on a deserted golf course, I certainly wouldn't deposit the weapon with the blood of the victim upon it within ten yards of the corpse. There is plenty of deeper undergrowth a good half-mile away. We were meant to find that club.

'And then your tendency to over-elaborate was helpful to us again. The clear print of Bill Birch's golf shoe was found as you intended by the body.' Lambert was interrupted by a sudden gasp and the scrape of Birch's chair as the Vice-Captain moved involuntarily: it was the first he had known of this. The Superintendent stilled him with a slight movement of his hand, but did not take his eyes off Parsons.

'Those shoes were worn by the murderer all right. And I remember how carefully you drew my attention to your shining city shoes when you returned to the scene of the crime with the ambulance. Size nine, I think; feet which would fit well enough into Bill Birch's size ten golf shoes, left like those of a hundred other golfers in our locker-room.'

'This is preposterous!' shouted Parsons. This time his articulation of the word had lost its precision. 'If you've indeed found a shoe-print beside the body of my friend Michael Taylor, then there's your murderer and it's time you arrested him!' He turned with an attempt at outrage towards the appalled Birch, but there was little menace left in him now, though Bert Hook tensed his muscles for action.

'Mr Birch couldn't have murdered Michael Taylor,' said Lambert with cold formality. Now he was moving securely upon a platform of fact, not conjecture, and the audience he had almost forgotten felt the authority of his words. 'Would you stand up for a moment please, Bill? Sergeant Hook, let's have that club for a moment.'

The Vice-Captain came gingerly forward as Hook retrieved Debbie Hall's club from the corner of the room where it had lain decently covered with a cloth. The club had already been checked for fingerprints, but he put it into the large hands of the Vice-Captain with all the reluctance of an officer relinquishing a vital exhibit.

'Now,' said Lambert, 'would you pretend to strike the stationary Sergeant Hook on the back of the neck, please?' Birch raised the club, then mimed an awkward blow to the back of Bert Hook's impassive head. There were gasps around the room as the purpose of the little pantomime became clear. There was no way in which the Vice-Captain could cut viciously into the back of anyone's head with this club, for he was striking with the smooth back of the club, not the cutting front edge.

For Bill Birch was a left-hander.

'It is as well after all that we played those few holes yesterday afternoon or I might not have remembered,' said Lambert, as Birch resumed his seat and Hook moved quietly behind David Parsons. All eyes were now on the Secretary, who was gazing sullenly at his hands, as if they had independently led him into such deeds. It was Birch who said to him, 'We were all glad to see Shepherd dead. But how could you kill Mike Taylor?'

There was silence for two, three long seconds. Then Parsons said in a weary monotone, 'I had no choice. He knew I'd killed Shepherd and he was never going to hold out under pressure. He told me he'd arranged to meet you this morning. I followed him when he parked his car.' Then he looked up and his eyes blazed. 'He was the kind of man who panics under fire. A rat who would run from the enemy. I killed him like a fleeing rat!' There was in his eye a psychotic gleam, in his voice an insane conviction, which made Lambert think that he might yet end his days not in Parkstone but in Broadmoor.

The confessed murderer was duly charged, and departed under discreet arrest in a police car. Cyril Garner positively revelled in the press conference he had arranged with such apprehension. John Lambert received a benevolent mention from his Chief Constable on television; his own tribute to his team got no further than the editing room.

By the evening of this eventful day, the extreme humidity had departed but the weather seemed set fair again. On the first tee, a strange four-ball assembled. It was Bill Birch's idea, and as the unfortunate decease of his predecessor had now made him Captain of the club, convention decreed that his word should be law in all golfing matters. The only way for golfers to dismiss the nightmare which had ended, he said, was to play golf: it was their duty to show the shaken membership that things were returning to normal. Being golfers, they found his logic irrefutable.

Thus those members in the newly reopened bar were surprised to see on the first tee Bill Birch, Mary Hartford, Debbie Hall and John Lambert. The Lady Captain, trim and unfussy, drove her ball down the middle of the fairway after the minimum of preparation. Debbie Hall settled over her ball and gave that preliminary swivel of the hips which made strong men weak with excitement; then she cracked the ball away, slightly pulled to the left but safe enough. The new Captain dispatched the majestic drive appropriate to his new status, long and high, with the controlled draw which took him as a left-hander well over the bunker on the right of the fairway.

John Lambert signalled the return to normality more clearly than any of them. There was a pleasing rhythm about his swing, a reassuring solidity about the contact of his driver with the ball. He looked up to see the ball arching high and proud against an azure English sky. Then it sliced gently away to the right, bounced once, and came to rest unerringly in the centre of the bunker which Bill Birch's ball had just cleared so easily.

Burnham Cross Golf Club might never be quite the same again. But some things did not change.